Cat
Between
Two
Worlds

Lesley Renton

 FriesenPress

Suite 300 - 990 Fort St
Victoria, BC, v8v 3K2
Canada

www.friesenpress.com

Copyright © 2017 by Lesley Renton
First Edition — 2017

ISBN
978-1-5255-0992-6 (Hardcover)
978-1-5255-0993-3 (Paperback)
978-1-5255-0994-0 (eBook)

1. JUVENILE FICTION

Distributed to the trade by The Ingram Book Company

Dedication:

To my two wonderful children,
Price and Gwen

Cat

Between

Two
Worlds

Clarion Review

Clarion Rating: 4 out of 5

On two legs or four, the colorful inhabitants of Tolk project a rustic charm full of whimsical folk- and fairy-tale elements, with just enough unique lore to be freshly compelling.

A young boy discovers a hidden portal to a magical realm, befriends a bevy of talking animals, and plans a daring rescue, all while staying mindful of making it home in time for dinner in Lesley Renton's *Cat between Two Worlds*, an innovative fantasy adventure that celebrates the extraordinary bonds of friendship and family.

When eleven-year-old Price Evans moves from Calgary to Clareburn, Alberta, he is amazed to discover a secret gateway into the enchanted Land of Tolk right in his own backyard. Trouble is brewing among its typically peace-loving inhabitants, and Price soon finds himself in the center of a rebellion that could shatter their idyllic way of life forever.

The Land of Tolk is populated with fairies, elves, giants, dwarves, and all manner of singing, dancing, glittering magical creatures, along with a cadre of anthropomorphic animals ranging from mice and squirrels to dogs, cats, bears, and birds, in waistcoats, trousers, and ruffled collars. On two legs or four, the colorful inhabitants project a rustic charm full of whimsical folk- and fairy-tale elements with just enough unique lore for a freshly compelling set of circumstances and intriguing new characters.

There is a classic dog-versus-cat rivalry between the king of Tolk, a loyal and fiercely protective German shepherd aptly named Noble, and a crafty and curious orange feline called Sinbad who is intent on stealing the crown. Sinbad plots to bring humans and technology through a portal with promises of luxury in the form of refrigerators, shopping malls, and bowls of milk.

Throw in a comedic sidekick made of pinecones, a fairy who is longing for affection, and a scheming cat, and for Price "it might just be the start of something exciting. And, whatever it was, he wanted to find out more." Upper-elementary and middle-grade readers will want to find out more as well as Price and his companions strive to bring peace and harmony back to the Land of Tolk in Lesley Renton's *Cat between Two Worlds*.

Reviewed by Pallas Gates McCorquodale March 1, 2018 "https://www.forewordreviews.com/reviews/reviewers/pallas-gates-mccorquodale/"

Acknowledgements:

I would like to express my appreciation to Carmen Wittmeier, my excellent editor, for her invaluable insights and suggestions.

And thank you, as well, to the FriesenPress editor, for such a supportive and encouraging review of the manuscript.

I'd also like to thank my son, Price Morgan, for the amazing cover design, lending this book an added measure of distinction.

And to my daughter, Gwen, thank you for helping come up with a great title. Also (though she doesn't remember, since she was only three years old at the time), for inventing the name "Octaruse Pinecone."

Prologue:
The Stone Wall

With gallant stride and head held high, a majestic German shepherd dog led the way across a grassy meadow. Strutting daintily beside him was a handsome cat, whose golden eyes and long russet fur had earned him the name of "Flame." The two stopped before one of the clusters of trees that spotted the meadow's green expanse. From where they stood, and only from that vantage point, a small section of stone wall was visible from within its shady depths.

"We're here, Flame. This is the place." The dog spoke with a reluctance that implied they might be parting ways.

"Ah. Very neatly hidden. I never would have found it on my own."

The dog pawed absently at the turf, as he considered what to say next. "Remember, you're taking a great risk," he said. "I have already warned you that coming back is not certain."

"Oh, but I won't go far, nor stay away too long. I'll be back before I have time to forget the way." Flame did not even look at the dog as he spoke. His golden eyes, ablaze with anticipation, were fixed intently on the wall, as though he were afraid to lose sight of it.

Disappointed, the shepherd dog looked away. "Then there is nothing left to say but farewell."

"Yes. Farewell it is, but not goodbye. I will see you again soon. You'll see. I'll be back before the new moon."

"Yes," agreed the dog, but he did not sound convinced.

Flame glanced at him quickly. "Do you doubt it?"

"I have no doubt you'll be back soon."

"Ha!" The cat tossed his tawny mane and laughed. "Then you must doubt that we'll be together again. That's nonsense."

"It means that I know that, from this day on, things will never be the same."

Flame did not bother asking his friend to explain. He was far too impatient to begin, and it was a foolish notion anyway. As he trotted off, he called over his shoulder, "I'll see you soon!" He did not look back.

But the dog stood and watched, unmoving, until his friend was out of sight, and even for quite some time after.

Part I:
The Summons

Chapter One:
Between Two Garages

The first thing Price did when he saw the huge poplar, shading a corner of the backyard, was climb it. It was twice the size of an ordinary tree. The old, gnarled trunk was so broad at the base that it looked as if two trees had grown together.

"This has *got* to be the biggest tree in town!" he said, contemplating this stroke of good fortune.

Plunking down on a sturdy bough, he began to idly swing his legs, but in the heat of the afternoon, the slightest effort made him feel hot; even in the shade it was sweltering. He blew out a puff of air and looked around. He noticed there were a number of good, solid limbs growing out from the trunk in all directions.

I could build a tree house, he thought. No doubt about it: This was a good move.

Leaning back, he could feel the rough bark through his T-shirt. He liked that, in the same way he liked getting drenched with rain on a hot day or having tired feet after a long hike. It felt real.

He glanced over at the house from this new, elevated perspective. It wasn't big, but it was old. It had stone facing and a peaked roof with cedar shingles. Inside, the floorboards had buckled in places and creaked with every step. He liked that too. It added to the character of the place, and it was spooky. He thought of the enormous tub in the bathroom that had feet with claws. He hadn't taken a bath in it yet, but knew that it would submerge him right up to his neck.

Grabbing an overhead branch, he pulled himself up to get a better view of the garden.

It was a big yard, entirely surrounded by a high wall made from the same kind of stone as the house. From the porch to the back gate, a straight walk cut across a broad, sunny expanse of lawn. The poplar grew near the back northwest corner by the garage. Its boughs reached over the wall, overhanging their neighbor's yard as well, but the dense foliage blocked that view completely.

Then he saw that he could get on the garage roof. Straddling the bough, he shimmied along, agitating the poplar leaves and stirring up hundreds of fragments of sunlight below. He was just about to swing down, when something caught his eye.

Their garage and the neighbor's stood side-by-side, and had been built on a lower level than the rest of the yard. Between the two was a shaded, sunken space. He couldn't see all of it; only a narrow strip of mossy ground was visible. Wildflowers and tall weedy tufts of grass grew against the neighbor's garage wall, but otherwise, it seemed to be completely empty and unused.

Almost at once, ideas jumped into Price's mind. His parents wouldn't be interested in the space, except maybe for storage. He would ask them about it. Perhaps it could be his alone—his hideout, a fortress. Unless, of course, he made a friend. Then it would be the perfect place to build a clubhouse. He liked that possibility.

But how do you get in there? he thought.

He wriggled along a bit farther, and just where the stone wall ended, there was a gate, perpendicular to the wall, connecting to the corner of their garage. So that was it. He hadn't even seen the gate behind the massive trunk of the poplar. Stretching out on his stomach, he could just see the other side. There were three stone steps leading down into the space.

Price clambered down the tree and hurried over to the gate. Eagerly he pulled on the latch. It didn't budge. He stretched an arm over the top, which was just about nose-high, and felt along the other side. His fingers grasped a metal object that he recognized at once as a large padlock. He gave it a couple of tugs, but it was locked.

Dragging over a lawn chair, he climbed up to get a better look. There was the padlock, all right, and not the combination kind like he'd had on his locker at school. He was going to need a key.

The space itself looked even more inviting close up. It was a good size: about twelve feet across and extending the length of the garages. And because it was so deep and sheltered, it would be out of the wind. That would be good when he wanted to sketch. A small section of stone wall closed it off at the back, so there was absolute privacy. No one would be able to see him in there. He thought again of the friend he might make. They could bring in foamies and sleeping bags and camp overnight. No fires, of course. His parents would never allow that, but they could have flashlights.

Pulling himself up, Price scissored his legs over the top of the gate and dropped down to the other side, narrowly missing the steps and landing heavily on a recent scattering of leaves over mossy ground. Glancing up at the leafy boughs of the poplar, he realized that somebody must have raked up all the autumn leaves. In fact, looking around, the whole place was about as neat and tidy as an empty shoebox.

Then he noticed that there was a second gate next to theirs, leading into the space from the neighbor's side. That gate, he saw, was not padlocked. This observation sparked a twinge of concern, which he quickly dismissed. No one was storing anything here—no tools, no discarded lumber, no junk—so it made sense that no one else was interested in the space, except to remove the leaves every autumn. And he would gladly volunteer to do that himself.

I could bring in some boards and a tarp, he thought, *and build a lean-to.* He could almost see the shelves he would make for all his stuff. But examining the long drop from the top of the gate to the ground, he knew he'd have to get that gate open.

Then he remembered that Mrs. Hudson, their realtor, had given his dad a key ring with a collection of old keys, for opening the various doors and locks on the property. There was sure to be one that would unlock the padlock. Without wasting any time, he scrabbled back over the gate and headed into the house.

He found his dad in the basement—or (more precisely) the cellar, for the walls were rough and dank and there was a distinct musty odor. He was trying to assemble some metal storage shelves and had discovered they were too tall to stand up in the squat, dark cellar. Price blinked, adjusting to the dim light of a single dangling light bulb, after being out in the August sunshine. The cellar was windowless, but at least it was cool. His father looked up.

"Price, you're just in time. Can you give me a hand with these shelves? I have to cut them down. See if you can find my hacksaw." His hands were occupied, so he gestured with an elbow towards a large packing box, on which someone had scrawled *TOOLS* with a black felt marker. Price rummaged through it, and after a few seconds, handed the hacksaw to his dad.

"Thanks. So ... what do you think of this dungeon? Pass me the tape measure. It's behind you."

Price looked around and sniffed. "I like the smell." He passed the tape measure to his dad. "It's like earth."

"You like it?" His father shook his head and began measuring about three inches off the end of each metal support.

"Dad?" Price began. "You know, next to the garage, there's this gate. It goes down into this kind of space. It's great! I want to go in there and sketch, but the gate's padlocked. Could I see those keys Mrs. Hudson gave you? Maybe I can get it open."

His father glanced up. "A gate with a padlock? Really? Sure. Let's get these shelves up, and then we'll go take a look. Here, hold this steady. So, what do you think of that old dinosaur over there?" This time he gestured towards an enormous black furnace that had about a dozen ducts radiating from its top.

"Wow, that's old. It's huge. It looks like a black, hulking spider riveted to the ceiling."

His dad chuckled. He recognized the comic-book lingo, born of his son's passion for drawing and creating adventures about superheroes. "There'll be lots of work to do around this place," he said. "I'd sure appreciate your help."

"No problem." Price glanced around. "Where're *my* tools?"

"Over there. Behind the furnace."

In the shadows, Price could just see one corner of the well-used toolbox—the old-fashioned, homemade variety that had two tent-shaped wooden ends supporting the long piece of heavy dowel that was the handle. It had belonged to his grandfather. Before he had died, two years ago, he'd given his old hand tools to the grandson who had always been his willing and eager assistant.

Price nodded. "Good."

Later, after supper, the two strolled together across the lawn to the hidden gate. The keys, dangling from his father's fingers, jingled softly as they walked.

"Let me try, okay?" Price jumped up onto the lawn chair, while his dad leaned casually against the garage wall.

Price examined each key. Some, of course, were obviously too large or too small or the wrong sort of shape. Only two looked like they might possibly fit the lock. But neither of them worked. Disappointed, the boy compressed his lips and looked appealingly at his father. "It'd be such a cool place to hang out. You wouldn't mind, would you?"

"Of course not. It looks like a great hideout."

"I could build a clubhouse."

"Sure." His dad nodded. "It's out of everyone's way. It'd be a fun place for you and a friend."

Then, taking the key ring, he looked them over himself. He could see at once that none of the keys would work. And he had also noticed the second gate. "It seems that we share this bit of property with our neighbor," he said. "I'll go over tomorrow after work and talk to him about it. It's a bit late for that now. In the meantime, I think you should stay out of there."

Price's face fell. "How come?"

"We haven't met our neighbor yet. And there's no point in needlessly ruffling any feathers, is there?"

It took Price a few seconds to reluctantly agree.

All this time, they were unaware of a big, rust-colored cat watching them from the poplar tree. He was stretched out along the same bough that Price had occupied earlier that afternoon. It made a nice, shady spot this time of day—a spot where a cat might catch a bit of a breeze and take a little nap. The shrewd golden eyes flitted from father to son and back again, almost as though he was following the conversation. And he continued to watch as the two ambled back towards the house. Then the cat shut his golden eyes and lay very still. But he didn't sleep. His tail twitched, first to one side, then the other, back and forth. Suddenly he was on his feet, and seconds later engulfed— the striking orange coat swallowed up in the leafy depths of the giant tree.

Chapter Two:
A Kind of Weed

"Whew!" His mother swiped a hand across the bridge of her nose and stretched out the crick in her neck. She and Price had just spent the morning unpacking boxes and moving furniture. "This is tiring. And dirty."

Dropping cross-legged to the floor, she leaned back on her hands. "Just imagine!" she said. "This is the *very* house your grandmother grew up in. The minute we heard it was for sale, we knew we had to buy it." She looked up at her son and smiled. "Even though I never lived here, the *idea* of it, you know, made it seem like the place where we belong."

Price knew the details, and he agreed.

"Your great-grandfather built that greenhouse in the side yard. Did you know that? And I'll bet he planted that big poplar." Mother flashed him another smile. Then pulling her phone out of her jean's pocket, she slid a finger across the screen. "Hey, it's noon," she said. "How about we take lunch to the park? It's just a couple of blocks from here. There's an outdoor pool where you can cool off."

"Sure," said Price.

Fifteen minutes later, they set out along the tree-lined avenue. Price liked the way the tops of the elms arched together over the road to create a Gothic canopy. He even liked the old, worn sidewalk with its tufts of grass and weeds growing in the cracks.

Nothing is new, he thought. *Around here everything is old and nothing really changes.*

The idea had a certain appeal.

They were just passing the old brick house next door, when they noticed an elderly man in the front yard.

"That, I believe, is Mr. Murphy," said his mother, slowing down.

Their balding neighbor was stooped over, adjusting his garden hose, apparently intensely interested in where to put the lawn sprinkler. He straightened his wiry body and rubbed his chin, eyes darting from one point to another as he studied the layout of his garden.

"I don't know him personally," Mother went on, "but he has the reputation of being a crank." She glanced sidelong at Price and smiled. "But nothing like that ever stopped me before. Maybe we can find out about that bit of 'land' you're interested in, Price." Without a hesitation, she waved and called out cheerily, "Good afternoon, Mr. Murphy."

Price watched with interest from the bottom of the walk. His mother, he knew, was the sort of person who approached strangers like long-lost friends she'd somehow just temporarily forgotten.

The man looked up, squinting. He did not reply or return the smile, but stared at Mother as though she was an unwelcome intrusion. She glanced around quickly. It was obvious that Mr. Murphy was an avid gardener.

"Mr. Murphy, what a beautiful garden!" She gazed about in admiration as she ventured up the walk towards him. "Just look at this hydrangea. And this rose bush! I've *never* been able to grow roses like that." She had reached him by this time. "By the way, I'm your new neighbor, Mrs. Evans," she said, smiling warmly.

Mr. Murphy, who'd been standing rigidly, watching her approach, suddenly relaxed. Price smiled to himself. His mom always had this effect on people. They just naturally seemed to like her. Of course, maybe that was because she just naturally liked people.

"Well now, it is looking pretty good, isn't it?" The old man nodded. "It's true that roses is tricky plants to grow— very finicky." He held up a crooked finger. "First, there's the soil..." Thus began a lengthy exchange, all about mulch, sunlight, and the best method and time to prune. None of it really interested Price. He took his time, moseying up the walk to where the two adults stood chatting.

After a few minutes, he was half-consciously aware that the conversation had turned to prize lilies, which it seemed Mr. Murphy grew in the back garden. He and his mother were like old friends now, and the old man was offering to show them the lilies. Mother, of course, was delighted. So Mr. Murphy took them around the side of his property, which led to a gate at the back of his house, connected to the stone wall next to their own yard.

Mother stopped at the threshold, rooted in silence. She gazed about in awe, while Mr. Murphy stood humbly to one side, his face aglow with modest pride. (Modest pride? That's the pride that comes with an achievement so amazing it simply transcends the creator—a thing apart, utter perfection. That was Mr. Murphy's garden.)

The foreground was a brightly colored collage of paving stones, patches of green lawn, and flowerbeds. An elegant weeping willow set off one corner at the back. Nearby, a fountain mushroomed up, its edges shattering in a shower of glassy drops that filled a small pool. Overflow from the pool tumbled down a collection of flat, mossy rocks, creating a miniature waterfall. The waterfall fed a larger, deeper pool with water lilies blooming on its surface. Large ferns and clusters of purple irises grew nearby in the shade, while luminous orange tiger lilies stretched their over-sized heads up into the sunshine.

Behind the fountain, where there was more sunlight, Price could see a small vegetable garden laid out with absolute geometric precision.

No weed would dare poke its head out of there, he thought. *It would get lopped off for sure.*

The boy stole a glance at Mr. Murphy. He looked pretty much like any other wizened old man, and yet, Price thought he could detect a gleam in his eye that was almost frightening.

At last his mother found her voice. "Mr. Murphy, I am amazed," she exclaimed. "There's nothing I could possibly say that would adequately praise this garden." She regarded the old man with undisguised admiration. The corners of his mouth twitched, as though he was struggling not to smile, and Price had a hunch that Mr. Murphy was not a friendly man at heart.

It was then that he noticed a large ginger cat lying in the shade on the back doorstep. "Hey, you have a cat," he said, pleased.

The old man frowned, and his eyes focused narrowly on the boy, as if he had just noticed him for the first time. "I'd advise you stay away from that cat," said Mr. Murphy. "Oh, he's a mean one all right."

Then he quickly addressed Mother again. "Still, he's a darned good mouser. 'Course, I see to it he gets his due reward. Fact is, I spoil him something terrible." He chuckled. "Keeps him loyal, you know. Ha!" He raised one bushy eyebrow. "I call him ... *Sinbad*," he said, as though it was an explanation. Price wasn't sure of what, but he made no attempt to go near the cat.

Then something else caught his eye. In the shade—directly under the poplar boughs that reached over the stone wall from their yard—stood two wooden garden gnomes. At least, he thought they were gnomes. A second look revealed a couple of weathered pieces of tree trunk that uncannily resembled gnomes. Dwarfs, that is, with domed bald heads and big chunky feet where the roots had been chopped off. Sappy old tree knots formed the droopy eyes, and clinging remnants of bark, the scruffy hair and beards. They had lichen eyebrows and enormous ears and noses, made of broken off branches and fungi. In spite of the vague features, they wore such startled, life-like expressions that they looked as if they were about to speak.

Mother noticed them at the same time. "Oh, aren't these incredible? Mr. Murphy, where on earth did you get them?"

"Well now, that was a bit of luck." The old man drew himself up. "It happens that I *found* 'em." He grinned. "Are you familiar with that bit of property there between our two garages?" he asked, tipping his head in that direction.

"Ye-e-s." Mother glanced at Price who was suddenly all ears.

"Well, the folks before you used to dump their junk in there." The old man clucked his tongue. "You can imagine how glad I was to get *that* mess cleaned up after they moved out." He grunted. "And there they were."

"They were?"

Price took a step towards the dwarfs and crouched down to get a better look.

Mr. Murphy stiffened. "Hey!" he snapped. "Don't you even *think* about touching those!"

At the same time, the orange cat appeared, positioning himself between the dwarfs, guarding his territory. He hissed softly.

Price had never intended to touch them. "I was just—"

"And you'd better not lay as much as a finger on *anything* in this garden, you hear me?"

Price stood up and stepped closer to his mother. He looked at Mr. Murphy and nodded.

"And I didn't clear out all that junk in there just so's some irresponsible kid could go and mess it up again ... you understand?"

Price averted his eyes and said nothing.

"Answer when I speak to you. You understand me, boy?"

"Mr. Murphy!" Mother looked steadily at the old man. But the fierce granite expression set in the old weathered face discouraged even her. She placed a hand on her son's shoulder. "Price is *not* irresponsible," she said evenly. "He wouldn't harm a thing."

The old man snorted. "Kids is all the same."

His mother was silent for a few seconds. Then she said, with icy politeness, "Those lilies, Mr. Murphy. We'd like to see them *now*, if you don't mind."

Mr. Murphy brightened at this proposal and gladly led them on a tour. But he ignored Price, who had no choice but to tag along.

I guess to Mr. Murphy, kids are just a kind of weed, he thought, and wished he was someplace else.

The walk to the park was quiet after that. Later, when they were sitting in the shade eating their lunch, Mother thoughtfully took in her son's somber mood.

She smiled. "Mr. Murphy certainly does live up to his reputation," she said. "Definitely someone whose heart is 'nothing more than a shriveled up pea,'" referring to a children's story that Price had loved when he was younger.

The best he could manage was a sort of lukewarm smile.

"But Price," Mother went on, "I'm sure we can find someplace in the yard where you can build a clubhouse. What about a tree house? That old poplar would be perfect, don't you think?"

Price forced another smile. "Yeah, it would."

"Then it's settled. Only it will have to wait until your dad and I get back from our trip."

Price shrugged. "Sure," he said. But when he thought about the space between the garages, and all its possibilities, he couldn't help feeling sour.

Chapter Three:
Octaruse Pinecone

Cool morning air wafted in through Price's open bedroom window—air that he knew would soon be stifling. Right now, stretched out on his back in bed, it felt like cool, phantom streamers slipping across his bare chest. He shut his eyes, savoring the sensation. No one else was awake yet. But, whatever was in store today, *he* was going to make the best of it. He quickly got up and dressed.

Downstairs, he took a banana from a bowl of fruit on the kitchen counter and went outside. As he crossed the lawn, Price was suddenly aware that he was being watched. Mr. Murphy's big ginger cat was perched loftily on the west wall. "Sinbad" the old man had called him. Well, Sinbad's shrewd eyes were fastened on him now. He reminded Price of a golden idol from an Egyptian tomb—a cat god. He seemed to be studying Price with the same kind of haughty indifference. The boy continued to eat the banana and stared right back.

But soon, left with a useless banana peel dangling from his fingers, he headed toward the old metal garbage cans he'd seen clustered together in the alley. One of them, he remembered, was lidless. Dragging a lawn chair to the spot, he climbed up, and leaning over the wall, dropped the banana peel squarely into the can.

Just at that moment, a German shepherd dog happened to amble by. Price had always wanted a dog, but pets weren't allowed at their condo in Calgary. He made a quick promise to himself to remind his dad that they now had a big yard. He whistled softly under his breath and the dog lumbered over.

"Stay," he said. "I'll be right there." Forgetting Sinbad, he jumped down from the chair, opened the back gate, and hurried into the alley where the dog was waiting.

"Hiya, fella." He stroked the animal's thick fur. "You're up early, too." The dog seemed to enjoy the attention, and the affection. He had that look of quiet joy that happy dogs sometimes have—just soaking it in, as though he had known all along that Price was his friend.

"Are you alone, boy?" It was obvious that the animal was well cared for, but Price noticed that he didn't have a tag, or even a collar. He wondered where he came from. Maybe he belonged to some boy his age, which reminded Price about the friend he was hoping to make. But there was no one in sight.

"I wish you could show me where you live," he said. The dog looked at him steadily. Then, nudging Price with his nose, he turned and began to walk away. He glanced back over his shoulder, as if expecting the boy to follow.

"Price," his mother's voice called through the open kitchen window, "are you outside?"

He looked longingly after the dog. But when his mother called a second time, he knew he had to go.

"Not right now, boy," he said. "But come back later. Okay? Soon." He hurried into the house.

"There you are," said Mother. She was wearing her blue bathrobe and fixing breakfast. She smiled. "We have to wash and vacuum out the car today. I'm going to pick up your grandma around eleven. I'll need you to come help with her bags."

"Sure," said Price. He didn't mind at all. His grandma was one of his favorite people. She would be staying with him while his parents were away on their vacation, planned long before the sudden purchase of their new home.

His mom smiled again. "You're up early. Where've you been?"

"Outside in the yard. There was this German shepherd in the alley."

Her eyebrows went up. "Well, I hope the dog is a more likely prospect than Mr. Murphy's cat!"

"Oh, definitely!" exclaimed the boy, laughing.

Mother placed a platter of scrambled eggs and toast on the table, "Here's breakfast," she said. "Now I've got to run and get dressed." She hurried off.

Later, Grandmother and Mother were sitting at the dining-room table over biscuits and lemonade. Never one to pass up freshly baked currant biscuits Price took a seat and helped himself. He spread thick strawberry jam on a warm biscuit and took a bite.

"Now Beth," Grandmother gently chided her daughter, "don't tell me you plan to head out on the first day of school and start looking for more things to do."

"You know me: a volunteer junkie," Mother joked.

"You'll wear yourself out, and this child will forget who you are."

"I'll do it in the mornings. Anyway, strange advice coming from *you*." She cast her mother a savvy look. "As I recall, unless you're crocheting or knitting, you can hardly sit still long enough to warm a cushion. Now, don't deny it." Grandmother was at that moment knitting a pair of slippers. Her speed and agility were amazing to watch, as though her fingers were motorized and someone had switched them to fast-forward.

"Oh, I'm not as spry as I used to be," she said. "More and more these days I find myself just sitting quietly, thinking about things. I guess it's because there are so many years to look back on ... and fewer to look forward to."

"Now, I'm sure you don't mean that," said the daughter, with her usual kind smile.

His mother, Price thought, could have been a younger clone of Grandmother, except that her eyes were brown, like his and Grandfather's. Grandmother, on the other hand, had the most unusual slanted gray eyes.

Those eyes turned to him now and crinkled into a smile. "Of course, I can look after Price whenever you want."

"Price is almost twelve now," said Mother. "Most of the time, he can take care of himself."

Price grinned. "That's okay, Grandma," he said. "You can look after me anytime you want. I'll take all the attention I can get."

"What was that, Price?" Grandmother was a bit hard-of-hearing.

He turned to face her. "I said you can look after me anytime. You know, my parents, they don't give me enough attention." He flashed his mother a grin, and she laughed.

"That reminds me." Grandmother's unusual eyes lit up. "I have something for you." She set down her knitting and began rummaging through her handbag, which was always hefty and crammed-full of paraphernalia. "Oh dear! I know it's in here somewhere. Ah...." Grandmother extracted a small package wrapped in white tissue. With a flourish, she set it on the table before Price.

"What is it?" he asked.

"Open it up," she said. "It's something I made myself. Kind of a whim."

Curious, Price removed the layers of wrapping. Inside was a strange sight indeed. Price stared at the object for some moments before he could properly respond to his grandmother's hovering expectancy.

It was a toy—a little man.

Grandmother launched into an explanation. "You see this," she said, lifting the shirt and exposing the belly of her creation. "I used one of those big, smooth pinecones for the body—from that spruce in my yard. The arms and legs I made out of twigs. See? Still green. They're attached with wire." She waggled one of the arms.

A polite "Wow" was the best that Price could muster.

"And look at this." She took one of the tiny, white-felt, gloved hands between her thumb and forefinger—amazingly all the fingers and even a miniature thumb were present. "What do you think of that?" she asked.

"Wow!" Price managed, with a bit more enthusiasm this time.

The little man was dressed in a white shirt, red vest, and green trousers, all sewn by hand with the smallest stitches imaginable. There were even a collar and cuffs on the shirt, and tiny pearl doll's buttons down the front. A bright yellow scarf, knit on the finest needles from the finest baby yarn, was coiled loosely around the peg neck. The feet were made from the halves of almond shells, and he could be made to stand up on them quite solidly. The head was a perfectly round wooden ball. A droll little face had been painted on it, with perhaps not the greatest skill, but certainly with considerable flare. And perched at an angle, over a puff of yellow cotton hair, was a tiny, black, woolen cap.

At first Price thought that he would much rather have had a new superhero action figure to add to his collection— this was, after all, dangerously close to owning a doll—but as he studied the strange toy, he changed his mind and decided that he liked it.

"Ha!" he laughed. "Boy, Grandma. What a face! If he could walk and talk, I'd like to see what tricks he'd be up to."

His mother laughed, too. "Now, Mother, are you sure he's not your alter-ego? I seem to detect something very familiar in that cheeky expression." She picked him up for a closer inspection. "He is charming. But you've certainly gone to a lot of trouble." She looked at her mother. "Whatever possessed you?"

"What was that? What possessed me? Oh, I don't know." Grandmother sighed. "Just a fancy, I guess. Perhaps he is my alter-ego, as you say." Her face had a faraway, wistful expression that Price had never seen before. He thought unaccountably of his grandfather. Perhaps Grandmother was missing him more than anyone realized.

"Well, I think he's great," he asserted, taking the toy carefully out of his mother's hand. His Grandmother had obviously put a lot of time and effort into this unusual project. "I'll keep him forever."

"Yes, you do that," said Grandmother. "I certainly had fun making him." She paused. "Wouldn't it be nice, though, if ..." Her voice trailed off and she looked down absently at her hands. Price was puzzled. He glanced at his mother, who was looking intently at Grandmother.

"If what?" Mother asked.

"You see, I made him with such devotion and care. He became almost real to me."

For once, Mother seemed to have nothing to say, and she never took her eyes off Grandmother.

Suddenly, the old woman laughed. "What am I thinking? A pinecone man! What a ridiculous idea."

Price felt relieved, but he noticed that his normally cheerful mom didn't laugh, or even smile.

But he was beginning to feel restless. "I think I'll go outside," he announced, standing.

"Yes," his mother agreed, "that would be a good idea."

In a second, he was heading for the back door.

"Perhaps you can think of a name for the pinecone man," Grandmother called after him. "He hasn't got one."

"Okay." Then he was gone.

Price had thought of taking a spin on his bike to explore a bit, but the afternoon sun was so hot that instead he climbed up to his favorite bough in the poplar tree. He laid the pinecone man across his knees and looked him over. Maybe he *would* try to come up with a name for him.

"Hm ... Nutty, Piney ... Coney, Cloney ... Clooney." He shook his head. "Nope." He decided to shut his eyes and just blurt out the first words that entered his mind. He screwed up his face and took a deep breath. "Octaruse Pinecone!" He opened his eyes and considered this unusual appellation of his creation. He laughed. "Yes! I like it. How about it, little guy? Octaruse Pinecone. I'll call you O.P. for short."

Having settled that, Price looked out across the yard and discovered that he and O.P. were not alone. A large, black squirrel stood upright in the middle of the lawn, watching them. Price thought about the currant biscuits in his mother's kitchen. He wished he could run in and get a morsel or two for the squirrel, but he knew that, if he even moved, the creature would be gone in a flash.

They continued to stare at each other for about a minute. Then the squirrel scampered away in the direction of the garage. Leaning over and pushing aside some of the poplar leaves, Price followed him with his eyes. From where he sat, he could just see the bottom of the gate that separated him from the space between the garages. In the blink of an eye, the squirrel had skittered underneath.

Price envied the animal his freedom. *I can't go in there*, he thought glumly.

Then suddenly, he jerked to attention. To his astonishment, he saw that the gate was slightly ajar. How could that be? And then, from the narrow opening beneath the gate, he saw two small black eyes watching him.

Chapter Four:
What the Note Said

Quickly, Price sidled back along the bough and slid down from the tree. He felt O.P. slip off his knees and land softly on the grass at his feet. Without even looking, he scooped up the toy and stuffed it into his short's pocket—all the while, his eyes never left the gate, just a few feet ahead of him. Then, on an impulse, he dragged a lawn chair to the west wall and climbed up. Cautiously, he peered over into Mr. Murphy's garden. It was deserted—no Mr. Murphy and no cat.

Price jumped down from the chair. *After all, it is half our property*, he reasoned. There was a brief blot on his spirits, when he remembered Mr. Murphy's warning. But he quickly tossed aside the thought. *I have as much right to go in there as he does. I just want to look around and see if the squirrel's still there.*

First, though, he checked out a small pile of debris that he noticed behind the tree trunk, against the stone wall—apparently the remains of a past tree-pruning operation. Price had an eye for things that might come in handy, and had soon extracted a good exploring stick.

With one quick glance behind, he slipped through the gate. In passing, he hastily examined the padlock and found that it was definitely hanging open. *Crazy!* he thought, shaking his head in wonder. He tiptoed down the steps, looking around for the squirrel. There he was, in a corner by the back wall, munching on some seedpods.

Price began poking around with the stick, being careful not to get too close. Then, under some dried leaves, he spotted a scrap of white paper. *Ah*, he thought, pleased to find something that even the fastidious Mr. Murphy had missed. He picked it up. It was a note with the tiniest scrawl: *Come to Riverbend, as soon as possible! Number 12.*

Laying down the stick, he sat on the mossy ground and leaned back against Mr. Murphy's garage. The squirrel had stopped eating and was watching him closely. Price studied the note. The tiny letters looked like a child's printing.

Some kid must have left it here, he thought. *Maybe they were having a scavenger hunt.*

Price felt a slight tug at his heart. *He* would like to go on a scavenger hunt. But he was puzzled. The note wasn't weathered at all. And he was sure that no children had lived in either his or Mr. Murphy's house for many years. And the space was so deep and sheltered; it seemed unlikely that the wind could have blown it in. He shrugged. Obviously there had to be an explanation.

Maybe the old lady we bought the house from had grandchildren, he thought.

Getting to his feet, he stuffed the note into his shorts' pocket. Not the same pocket where he had so absent-mindedly put O.P. a few minutes before, but into the other one: the left-hand pocket.

It was at this moment that a very strange and remarkable thing happened—something so rare that it's almost unheard of.

When Price looked up again, the squirrel had gone. And to his great surprise, he saw the German shepherd dog standing just beyond the corner of their garage watching him. Instinctively, Price reached out a hand and stepped forward into the sunshine.

Suddenly everything was a confusing jumble. The back wall of the space seemed to have disappeared, and then reappeared, and Price was now somehow on the wrong side of it. Had he walked right through it? And where was the alley? More to the point, where on earth *was* he? Frantically, he swung around, trying to locate the space and the gate. He could see the wall plainly enough, buried in the shade of some trees. And he—why ... he was standing at the brink of a great meadow!

But he hardly had time to reflect on this incredible event when he received yet another shock. Of all things, there seemed to be a mouse in his pocket! He could feel it writhing and wriggling around, and could hear it squealing.

"Ach!" cried Price, "Ach!" careening backwards, as if he could back away from it. Frantically he pulled off his shorts, grabbed the bottoms of the legs and shook them out—as far away from his body as he could get. The creature dropped out of the pocket and plopped onto the ground.

Price did a double take. It was not a mouse. He had completely forgotten that in his right-hand pocket, placed by his own hand, was Octaruse Pinecone. And there he lay, flailing about on the grass, moaning.

"Ow, ow, oooo! You didn't have to do *that!*" he wailed. "Oh, my head! You didn't have to put me down so hard! Ow-w-ooo!"

The shock of finding himself not only in this *place* but in this place with this *thing* was too much for Price. He dropped to his knees, staring at the creature.

The little man carried on like that for one or two more minutes. Finally he settled down, most likely tired out. He lay on his back on the grass, panting, his head bobbing up every few seconds to look nervously around.

The dog sidled over and licked Price's ear.

"Oh there you are," said the boy, coming to himself. He reached an arm around the animal's neck and held on.

Suddenly, the little man hopped to his feet, no doubt to get a better perspective on what was around him. Of course, considering he was only about eight inches tall, that perspective was rather limited.

"Where in the world am I?" he said. His voice was thin and high-pitched, like the whine of a fiddle—on the first lesson.

Price blinked and shook his head in disbelief. "You can talk!" he exclaimed, "And move around!"

"What's that? Talk, did you say? Move? Ha, ha! So I can!" He lifted an almond-shell foot and shook it. "Ho! Hee-ha!" He laughed and began to dance around. "Why, this is wonderful! Walking and talking, dancing and singing. Tra-la-la-la. And jumping. See, I can jump! Whee-hee!" He began hopping in a zigzag.

The German shepherd made a sound like a chuckle deep in his throat.

"It's okay, boy," said Price. "He-he's harmless..." After all, his grandmother had made him. Didn't that make it all right?

Until that moment, O.P hadn't noticed the dog. The small wooden body instantly froze. He looked (dare I say it?) like a veritable stick man.

"Aw-w—" the boy said kindly. "Don't be afraid. He's friendly. See. He won't hurt you." To make his point, he affectionately stroked the animal's thick fur coat.

But O.P. was not reassured. His small, painted mouth and painted eyes formed small round painted o's. And he seemed to have lost the power to move (so recently acquired). In a tinny sort of voice, he said, "Please—put me back—in your pocket."

Price laughed. "How about I put you in my shirt pocket?" he said, at the same time remembering that he was still kneeling on the grass in his underwear. "You can stand up in there and look around."

"Is it safe?"

"Absolutely."

Jumping up, he grabbed his shorts and pulled them on. Then he carefully picked up the pinecone man and settled him in the breast pocket of his T-shirt, which happened to be a nice roomy one. Of course, this brought O.P. even closer to the dog. At first he cowered down, deep inside the pocket, but when it was obvious that nothing bad was going to happen, he cautiously poked out his head.

"There. You see?" said the boy. "You're perfectly safe."

The dog emitted one sharp bark of approval.

"Well, now that I know I'm safe, I'd like to know *where* I am." He bent one of his flexible arms and scratched his forehead. "*And* what I'm doing here." O.P., of course, did not have any elbows, or knees either, for that matter. It was lucky that the twigs Grandmother had used to make him were green and pliable, or he would have been as brittle as a raw noodle. "I do seem to remember that I have a ridiculous name." He rolled the round-dot eyes so that they looked like bouncing periods. "Octaruse Pinecone! Can you believe it? Oh, *please*, won't you call me O.P.?"

"Sure," said Price, surprised. "But—how did you know?"

"Know what?"

"Your name."

O.P. looked at the boy as though he had just sprouted grass on his head. "Doesn't everybody know his own name?"

Price thought it would be better not to mention that *he* was the one responsible for the unusual appellation. As long as O.P. wasn't aware of it, it seemed better to keep that to himself.

"Now, as to where we are," said the boy, "that's ... a good question." He looked around in awe. "You see, O.P. That's where we came from: right there." He pointed to the wall, buried in the shadows. "But," he frowned, "I have no idea where we are now."

The little man looked up at him doubtfully. "Well, if you don't know where we are, then who does?"

Price shrugged. "It's too bad you can't talk, boy," he said to the dog. "You could probably tell us what's going on."

Now, Price was someone who did not easily doubt his senses. He knew that something remarkable had happened—was happening, right at that moment. He knew that this something defied logic. But he also had sense enough to realize that it was real, and that, in fact, it might just be the start of something exciting. And whatever it was, he wanted to find out more.

Suddenly the dog pulled away from them. His ears pricked, and he lifted his majestic head into the passing breeze. His nostrils quivered as though he had caught a suspicious scent. It even seemed to Price that a real frown puckered the intelligent canine brow. Without warning, the dog bounded away through the tall grass.

Price and O.P. looked at each other. It seemed they had been left entirely to their own devices.

Chapter Five:
A Riddle

"Well, what d'you know about that?" said O.P. "Gone. And without even a fare-thee-well. Can't say I'm sorry, though. Too big by half, that fella. And hairy! Did you notice he was wearing a fur coat? On a day like this! Hee, hee."

"Aren't you wearing a wool scarf?"

"Nope," responded the little man. "Took it off. Do you think I'm a blockhead? I put it right here—in my pocket."

Price pushed his chin down to get a better look at the small, wooden curiosity. "*Your* pocket?" he said, but decided not to argue the point. He eyed O.P. with interest. "*I'm* big," he said, looking out again over the meadow. "You're not afraid of me, are you?"

"Of course not. *You* don't have fangs."

Price was scanning the place where the dog had disappeared into the tall grass. For just one second, he thought he caught the hint of a shadow (or was it just a ripple?) far off to the right, but it vanished before he was even certain it had been there at all.

O.P. was leaning out of the pocket as far as he dared, trying to get a better look at Price, who was surprised to see that he could rotate his round head a full 180 degrees, like an owl. The painted eyes had become tightly painted slits, as O.P. squinted up into the sunlight.

"Who are you anyway?" he asked. "I don't remember ever seeing you before. Come to think of it, I can't recall seeing *anybody* before." He looked puzzled, but only briefly. "But that doesn't matter. What I want to know is who *are* you?"

Price took O.P. out of his pocket and set him on his palm, so that they could look at each other more comfortably.

"My name is Price Evans. And I live in a house on the other side of that wall." He pointed. "You can see the wall from here. We just moved there, from Calgary to Clareburn, Alberta."

"Ha! Price! What kind of name is that? What are you— some kind of price tag or something? Haw, haw." O.P. was obviously greatly amused by his own wit.

But Price didn't laugh. He'd heard the joke many times before from classmates at school. "It's a family name," he explained patiently. "When my grandmother was a kid, her last name was Price."

"Your *grandmother!* Ha! It's a bad enough name for a boy, but for a *grandmother?*"

"It was her *last* name. Don't you know about first and last names?"

"So," said O.P., ignoring the question—the painted eyes tilted upwards as he studied the sky for a second—"when you think about it, wouldn't that mean that my first name is O. and my last name is P.? Ha, ha, ha!"

Price snickered in spite of himself, but he had other things to think about. "O.P.," he announced, "I'm putting you back in my pocket, so I can take a look around."

"Wanna see me take a look *around?*" O.P. proceeded to do a full rotation of his head on his stump-of-a-twig neck. "There. Now *you* do it. Ha, ha."

Price obliged him with a vague smile, but at that moment he was more interested in finding out where they were and what they were going to do about it. He carefully placed O.P. back into his pocket, and shading his eyes with his hand, looked in all directions.

The meadow stretched out to the front of them as far as he could see. Ripening gold had begun to bleach out the green of early summer, and here and there the landscape was daubed with groves of trees. In fact, the stone wall and his backyard seemed to be somehow connected to (or part of) such a grove. He wasn't sure how far back the trees extended, or if even perhaps the whole countryside began just where he was—like the edge of a page.

To the right, what would have been east if he'd been standing in his own yard, was a much more extensive wooded area. It consumed the entire eastern horizon and disappeared over the rim of—well, what he would have called the Earth, but he wasn't even sure about that. To his left, along the western horizon, ran a range of mountains. Not majestic stone edifices like the Rocky Mountains near his home; these were more like immense wooded hills.

The only other feature of note was a large grassy mound about a hundred yards to the west. It reminded him of the native burial mounds he'd seen on the prairies, only much larger—so large that he thought it must be a natural phenomenon. It was flat on top and tapered down to the bottom, like an overturned laundry basket. There were no signs at all of any man-made structures—no fence posts, no vehicles, no equipment, no buildings of any kind.

"Let's head over to that mound, O.P.," Price said. "We might be able to see more from there."

But instead, he dropped to his knees and began to empty the remaining contents of his right-hand shorts' pocket onto the grass. He tried not to bend too far forward in doing this, realizing that O.P., who was already leaning a little dangerously out of his pocket, might take a tumble.

"Hey!" O.P. frowned impatiently at this delay, but curiosity got the better of him, and soon he was watching with interest.

It was a deep pocket and always contained a few items that Price had collected from gutters or small piles of debris that he happened to come upon. His selective eye was trained to pick out things that might prove useful—which was why his mother always bought him pants and shirts with lots of roomy pockets. Today, there was a length of yellow cord about fifteen inches long, a large rusted bolt with the nut still on it, a big safety pin, the stub of a pencil, and some fishing line that he himself had coiled into a tight little wad.

"So *that's* what I was sitting on!" complained O.P. "No wonder it felt like I was trapped inside a bag of spare parts!"

Price shrugged. "I'm sorry, but I didn't know then, did I?"

"Didn't know what?"

"That you were a real person."

"Didn't know I was real?" The little man was suddenly livid. "Didn't know I was *real?* What did you think I was—a piece of your mind, a page out of a book? How would *you* like it if I said *you* were a mere figment of the imagination—a mirage. Hm?" The painted eyes squinted up at him accusingly. "Maybe even a bad dream! What *are* you doing anyway?"

Price had taken the piece of yellow cord and was tying it to a bush next to the stone wall. "It's a marker. I want to be sure I can get home again," he explained, ignoring O.P.'s little tirade, which he attributed to nothing more than the 'terrible two-minutes.'

"Now, let's get going," he said.

The tall meadow grasses rustled like paper streamers as they brushed against Price's legs. He thought about taking off his shirt and putting it over his head for protection from the sun, but of course, with O.P. tucked in the pocket, he couldn't do that. And, oddly enough, he didn't seem to need to. "You know, O.P.," he said, "It's not nearly as hot now as it was earlier."

O.P. did not reply and was mostly silent as they plodded along. When he finally spoke, it was in a meek voice. "You wouldn't hold it against me, would you?"

"What d'you mean?" asked Price. "What're you talking about?"

"I mean, you are bigger than me, as you say."

Price chuckled. "Actually—I'm considered pretty harmless," he said, remembering his mother's comment to Mr. Murphy.

O.P. looked relieved. A few minutes later, Price noticed that he had disappeared inside the pocket. And he could hear a sound, like someone puffing softly on of one of those wooden train whistles sold in hobby shops. Could it be snoring? Price took a peek. Sure enough, the flexible arms and legs were curled up, the painted mouth had puckered into a small round 'o', and the painted eyes had disappeared altogether. The boy smiled. Maybe there had been just too much excitement for O.P. on this, his very first day of existence. Perhaps he was just a baby after all.

Soon they'd reached the top of the mound. Looking around, Price could see nothing more than what they'd already seen from below. Except that there was a thickly wooded area behind the mound, which hadn't been visible from their original point of view. Also, there was a large, flat rock protruding near the front, right at the top. But there was nothing to shed any light on where they were or what kind of place this was. Price was disappointed.

Nearby, a prairie meadowlark suddenly broke into song. The boy looked around, but the bird was hidden somewhere in the tall grass. Now, in all the world there is no more joyous sound than the lilting warble of a meadowlark. Price held his breath and listened. Over and over, in rippling strands of silver sound, the small, yellow-crested bird trilled its beautiful melody.

Then Price's eyes widened in amazement. He had thought that he was hearing simply the musical tones of the bird call, but suddenly he realized that the tones had words. Words! And the little meadowlark, in his fluent piccolo voice, was repeating the same words over and over. Price shivered from crown to toe as he listened.

> *"For a door to open, first you must knock on it.*
> *Toora-lee, toora, toodle-lee.*
> *To get to the treasure, you first must unlock it.*
> *Tweedle, tweedle-dee, tweedle-lee.*
> *The key to this riddle is deep in his pocket.*
> *Toora, tweedle-lee, toora, tweedle-lee.*
> *Deep in his pocket."*

Price was puzzled, but then he gasped. Of course! The slip of white paper! The note with the tiny writing. He'd put it in his pocket. He'd forgotten all about it. Quickly he snatched it out and read it over several times. Riverbend. But there was no sign of a river anywhere that he could see. Or was there? That long stretch of woods that ran the length of the eastern horizon could be hedging a river. Trees very often grew more thickly along a riverbank. Price shook the little bundle in his pocket.

"O.P.! O.P.! Wake up!"

Chapter Six:
Into the Woods

"Wha-? What is it?" spluttered the pinecone man. Price had pulled open the rim of the pocket and was peering down at him. He looked up at the boy through bleary eyes. "Who are *you?*" he said, straightening his legs and pulling himself to his feet. "Ah yes," it came to him. "Now I remember." Then he shook the slumber out of his round head so vigorously that the line of his mouth reached from one painted ear to the other.

"*Why* did you have to wake me up?" he asked. "I was dreaming about a dear old lady with wrinkles and white hair and..." He stopped. A small painted furrow appeared on his brow. "And really quirky eyes! Her hands were soft as velvet." The painted mouth stretched into a happy smile.

"That was my grandmother," Price explained.

"What?" O.P. was startled, then indignant. "Oh no. I refuse to believe she was any relation of yours."

"She made you," Price said, ignoring the jibe.

"Made me!" O.P. seemed taken aback. In fact, he was apparently so amazed at this unexpected piece of news that he was temporarily at a loss for words.

Price took advantage of the silence. "O.P., there's something I have to show you. About this note..." He produced the scrap of paper. The pinecone man stared at it blankly.

"I forgot about it," Price went on. "But I found it just before we got here. Listen to this: *'Come to Riverbend, as soon as possible! Number 12.'* See those trees on the horizon? I think they might run along a river. I want to check it out."

"What d'you mean, you *forgot* about the note? How could you forget something like that?"

"There was this squirrel, in the space," Price explained. "That's where I found the note. Then when the dog came along, I put it in my pocket and I just forgot ... that's all. Until now."

O.P. shook his head in disgust. "Are you always an absentminded fumble-brain?"

Price smiled and shrugged. "I don't think so." He glanced sidelong at the little man. "Anyway, I have you to help me now."

The small round eyes grew larger, and if possible, slightly rounder. "Well yes. I see your point." He pulled himself up.

"So, what d'you think?" asked Price.

O.P. frowned. "I don't know. It might be dangerous. And what about the squirrel? *And* the dog?" He shuddered. "What happened to them? And that note, you know, could have been left there for *any*body."

"True," Price considered, "I don't really know that the note was meant for me."

O.P.'s frown deepened. "Here, let me see it," he said.

"Can you read?" asked Price in surprise.

"Can I read? What do you *think?*" O.P. reproached him irritably. "Do you think I was born yesterday?"

"No-o," Price smiled. "I don't think you were born *yesterday.*" He handed him the note.

O.P. studied it in earnest. Price had to laugh. He looked so intense—like a miniature old man engrossed in the newspaper.

The little man glared up at him. "What's so funny?"

"Nothing," Price said, putting on a straight face. But then he thought about what O.P. had said. "You know—you could be right about the danger part."

"What! Where's your spirit of adventure?" O.P. sniffed, and then cast the boy an oblique look. "Don't tell me you're afraid."

Price laughed again. "Well, I'm not afraid of dogs with fangs, anyway."

A small, red-painted splotch appeared on each of O.P.'s cheeks.

"Hey!" declared the boy in real amazement. "You can even blush!"

This time O.P. made no response. With great dignity, he folded the note and slipped it into the shirt pocket. Then he said, "For your information, a stick man has a lot to fear from dogs. A dog likes fetching a stick, you know, to the end of trapping it in its jaws ... usually when sporting with some careless boy." He eyed Price suspiciously.

Price realized that this was true. Dogs did chase after sticks. "I never thought of that," he said. "But only if the boy throws the stick first," he added. "Suppose I give you my word of honor that I'll never do that?"

Price was almost sure that he saw a look of relief settle on the painted face. "All right," O.P. agreed with a nod. "I'll trust you on that."

But Price was eager to get going. "Here's what I'm gonna do now, O.P.," he said. "First, I'm going home and I'll tell my mom—hm ... she might not believe the exact truth. Well, I'll tell her something, but not a lie. Then I'll get my bike and some food, and I'm gonna to see if I can find Number 12, Riverbend. You can come with me or not. It's up to you."

"What d'you mean? Of course, I'll come. Do you think I'm a baby?"

Price decided it was better not to comment on that. "I just hope Mr. Murphy isn't there," he said, feeling a sudden prickle of worry. "And I hope we *can* get home. And I hope we can get back here."

"Mr. Murphy?"

"Yes—I'll explain about Mr. Murphy on the way."

About twenty minutes later, thanks to his yellow marker, Price had again located the grove of trees. As soon as he stepped towards the stone wall, the space between the garages conveniently opened to his view. He slipped quietly through the gate and into his backyard. O.P. was still standing upright in his pocket, but to Price's dismay, was once again as stiff and lifeless as a corn shuck. He hurried into the house.

Grandmother had gone up to the spare bedroom and was unpacking her bags. Mother was sitting on the sofa in the living room, checking her list of all the last minute things to be done before she and his dad left the next morning for the airport. She looked up and smiled when Price entered the room.

"Mom, I'm going to take my bike and do a bit of exploring," he said. "I want to check out the river." Like most small towns, Clareburn had evolved around a source of water: A river ran through it.

"All right..." She hesitated. "There's a park there. Riverbend Park." Mother frowned. "You're not thinking about going swimming, are you? You'd better not. The currents in that river are pretty strong."

"No, I won't swim. I just want to explore."

"Fine, then." Mother laughed. "I see you have a pal in your pocket. Be careful not to lose him. Grandmother went to a lot of trouble to make him."

"I'll be careful."

Price dashed off. He got his cap from the hall closet. In the kitchen he put two—no, four—currant biscuits into a plastic bag and filled a water bottle with cold water. These all went into his backpack.

Outside again, he climbed up on the lawn chair and surveyed the neighbor's garden. He suspected Mr. Murphy had gone for the day, maybe leaving the cat inside. He dragged the chair away from the wall and got his bicycle out of the garage.

Once in the space, Price wasn't sure what to do. He could see the stone wall at the back—looking very ordinary and solid. Finally he shut his eyes, took a deep breath, and walked right into it, bicycle and all. It was a great relief when he reopened his eyes to the sight of tall meadow grasses flowing in waves across a sea of gold and green. He was even more relieved to hear a small angry voice emanating from his shirt pocket.

"Now where did *that* come from?" complained the voice. "One minute we're going to *get* the bike and the next thing it just appears out of nowhere. What kind of tricks are you up to anyway?"

Not knowing what to say, Price pointed the bicycle due east and started to mount.

"Hey! Wait a minute. What about the food? You *said* you were going to get us something to eat."

Price sighed. He knew that an explanation was inevitable. "O.P., I hate to tell you this—" He took the little man out of his pocket and set him gently on his palm. "But we've already been home and come back again."

O.P. opened his mouth to protest, but Price motioned him to silence. "We were gone about fifteen minutes. I-I don't know how to say this, but when we got there, you … you became nothing more than a lifeless toy, just like when Grandma first made you."

The little man stared at him, not seeming to understand. Then he vehemently shook his round head. "I don't believe you!" he retorted.

"Sorry, but it's true. It's only when we come here, through that … that wall and into whatever this place is that you come to life."

O.P. blinked his round dot eyes a couple of times but said nothing.

"Listen, if it makes you feel any better, I don't understand it either."

Carefully Price put him back into his pocket. "Well, here goes," he said, and they set off across the meadow.

It was tough going, pedaling through all that grass, but Price knew it would be quicker than hiking. And the bicycle tires left a convenient line in their wake as they parted the grasses, like the tail of a comb running through a thick brush of green hair. It would help him find his way home.

O.P. was silent and Price felt sorry for him. After all, the little guy had only been alive for about an hour and had had a lot to take in.

At last a small voice said, "You could have left me behind, you know. You didn't have to bring me back. Why did you?"

"Sure I had to bring you back. You have as much right to live as anyone. And besides, I like your company."

"Really? You like me? But, I thought…"

Price glanced down and was surprised to see what he thought was an infinitesimal tear, the size of a pin tip, glistening on his cheek.

"I-I'm glad you like me," continued the pinecone man in the same small voice. "I'm sorry I've been so cheeky. I can't seem to help myself."

Price wasn't sure how to respond to this humble gesture. Finally, he said, "That's okay. Besides, I like your cheeky ways."

O.P. was pleased. His mouth stretched into a happy smile. He sniffled and wiped away the tear with his sleeve.

They had come to a slope, and as they bounced along, began to gain speed rapidly. "Hey! Slow down!" O.P. complained loudly, apparently quite himself again, "I feel like I'm in a b-b-blender!"

Then they heard a sharp bark. It was the German shepherd, running alongside them about twenty yards to the left. Price smiled and waved. The dog barked twice again, before veering even more to the left. Price angled his bicycle and followed, and rather than slowing down, they went even faster.

"Whoa! Whoa!" shouted O.P., but Price paid no attention.

It wasn't long before they reached the wood. Price braked and dismounted. He leaned his bike against a tree trunk, and out of habit, got out his chain and locked it up. The dog had vanished. As suddenly as he had appeared, he'd disappeared, and neither Price nor O.P. could see any sign of him.

An exasperated O.P. clutched the cap on his head with both hands. "How could you just blithely follow that dog— without even knowing if he's friend or foe? Now do you see what's happened? The cunning beast has deserted us again. For all we know, he may have been leading us into a trap."

"A trap? What for?"

"What for! Why ... well ... I don't know. But I think you're far too trusting."

"I do trust him," the boy stated. "I think he's looking out for us. You worry too much."

The river was not visible from where they stood, but they could hear the distant babble of water from the other side of a dense screen of trees and bushes.

"I guess the next thing is to get to the river and look for a bend. Hey, are you hungry?" Price began rummaging through his backpack and pulled out the bag of currant biscuits. He took out two, broke off a morsel, and made to hand it to O.P. Then he hesitated. "Do y—" He was about to say 'Do you eat?' but the venomous look shot at him made the question irrelevant. He handed the piece of biscuit to the pinecone man. He'd made sure that it contained a couple of juicy currants. Then he began to munch on the remainder.

"Say, this is pretty good." The food cheered the little man considerably. "Especially these prunes."

Price laughed. "Those aren't prunes, O.P. They're currants."

"Don't be ridiculous," the little man retorted. "Everybody knows that currants are very small. Mm. Delicious."

They had just devoured the last bit and enjoyed a generous swig of water—O.P. drank his from the bottle cap—when Price looked up sharply.

"Listen O.P. Did you hear that?" He pointed to some dense brush just ahead of them.

O.P. was licking his white-felt fingertips. Price was amazed to see that he had a small pink tongue. He quickly decided not to mention it. After all, everybody has a tongue, don't they?

"Nope. Can't say as I did. You must be hearing things. Now, let me tell *you* about something. It's called a 'breeze.'

Sometimes it blows through leaves and grass and makes a noise. Hee, hee."

But Price wasn't listening. He'd moved closer to the source of the sound and was staring intently into the bush. Everything was still and quiet. But then, just for an instant, deep in the underbrush, he was almost certain that he saw a flash of orange. He strained his eyes and ears, but everything was silent and unmoving and green once more.

He had just decided to go and investigate when he was startled by another sound. This time there was no mistaking it. It came from the direction of the river and could be heard plainly over of the babble of water. It was the sound of someone sobbing.

Chapter Seven:
A Pouch is Retrieved

"D'you hear that, O.P.? Someone's crying."

"*Do I hear—? * My ears may be flat as egg shells, but they *can* hear."

Price smiled and shook his head. "Just stating the obvious," he said.

Then, facing the river, he walked up and down the line of dense brush and trees several times, looking for an entry. Finally, he discovered the start of a narrow trail hidden under some groundcover. They set off immediately.

The path led down a gentle grade through a thick wood of aspen and evergreen. The closer they got to the river, the larger the pines grew, casting such a deep shade on the forest floor that the underbrush began to thin out. Soon they caught glimpses of sunlight dancing on water, and finally they could see the river itself—at this distance hardly more than an over-sized stream.

Then they spotted a small figure. Sitting on a large, flat rock near the bank, completely surrounded by water, was a girl. Although she sat facing them, her knees were drawn up and her head was buried in her arms. She was crying openly, unaware that she was being watched. With each fresh sob, her small shoulders heaved. Price and O.P.

approached slowly, but the girl, apparently, was so absorbed in her misery that she was beyond noticing them. Soon they were near enough to see that she wore a silky white dress, cinched at the waist with a silver cord, and that she had silver shoes on her feet.

It's a little kid, thought Price. *And she's dressed for a party.*

By now they were so close that they didn't dare go any farther.

Price felt awkward standing there watching a stranger cry. He had just made up his mind to say something when the girl raised her head. She saw him at once. In the same instant, she stopped crying and jumped to her feet.

Price was astonished to see that she wasn't a young child after all. She was older, but her face and features were so small... He was baffled.

There was one suspended moment of silence when no one moved or spoke, and time seemed to have stalled. Then there was a sudden sharp billowing sound, like the thwack of a sail being flung open to a stiff breeze. Price stared, absolutely stupefied, for the girl had just unfurled a set of beautiful transparent wings. For about three seconds, she held them poised, like a flower with four large glistening petals. Then the wings began to vibrate so rapidly that they made a silvery-blue mist behind her back. Price could hear them hum, and could feel a faint draft blowing against his face as the wings lifted her gently into the air. Like a bubble, she floated up before their eyes.

Price was so astonished that his knees buckled under him, and he found himself sitting squarely on the turf.

"Hey!" complained O.P., holding onto his head. Then his eyes widened. "By gosh, it's a fairy!" he said. "I've always wanted to see one. Ha! How do you do, Miss Fairy, whatever-your-name is?"

A fairy? But there were no such things as fairies.

The fairy had not noticed O.P. until he spoke. She drifted in a bit closer to get a better look, staring openly, as if she couldn't quite believe her eyes.

"My name is Winifred," she said, looking down on the pinecone man. "Winifred Fairchild. But usually I am called Freddy." Her voice was soft and sweet.

"How do you do, Freddy? My name is, uh, O.P.—I won't tell you what that's short for. And this person—who apparently doesn't believe in fairies—" he eyed Price doubtfully, "is Price."

Freddy's attention diverted back to the boy, still sitting on the ground, gaping. Suddenly feeling embarrassed, he stood up awkwardly. The fairy floated down and faced him, her feet about a foot off the ground. But she kept at arm's length and could have flitted away in an instant if she had wanted to. She looked fully into his eyes, and rather shyly, Price gazed back into hers.

She had a perfectly oval face, framed with golden curls. Her lips and nose and brow were very fine and small. But by far, her most striking feature was a pair of large, slanted gray eyes. This startled Price—they were so much like eyes that he already knew. Only, these eyes were not old; they were young and fair. It was impossible to guess what age the fairy might be. She was tiny—hardly more than three feet tall—and very slender, but she looked as though she could be about his age. But then this was his first encounter with a fairy. For all he knew, she was as old as time.

"You don't believe in fairies?" she asked, her unusual eyes wide with wonder.

Price blushed. "Well, I've never met one before." But when he looked again into those large unearthly eyes, so strikingly familiar, he wondered.

"I am a fairy," she explained. "But who are you?"

Price cleared his throat. "M-my name is Price Evans."

She frowned, as if this was not an acceptable answer. "But ... *what* are you?" she asked.

"What do you mean?" He shrugged. "I-I'm a boy."

Freddy gasped, and for a second, her remarkable aerial suspension faltered, as though she had lost her balance. "A boy!" she exclaimed. "But what are you doing *here?*"

"Well—I'm not sure," confessed Price, looking around. "Just where is here?"

"Why, this is the Land of Tolk, of course."

"Th-the Land of Tolk? Is that where I am?"

"Didn't you know?"

"No. No, I don't know anything about it."

"Then how did you get here?"

"Well, there was this squirrel and a German shepherd dog. And—"

"You mean King Noble?"

"Who?"

"King Noble. The dog. He is the king of Tolk. *He* brought you here?" Like a speck of dust caught in a sunbeam, Freddy drifted down and touched lightly to the ground. Her wings suddenly became still and folded on her back, much like a moth's. Price was surprised at how compact they had become.

"I-I guess so."

"This is incredible!" exclaimed the fairy. "No one from the outside world *ever* comes to Tolk."

Price was beginning to gather his wits. The shock of meeting the fairy was quickly being replaced by a burning curiosity.

"I've never heard of this place. What is the Land of Tolk? Where is it ... where are we?"

The fairy gave him a measuring look. "We?" she asked. "Yes, I was wondering about that."

She frowned, and leaning forward, brought her face up to O.P. She studied him with interest. "What a strange looking creature you are." The little man reddened, but was obviously pleased to be the beautiful fairy's focus of attention.

"You mustn't mind the boy," he declared grandly. "After all, he's just a kid. Hee, hee." Then he spoke sternly to Price. "I can't believe you don't know about the Land of Tolk. Why, everybody knows about Tolk."

"Do *you*?" asked the fairy, surprised. "I've never seen you here before." Then she giggled, "If I had, I would certainly remember." Her laughter was enchanting, like the sound that bluebells swaying in a breeze might make, if they weren't mute.

"Yes, that's true." The little man removed his cap and scratched his head. "And I didn't know it myself until I heard the name. Then all of a sudden it came to me, like remembering a dream the morning after."

"But O.P., how could you possibly know about this ... place?" Price was beginning to feel exasperated. "Just an hour ago you were nothing but a lifeless toy that my grandmother made. You've never even been here before."

"I *have* heard of such things," the fairy mused. "It's *very* rare, but it has been known to happen. Someone from your world makes something out of materials found in nature. And, if the creator imbues it with a personality of its own, it can come to life here. It takes on the same identity." Her voice was as soft as raindrops sifting down on a glassy pool. "There is a small marble pony, I've heard, that lives amongst the elves."

Price shook himself. What was this girl talking about? He wanted to sit down again, so he did. At this, the fairy daintily lifted the hem of her dress and set herself upon a mossy rock.

"But such things are very rare," she went on, crossing her legs. "Almost unheard of."

"Elves? I don't know what you're talking about." Price looked away and shivered.

"Well, you see," the fairy went on, "even though Tolk is almost completely unknown to the outside world, we are connected."

"What d'you mean 'connected?' You mean, like how I got here?"

"I don't know about that. But if the Earth had a mind and a soul, then you might think of Tolk as part of its unconscious. You might say ... veiled."

"I don't get it," Price felt completely adrift. "If we don't know anything about Tolk, then how come you seem to know about us?"

The fairy ignored Price's question. She looked directly at O.P. and seemed puzzled. "And it doesn't explain how *you* know about Tolk. After all, you couldn't know anything that your creator didn't already know herself."

"Boy, now you've really lost me," said Price. "How could my grandmother possibly know anything about ... this place?"

Freddy blinked her large eyes twice. "How did you come to meet King Noble?"

"Don't you ever answer a question when you're asked?" Price was annoyed.

The fairy looked surprised. But then she laughed again—that light, tinkling laugh—and the boy's irritation promptly melted away. "I'm not used to answering questions," she said. "We fairies generally keep to ourselves. But I hardly know anything about your world." She studied

Price for a couple of seconds. "I've heard that humans can be mean and wicked, but Tolk is always peaceful. We don't *want* our existence known amongst humans."

The fairy suddenly bit her lower lip. "Oh—" She stood up abruptly, glancing around, as if afraid she might have said too much. Her wings opened again, but quietly this time. She did not fly away, but the wings fluttered, as a butterfly's do when it lights upon a blossom.

Price couldn't take his eyes off Freddy's face, now pinched with worry. No one spoke for several seconds, until O.P. broke the silence.

"Uh, Miss Freddy—Miss Fairy-lady, I have a question."

The fairy glanced at the pinecone man. She didn't say anything, but her look implied, 'You may ask, but don't necessarily expect a reply.'

"Could you take me for a ride? A fly, I mean? I've always wanted to."

Her face brightened. "Why yes, I ... Oh." Again the smile collapsed, as though she had just remembered something tragic. "I-I can't. Something has happened."

"What is it?" asked Price. "And why were you crying just now?

Fresh tears welled up in the fairy's eyes, and Price almost regretted his question. "You see," she said, pointing, "I've dropped my little pouch in the river."

"Your pouch? What's that?"

"It's a small bag that I wove myself—out of spider silk. It holds a beautiful jeweled comb that I was taking to Laefay. She was going to wear it in her hair tonight at the Bower. She will be so disappointed, and so will Elaine. It was Elaine who asked me to take it to her." She struggled to hold back the tears.

"Is that all?" Price was relieved. "The way you were carrying on, I thought you'd lost your mother or something."

The fairy looked at him in surprise. "But, of course, I don't have a mother," she said.

"Oh. I-I'm sorry," said Price, wishing he could take back his words. "I didn't know."

"What didn't you know?" She looked at him again with those wide, wondering eyes.

Price shook himself. Fairies certainly were confusing people. "Never mind," he said. "Show me where you dropped your pouch. Maybe I can get it for you."

Freddy looked him over doubtfully. "Do you really think you can?"

"Maybe."

"Well. Then boys must be more clever than they look," she said.

The wings opened and began to flutter rapidly, and the fairy lifted off and drifted towards the stream.

"Follow me," she called. Soon she was hovering over the water, near the large rock where they'd first seen her. "Here," she said, pointing down.

Price sloughed off his sneakers and waded out to the rock. He climbed up and peered over the far side. There, at the bottom of the stream, in a small recessed pool, he could plainly see a drawstring bag under the clear water, apparently made of the same silvery fabric as Freddy's dress. And it was definitely out of reach.

"I could dive for it," he said, looking up at Freddy. "But I promised my mom I wouldn't swim in the river."

"Can you swim then?" she asked in surprise.

"Sure. Can't you?"

O.P. groaned. "You'll have to forgive this ignorant human boy, Freddy." He shook his head sadly. "Honestly, Price, what is that *thing* attached to your neck? Is that a head? You really should use it. Don't you see that Freddy has *wings?* Fairies can't swim in water. They don't even like to go out in the rain."

Price looked questioningly at the fairy.

"Oh yes, it's true." She nodded and her face was grave. "I couldn't fly if my wings were wet. It's the one thing that I fear."

Price thought about that. "I don't think I'd want to fly, if it meant I couldn't swim." Then he shrugged and smiled up at the fairy. "But I guess it doesn't matter, because I can't fly anyway." Freddy laughed her sparkling little laugh.

Sitting down, Price sidled over to one side of the rock, leaving a flat area exposed. Onto this surface, and for the second time that day, he emptied the contents of his right-hand shorts pocket. He took the fishing line and tied one end of it securely to the rusty bolt that still had the nut on it. This was to be the weight. He left about ten inches of line dangling from the knot. Then he opened the large safety pin and bent the tip to give it more of a curved point. This was to be the hook. He attached it to the short, leftover end of the fishing line. He turned to Freddy and grinned.

"It's ready," he said.

"What is it?" she asked, her face bright with curiosity.

"Watch this."

Price tossed the device several times into the pool, until at last the safety pin caught on the pouch. He pulled it out of the water, dripping wet. "Tada!" he exclaimed in triumph.

Joyfully, Freddy clapped her hands, and her happy laughter rang through the air like the music of a wind chime.

"How's that for using my head, hey O.P.?"

For once, O.P. was speechless. Then he let out a whoop. "Whoo-hooo! I guess that head of yours is good for something after all!"

Price carefully detached the silken bag from the safety pin and stuffed his wet 'gear' back into his pocket. He handed the pouch to Freddy, and still suspended in the air, she fastened it to her sash.

"Thank you, Price," she said. It was the first time the fairy had called him by name. For some reason, it made Price feel special.

Chapter Eight:
Giants, Goblins, and Bears

Price waded back to the bank, and sitting down on the mossy ground, picked up a sneaker and began putting it on a wet foot. Freddy fluttered down and sat beside him.

"What is it like where you live?" she asked.

"Where I live? Well ... in the country, it's like here. But in town, there are lots of houses and stores." He glanced up from tying his shoelace to see if she understood. "Buildings, you know?"

Freddy nodded eagerly. "The giants live in houses. They make them out of tree branches, latched together." She said this by way of explanation, so that Price would know she had caught his meaning, but his fingers immediately stopped in the middle of tying the bow.

"Giants?"

Freddy nodded.

Price was silent for a few seconds. Then he asked, a bit too carelessly, "Where do the giants live?"

"In Drumbleton," she replied. "It's quite far from here. But, of course, giants travel very quickly. They take such long strides."

Price's fingers still hadn't moved. "Just how big *are* these giants?" he asked.

Freddy looked Price up and down. "Much bigger than you. I'd say at least four times your size."

Price quickly turned his attention to the other foot. "Are they dangerous?" He tried to focus on his sneaker.

Freddy laughed and so did O.P. "Dangerous?" he chortled. "Are sofa cushions dangerous? Is a sack of potatoes dangerous? Hee, hee, hee. Only if one accidentally falls on you. Ha, ha!"

"I don't know what you mean," Freddy said. "Giants are very dull, though they're harmless enough. The head giant's name is Bran. But I don't care about giants. I want to hear about where you live."

Price wasn't sure what to tell her, and he was having difficulty directing his thoughts away from giants. "Well ... uh ... we have things like cars, TV, smart phones, and computers. I go to school most of the year, but right now I'm on summer vacation."

Freddy frowned and shook her head. "Now you are talking gibberish."

Price had finished with his shoes. He sat up straight and looked at the fairy. Apparently she didn't know about any of these things. But he was at a loss as to how to explain them.

Freddy's eyes suddenly grew dark with mystery. She brought her face close to his. "Do you know anyone *bad?*" she asked quietly.

Price gave her a blank look. What kind of question was that?

"You must have a pretty low opinion of humans," he said. "Actually, most of the people I know are pretty decent." He thought about his last year's science teacher. "Like Mr. Bunnage," he said. "He took a group of us kids, those of us who weren't much into sports, and on his own time helped us build a racing car." He smiled, pleased at the recollection. "I like Mr. Bunnage." The smile faded. "But then there *was* Leroy."

"Who's Leroy?" Freddy and O.P. chimed in unison—an odd duet, dry reed and fairy bell sounding together.

"Leroy? A very big guy ... and mean. He used to steal kids' lunch money. We all knew about it, but nobody ever said anything, because we were afraid of him."

"What happened to him?" asked Freddy.

Price shrugged. "Not much. Mrs. Kubas, our principal, found out that he had no dad and his mom was hardly ever home. So now he lives with his uncle."

"Oh." Freddy seemed disappointed. And she looked puzzled. "When I'm hungry, I eat blueberries or watercress. Don't you have any where you live? What do boys eat, anyway?"

But Price wasn't listening; he was deep in thought. "You're right," he said after a moment. "Where I come from, there *are* people who do bad things. But I've been lucky, and I don't think much about them. Isn't there anyone like that here in Tolk?"

"Oh no," replied Freddy. "No one here is ever really bad, or really very good either ... or so I've been told. Except for King Noble. I believe that he is very good."

"Really? Then this must be a nice place to live."

Freddy brightened. "Yes, it is." But then her face fell. She glanced around furtively. "But lately," she said, "something strange has been happening."

She leaned closer to Price, so close that he could feel fairy breath against his cheek. She spoke in a whisper, but articulated her words carefully. "I've heard rumors that there are some who have been holding secret meetings at night."

"Really?" asked Price. "Is that bad?"

"No," said Freddy, sitting back again, "but it's very unusual." She shivered.

"Who else lives in Tolk?"

"Oh, there are the other fairies, of course, and the dwarfs and the elves and the beautiful Peri dancers, who come down out of the sky at night. They are fairies as well. And there are all the small animals and birds. The only big people here are the giants and the bears."

"Bears?" Price didn't like the sound of that.

Freddy laughed. "What's the matter? Are you afraid of bears, too?" she asked. "I've never heard of anything so foolish."

"Hee, hee." O.P.'s reedy laugh echoed Freddy's. "Imagine being afraid of a roly-poly bear. Hoo, hoo!"

Price scowled. He decided not to remind O.P. about his fear of dogs with fangs. "The bears where I come from are wild," he said. "They could even kill you."

"Oh well, then you are fortunate to be here!" Freddy exclaimed. "To begin with, the bears here are friendly. In fact, they can be a lot of fun. Moreover, there is no death in Tolk. We are all immortal, and ..." she straightened her small shoulders, preparing for the grand pronouncement, "as long as you stay here, you are too!"

Price didn't know what to say. Immortality? He'd never given it a thought. On Earth, of course, death was inevitable, but it seemed like something such a long way off that he'd never really considered it. But then he thought of his grandfather. If *he* had come to Tolk, he would still be alive, right this minute. Price felt a sudden throb of grief and found himself missing his grandpa. Whenever Grandma spoke of him now, it was as though he *was* still alive—not in the same room, exactly, but somewhere nearby, so that Price had begun to see it that way too. It was all very confusing.

He shook his head, dismissing the sad feelings. "I don't really think about dying," he said.

Freddy seemed deflated, as though she had offered him a piece of gold and he had turned it down point blank, not even recognizing it for what it was.

But O.P. was impressed. "Live forever? Ho, ho! Now I could get used to that! Think of all the mischief I could cause in an eternity. Ah ... the possibilities. But enough of this heavy talk. What about that 'fly?'" He folded his arms and the painted mouth actually formed a pout. "You as much as promised, you know."

"Oh!" said Freddy. "I'd forgotten. Come then. We can go at once."

She lifted him out of Price's pocket, and after a few seconds of deliberation, tucked him into the sash at her waist. His arms waggled out at the top, and his feet dangled down from the bottom.

"There now. Are you snug?"

"Oh yes," he replied, rubbing his hands together in anticipation.

"Then here we go." Even before she had finished speaking, the wings had unfurled. They fluttered briefly, then vibrating rapidly, began to hum. Rising straight up into the air, they were soon well above the trees, looking tiny. Free from obstructions, the fairy flew off on a horizontal path, like a hummingbird, and soon they were out of sight. Price couldn't help feeling a bit envious. Freddy would never be able to give him a ride like that.

Left with some time to himself, Price picked up a stick and began to absently draw in the dirt on the path. Then, recalling how he'd poked around with a stick earlier that day, he reached into his shirt pocket where O.P. had left the small piece of paper. He pulled it out and stepped closer to the stream, scanning the bank. *Riverbend*. Well, the river did curve to the right just ahead there. When Freddy and O.P. came back, they could explore. Maybe Freddy already knew where Riverbend was.

As he stood there, plotting their next move, Price suddenly caught sight of the upright tail of an animal, maneuvering towards him through some ferny undergrowth. He couldn't see the body attached to it, but the tail was orange. He slipped the note into his shorts' pocket, just as the animal emerged from behind a juniper bush. To Price's great surprise, it was Mr. Murphy's cat, Sinbad. Their eyes met at once.

Sinbad visibly started and actually froze with one foot poised, ready to take a step. Then slowly he lowered the paw and ambled over to Price. He sat down directly in front of him.

"So, he brought you here, did he?" His voice was like chalk on slate, soft and raspy. "Now, why would he do *that*, do you think?"

Sinbad began licking a paw. He had asked the question as if he himself already knew the answer, but wanted to learn if Price did—the way your mother asks who ate all the chocolate chip granola bars, when all the time she knows it was you. Price did not reply.

"So … that's the way it is then," the cat continued, between licks. "I suppose … hm. But perhaps not."

Now, Price had been unable to answer, not because of what Sinbad had said but because he had *said* anything at all. In spite of all the other remarkable events of the day, Price was still dumbfounded at hearing a cat speak—especially Mr. Murphy's cat.

Sinbad stood up and stretched. Slowly, he circled the boy. "I saw you with him this morning. I wondered what he was doing there ... in death's domain."

"Y-you mean King Noble?" asked Price, finding his voice.

The cat stopped in his tracks. "Oh, so then you *do* know."

"Know what? What do I know?" There was a nervous edge to Price's voice that he immediately regretted. He didn't trust Sinbad. And he wasn't about to expose his ignorance.

The animal narrowed his golden eyes, as if to probe the boy's thoughts. "Why, you know King Noble, of course. You know about this place?" He looked around.

"Of course, I know. Th-this is the Land of Tolk."

The cat went silent. His tail twitched slightly, in irritation. "Then he *has* spoken to you!"

"No. No, he hasn't," the boy answered truthfully.

Sinbad hissed. "You're lying!" he said. "Besides, what does he think *you* can do? There is absolutely *nothing* you can do about it."

Price, of course, had no idea what he was talking about, so he made no response.

The cat began to pace. "Unless you want to make some kind of ... uh ... an arrangement, you know, between you and me."

Price swallowed. "But what ...? I don't ..." His eyes flickered uncertainly.

The cat watched him closely. "No. I suppose not," he muttered. Then he sat down again, and with his tongue, began to preen his mane. He glanced up. "You *do* realize that this is a dangerous place. I'll wager he didn't warn you about that. This is wild country! There are bears with teeth and claws like daggers and wild men as tall as trees." The cat jumped to his feet. "Not to mention the goblins. Wicked creatures those! Tear out your heart as quick as say good morning—no questions asked. Did ... uh ... King Noble—as he calls himself—did he happen to mention any of this?"

"No," answered Price, who had (of course) never actually had a conversation with the dog.

"Then you admit it!"

"Admit what?"

Sinbad snorted. "Then he *has* spoken to you. Well, if you want *my* opinion, I think he intends to *use* you ... use you for his own purposes, simply to appease those *wicked* goblins. Then he'll eat you. Yes, that's what *I* think." The cat eyed him levelly. "What do *you* think?"

"But, I ..." Suddenly Price wasn't sure what to think. *Vicious bears? Wicked goblins? Wild men as tall as trees?* Freddy had said that the giants and bears were harmless.

But there was one thing Price did know: He knew that he didn't like this cat. He laughed disdainfully. "Sinbad," he said, "you're really not a good liar."

The creature spat in anger and flattened himself against the ground, ready to spring. Price was startled, but then remembered that he was still holding the stick. He pushed the point firmly into the earth, squarely between him and Sinbad and leaned down on it, glaring at the animal. The cat's tail whisked angrily from side to side. But then, all at once, he relaxed and rose serenely to his feet.

"I see," he said. "So, this is how it's going to be." Taking his time, he stretched out his feline spine. Then, turning his back on Price, and without any hint of concern or hurry, he began to walk away. Just before he disappeared into the bush, he glanced back. He grinned. "Don't say I didn't warn you."

Price watched the orange tail wend its way through the greenery until he was gone.

Chapter Nine:
A Mouse House
and Acorn Loaf

Price was baffled. Without a doubt, that was the strangest conversation he'd had all day. Even O.P. and Freddy made more sense. But he had little time to think about it. A pinecone suddenly came hurtling through the air and hit him on the head. Annoyed, he shook out his hair, even though the pinecone had already bounced onto the moss at his feet. Then a second pinecone hit his shoulder. He looked up. High above, trying not to laugh, Freddy and O.P. were sitting on a bough of an enormous evergreen. When they realized he'd seen them, they waved and laughed outright.

Price shook a fist at them in mock threat. "Okay, you guys, come down here!"

"All right," called Freddy and stood up.

Balancing effortlessly on her toes, the fairy bent her knees and sprang lightly into the air. O.P. moaned and covered his eyes. Just at that instant, when they hung suspended between rising and falling, the wings fluttered open and they floated gently to the ground. The fairy landed daintily on the points of her silver shoes.

"There," she exclaimed brightly. "Wasn't that fun, O.P.?"

"Oh, sure." The pinecone man's reedy voice was trembling. "Great fun, if you don't mind having nothing between you and solid ground but a thin piece of gauze and a hundred yards of invisible gaseous matter. It was those moments when we were hanging in mid-air *without* wings that really got me. I thought I was going to 'drop dead,' if you know what I mean."

Freddy laughed. "O.P., surely you know that fairies must be careful when flying around trees. What if my wings got caught in some branches? Think what might have happened. You are such a nut!"

"*Nut?* Who're you calling a nut?"

Again Freddy laughed her music-box laugh. She released the little man from her sash and carefully put him back into Price's shirt pocket.

"Well, aren't you?" she said, bringing her face close to his and shaking her golden curls at him. "Just look." She poked the pinecone stomach with a small, slender finger. "Anyway, remember? You can't 'drop dead' in Tolk."

"Maybe not, but all the same, I *would* like to stay in one piece."

Freddy's smile suddenly vanished, and she looked up at Price. "What did the cat want?" she asked.

"You saw him?" Price shrugged. "Mostly he wanted to know why I'm here. But *I'd* like to know what *he's* doing here. I thought he belonged to my next-door-neighbor, Mr. Murphy."

Freddy's eyes widened in surprise. "Oh no. He lives right in Tolk. At one time he used to wait upon King Noble. But..." She reflected a couple of seconds. "I haven't seen them together for quite a while. But then, fairies generally keep to themselves. What did you say to him?"

"I didn't tell him a thing. I don't like him." Price frowned. "Is that possible, Freddy? Is it possible that he lives in both places? I mean, in my world and here, too?"

Freddy gave this some thought. "Perhaps..." she said. "In a way, we Tolks can leave any time we want. There are places, portals, where we can get in and out of Tolk. King Noble knows where all of these portals are. But of course, no one ever really wants to leave. And I've heard that getting back is not as easy as you might think."

She paused again, thinking. "Except, there was someone once... Rumor has it that many years ago, a fairy *did* leave Tolk. They say that she was unhappy." The fairy looked genuinely puzzled. "How could anyone *not* be happy in the Land of Tolk? I am *always* happy." To prove it, she smiled. "But that was before my time, and I don't know whether it's true or just a story."

"You weren't happy when you lost your pouch," O.P. reminded her.

"That's true," said the fairy. "I'd forgotten that. But everyone was counting on me. And it's such a nice pouch." She glanced down at the object and patted it affectionately.

Price wasn't interested in Freddy's pouch. "What do you mean it's not as easy as you think to get back into Tolk?"

"It took me six days to collect all that spider silk," Freddy went on. "That's very tricky business."

"Freddy," Price insisted, "what do you mean it might not be easy to get back into Tolk?"

"Oh—I don't really know," said the fairy. "I think that maybe you forget the way, or change your mind. I couldn't say. I've only heard tales. I'll tell you one thing though, that cat was right to wonder why you're here. Strangers *never* come to Tolk. Each of the gateways is a carefully guarded secret. There are very few Tolks who even know where they are—or care, for that matter." She began doing a little skipping dance on her toes.

Price was mystified. Portals, fairies, Mr. Murphy's cat … talking! It was all so confusing. He shook his head to clear out the cobwebs.

Then for the third time that day, he remembered the note. "Freddy," he said, pulling the now crumpled paper out of his pocket. "Do you know where Riverbend is? Number 12, Riverbend?"

"Riverbend?" The girl shook her head. "I've never heard of it."

"Oh. That's too bad." Price was disappointed and made a face. But then he noticed the fairy's large gray eyes watching him. He tried again.

"You see this note?" he said. "I found it just before I got here."

Freddy glanced at the paper. "I don't read human writing," she said. "Although many Tolks do. King Noble has taught them, you see. But we fairies have our own script that only we can read."

Once again, Price read the note aloud. Then he said, "I want to find Number 12, Riverbend. Would … would you like to come along?"

"Me?" the fairy asked.

"Sure. Don't you want to?"

She hesitated, looking uncertain, but then quickly made up her mind. "Yes," she said, "I would like to come." But there was a slight quaver in her voice, which Price did not notice.

"Then look," he said, "See there?" pointing downstream, "Where the river curves off to the right?"

"Yes, I see," said the fairy.

"Let's try there," said Price

Freddy's wings instantly flew open and she launched into the air. At the same time Price began clambering along the bank, over rocks and roots and the slippery, mossy ground. It made a rough ride for O.P., much to his chagrin.

"Take it easy!" he griped. "I feel like I'm being jogged along in a sack."

Freddy flew over the stream, clear of the trees. "I hardly ever walk," she called, observing them from several feet above.

Price glanced up at her. "I don't blame you," he said. "Flying would be awesome."

"Yes, it is. It's one of life's greatest pleasures." Grinning, she spread her arms and did a loop-de-loop.

Then suddenly, as if on an impulse, Freddy flitted down to the ground. She smiled. "Just for today, I'm *not* going to fly."

"Really?" said Price. "Thanks. It'll be nice to have company."

Freddy blushed, and then seemed surprised, as if it had been an entirely new and unexpected sensation. Instinctively, she touched a hand to her cheek.

"And exactly what do you call *me?*" cut in an irate voice. "If I'm not company, what am I? A decoration on your pocket?"

"I mean, it'll be nice to have more company, O.P. *More* company."

Fifteen minutes later they were standing at the place where the river meandered to their right, taking a more easterly course. Here they found a narrow but well-used path leading up from the stream to higher ground.

"There's nothing but rocks down here," said Price, looking around. "I think we should follow this trail."

"Did you hear that, Freddy? Why, this boy has a mind like a steel trap. Hee, hee. Have you noticed his uncanny knack for spotting the obvious?"

Price rolled his eyes. Glancing at Freddy, his lips twisted into a smile, and she giggled.

They soon discovered that the trail ended where it intersected another, broader path, running parallel to the river.

"This looks promising," said Price. But after several attempts, with Freddy going one way, and Price and O.P. the other, they still had found nothing.

Price leaned against the trunk of a large tree to think. Freddy joined him, and a little tired from all the walking, sat down nearby on the ground, chin in hand.

"Price. Look at this." With the toe of a shoe, she pointed to the base of the tree. Near her foot was a small, rudely carved number 7. Price immediately got down on his hands and knees to examine it. Then he saw what appeared to be a door, about ten inches high, hidden in the crook where a big root connected to the trunk.

"Hey, there's a door." He stared at it for a few seconds. "Do you think I should knock?"

O.P. hooted and Freddy laughed.

"Well, if you don't, I will," said the fairy. But then she reconsidered. "I have a better idea! Why doesn't O.P. knock? He's the right size."

The pinecone man beamed at this suggestion. Price lifted him out of his pocket and set him on the ground. With chest out and a thumb caught nonchalantly in an armhole of his vest, O.P. strode over to the door and rapped lightly. His small, white-felt fist produced only a muffled sound. They waited. He knocked again, much harder this time.

Finally, just when they were beginning to think no one was home, the door opened slowly outwards. A lady mouse—the largest mouse Price had ever seen—peered out. She was wearing a dust cap and a frilly apron and holding a tiny broom in her hand. The mouse took one look at O.P., squeaked loudly, and slammed the door in his face.

"Oh no," moaned Freddy. "I'm afraid you've frightened her, O.P."

"I-wha...?" The pinecone man stood staring at the door, flabbergasted. Then he began pounding on it with both fists.

"Open up, you confounded rodent! Who do you think I am? An alien? The secret police? Open this door!"

"O.P., O.P.," coaxed Price. "You'll only scare her more." Finally he had to pick him up and stuff him, squirming and yowling, into his shirt pocket. Immediately the protests stopped and O.P.'s head appeared over the rim.

Freddy knelt before the door.

"Mistress Mouse?" she called softly. "Don't be afraid. This is Winifred Fairchild, one of the fairy-folk. Won't you come out? We want to ask you something."

A couple of seconds later, the door reopened and the mouse cautiously poked out her head.

"What is it?" she asked in a small, fluty voice. Then she happened to glance up at Price. "Oh my!" she cried, throwing up her tiny mouse paws with their long, bony mouse claws. The broom clattered to the ground, and for the second time, she ducked inside and slammed the door shut.

"Oh dear!" sighed Freddy. "Now what do we do?"

The words were hardly out of her mouth when the door opened again and the same mouse's head appeared. This time she looked directly up at Price.

"Are-are you the one they sent for?" she asked.

Price, of course, had no idea what she was talking about. He shrugged. "I don't think so. We're trying to find Number

12, Riverbend." He pulled the note out of his pocket and showed it to her. "Is this Riverbend?"

"Oh. Then it *is* you!" She nodded eagerly and clasped her bony claws together. "Meepy! Meepy!" she called to someone in the dwelling, just behind her. "Oh, I am *so* sorry. I feel so ashamed. I'd like to invite you in for a bite, but of course..." She fussed apologetically, tucking one of three protruding stray hairs under her dust cap. "I'm afraid you wouldn't fit! Tee-hee."

At this, O.P. stretched his twig arms over the top of the pocket and leaned forward. "*I'm* the right size," he piped up.

The mouse abruptly drew back, emitting a short, frightened squeak. "W-why, yes," she stammered. "But-but who ... *what* are you?"

"*What* am I?" O.P. was obviously offended. "Why, I'll have you know that I am O.P. and I..." The mouth was opened, ready to expostulate, but no words came out. "Now that you mention it, I'm not exactly sure what I am."

Price chuckled. "That's because you're unique, O.P. You're one of a kind."

As soon as this idea had sunk in, the little fellow glowed—literally beamed with pleasure. "By golly ... I am! One of a kind!" Then he added, with a note of triumph, "And that's more than any of *you* can say. Ha!"

"Don't mind O.P.," Freddy explained to the mouse lady. "He just takes a little getting used to. What's your name?"

"I-I'm Millie Muskin," she replied, keeping a dubious eye on the pinecone man, who was rubbing his hands together.

"Now that we've been properly introduced, how about that bite?" O.P. said. "You did say something about a bite, and I am just a little peckish, now that I come to think of it."

"Uh ... won't you please come in?" The mouse spoke politely, but Price was certain that, if she weren't already wearing a gray fur coat, her face would have been white.

O.P. aimed a knowing look at Price, who recognized his cue. He lifted the little man from his pocket and set him on the ground.

It was then that they noticed a strapping young boy mouse standing in the doorway behind Millie.

"Oh," she said. "This is Meepy. Meepy, meet Winifred Fairchild, one of the fairy-folk. And this is O.P. and ... I'm sorry; I don't know your name, dear."

"I'm Price Evans," he said, smiling. "Hi."

The young mouse squinted up at him and nodded.

"Meepy, Price needs to find Number 12, Riverbend," said Millie, emphasizing the words as though they carried some special meaning that Meepy would immediately understand. "I want you to take him there."

Meepy nodded again. Thrusting his hands into his trouser pockets, he grinned up at Freddy and Price.

"Well..." The mouse lady began fussing with her apron and sighed, as if to say 'Now *that's* done.'

O.P. was watching her eagerly. Her face fell when she recollected the invitation, but she seemed resigned to her fate.

"Won't you come this way?" she said, stepping to one side and presenting the open doorway.

"Should we wait around, or should we go on without you and come back later?" asked Price. O.P. stopped in his tracks. He shot the boy an indignant glare.

"Wait for me, of course."

Freddy and Price exchanged a look. Freddy giggled, and Price was wishing he hadn't left the remaining currant biscuits behind with the bicycle.

About ten minutes later the door opened again. O.P. and Meepy emerged together.

Standing behind them in the doorway, Millie Muskin tittered, "Why, thank you *so* much, Mr. O.P. It's been my pleasure, I'm sure. I'm so glad you enjoyed the acorn loaf. It's an old Muskin recipe. Next time I see Maebella, I'll tell her what you said." Then, in the manner of all good mouse-keepers, she set to scolding them soundly before the fact.

"Now, mind you two, don't let that orange cat see you. I wouldn't trust him any farther than a giant's wit. I dare say he's learned some bad tricks out there in that wicked place—from what I've heard. Meepy, I'm counting on you to see that our friends have safe passage … you hear? Now … if you don't mind, I have work to do." She looked up at Price and Freddy and grinned, revealing two prominent little mouse teeth.

Price wondered what had transpired behind that small door in so short a time to produce this change of heart in Millie Muskin. He caught Freddy's eye and could tell that she'd had the same thought. O.P., it seemed, must have some hidden charms of which they were not aware.

The lady mouse disappeared inside the mouse hole and shut the door. Price looked down at the two small creatures on the ground. "I can take you both in my pocket if you want," he offered.

"Go in your pocket?" O.P. looked shocked. He shook his head as though he had never heard of such a thing. "I never ride in pockets," he said.

He lifted his chin (of course, O.P. didn't really have a chin, but I think you know what I mean) and linked arms with Meepy. The two then strode off together along the trail. All went well until Meepy dropped down on all fours, picking up the pace. Now the going was much harder for

O.P., but he did his best, and soon they were moving at a good clip, off to find Number 12, Riverbend.

Chapter Ten:
Number 12, Riverbend

Soon Meepy halted before a dense growth of shrubbery. By this time, O.P. was chuffing away like a small steam engine.

"Whew!" he panted. "Are we here already? (*Puff, puff*) So soon? I thought it would be much (*puff*) farther than this."

Meepy emitted a kind of warbling sound that might have been a snicker. He leaned carelessly against a slender woody stem and stuffed his hands into his pockets, giving O.P. a moment to catch his breath.

Price looked around. He couldn't see any particular reason to stop. "Are we ... taking a break?" he asked, although he was pretty sure that this was not the case.

O.P., who had flopped down on the grass, looked up in alarm. "You mean this *isn't* the place?"

Meepy made another sort of chirping sound. Then, without a word, he disappeared under a large bush.

Price looked questioningly at Freddy, but she only shrugged.

So he crouched down and pulled aside some of the tangle of leaves, trying to locate the mouse.

"There's a hollow space behind here," he said. "But I can't see Meepy anywhere."

He lowered himself nearly onto his stomach and found that he could just squeeze under the branches and into the hollow. Once inside, he discovered that there was a tunnel, completely invisible from the outside, which burrowed through the thick mesh of brush. He turned himself around and poked his head back out. "Come on. There's a tunnel here."

Price struggled to raise the mangle of vines and leaves as high off the ground as he could, to accommodate Freddy's wings. Although folded compactly on her back, they could still possibly get caught.

But it was O.P. who strode nonchalantly on through. "Why, I thank you," he said, with exaggerated courtesy. "Of course, that was quite unnecessary. But I know it's easy to forget how small I am when I have such a large presence."

"Yup. That's true," Price agreed. He looked out through the opening and smiled encouragingly at Freddy. She hesitated, as though unsure of what to do.

"Come on," Price repeated. "There's enough room. My arms are getting tired."

The fairy sunk down onto her belly and wriggled through into the hollow. Upon standing, she looked down at her now rumpled and dirty dress. "Oh no!" she exclaimed, and with her two hands pulled down the hem at the bottom to get a better look. Then, unexpectedly, she laughed. In fact, she seemed almost pleased at the sight.

The tunnel was not completely dark. Pale freckles of sunlight filtered in through the tangled walls. It took a few minutes to adjust to the dim, fluctuating light as they crept along.

Soon they came to a wooden door about three feet high. A number 12 was carved into the center, under a tarnished copper doorknocker. They could hear the muffled sound of voices coming from the other side. Meepy was standing off to the right, in the shadows, and when they were all assembled, he reached up on tiptoe and applied the knocker. Then to Price's surprise, the mouse scampered away, having accomplished his errand without saying one word.

But there was no time to think about that. As soon as the knocker sounded, the voices inside, which Price was pretty sure were not human, went quiet. Then he heard some muttering, the scraping noise of a chair being pushed back, and the shuffle of approaching feet.

The door opened slowly and a dim light spilled into the tunnel. Price blinked. He saw the silhouette of what he thought was a very large, plump gopher—nearly fifteen inches tall—squinting up at him. The creature had on a white shirt, open at the neck, with the sleeves rolled up. Over that he wore an unbuttoned waistcoat. He stared silently at the odd party, as though he couldn't quite make out who or what they were.

Price reached into his pocket and produced the note. "Uh, is this Number 12, Riverbend?"

Immediately the gopher's face lit up. "It's him! He's found us after all! Oh, do come in, come in!" He went down some stairs into a passage, making room for them to follow. "Mind, watch your step now."

Bending to get through the doorway, Price stepped cautiously down the small stairs, being careful not to trip on his feet. But the stairs were much too steep for O.P., who stood helplessly at the entrance. "Ahem. Price?"

Turning around, the boy saw a pair of forlorn painted eyes looking up at him. He could see that, finding himself in a predicament, O.P. was begging forgiveness. Never a grudging boy, Price simply picked him up and put him into his shirt pocket. Tired and contrite, O.P. hunkered down and shut his eyes.

Price couldn't quite stand up in the passage; he had to walk just slightly stooped over. The light he'd seen came from a single candle in a copper dish, hooked onto the wall. On the right was a coat rack with a couple of gray, baggy-looking garments hanging on it. A straw mat lay on the packed earthen floor beside it. Several pairs of well-worn woolly slippers had been neatly arranged on the mat, including a couple of pairs that looked distinctly feminine. On the opposite wall, a wooden bookcase held a number of well-thumbed volumes. And tacked up over the bookcase was a charcoal sketch of a young lady gopher in a flowered bonnet. Next to that was a dim, rippled mirror in a plain wooden frame. Price felt as though he had stepped back in time about four hundred years.

The gopher hurried ahead through an open doorway at the end of the passage.

"Aha! What did I tell you? The boy has arrived after all!" he said, speaking to someone in the next room. The announcement produced some mutterings and exclamations of surprise; it was hard to tell if they were favorable or not. Price turned to Freddy, but to his surprise, she wasn't there. Then he saw her still kneeling by the door, looking in. He motioned to her. "Come on."

She hesitated briefly, and then carefully tiptoed down the stairs.

"Come, come!" the gopher called jovially. "We are all in here."

Price stepped into the room. It was much larger and brighter than the hallway and he could stand up straight, although the top of his head was actually just brushing the ceiling. In the center was a big square table, and gathered around it was the oddest collection of beings he had ever seen.

The most prominent of these was a very fat, very haughty-looking muskrat. She wore a voluminous purple dress with a big, ruffled collar. Sitting down as she was, her plump body pushed the collar right up to her chin, so that it looked as if her head was on a platter. On her right slouched a big black cat, and next to him, grinning ear to ear, stood the gopher whom they had met at the door.

But it was the two glum-faced dwarfs, seated to the left of the muskrat, that caught Price's eye. He couldn't help himself; he did a double take. He immediately recognized the long beards, enormous ears, and domed bald heads. The only difference was that these dwarfs were not lawn ornaments. They were living, breathing flesh and bone.

All eyes were fixed on Price.

"Welcome, welcome!" the gopher exclaimed happily. "Now, let me introduce everyone."

Suddenly the muskrat lady squawked. Craning her neck forward, she squinched her eyes at them. (It could be argued whether she actually *had* a neck. At any rate, her round head rotated a little more to the front of its frilly perch.)

"Is that a *fairy* I see lurking back there?" she asked sharply.

"Oh well, I don't know," murmured the gopher. "Is it now?" Everyone looked at Freddy. She shrank back into the shadows just behind the doorframe.

"There will be *no* fairies at this meeting!" The muskrat made a fist and hit it soundly against the table. "We all know that fairies are unreliable. One can *never* trust a fairy to keep a secret. They are too flighty by far."

Both dwarfs nodded and grumbled their agreement.

"Aye," spoke the largest. "You can't trust a fairy to keep a secret." His voice had a surprisingly deep pitch for someone so small.

"Tch, tch." The gopher shook his head. "I suppose I didn't notice her come in. Miss, I'm afraid you cannot stay. This is no place for a fairy. I'll see you to the door." He began to shuffle towards her. "And mind you don't tell *anyone* what you've seen here today."

"Wait!" Price straightened up as much as he could. "This fairy is my friend. If she goes, I go too."

A shocked silence hung over the group. Six pairs of startled eyes leveled at the boy.

"Freddy's not unreliable," he went on. "She can keep a secret as well as anybody."

The muskrat lady's lower lip dropped down in amazement. The gopher began to fidget nervously. He cleared his throat.

"Well, ahem, since you put it that way, I suppose she can stay after all. Uh ... won't you come in, miss? Now, what did you say your name is...? Freddy, is it? I'll pull up a couple of chairs for you both."

"But..."

"Silence, Priscilla! You heard what the boy said. Keep in mind that we *desperately need his help!*" He turned back to Price and Freddy. "Now, won't you both sit down and make yourselves at home? Are you hungry? Dot, can you bring our guests some of your famous apple tart and berryade?"

In the corner nearest them, a she-gopher sat in a large stuffed chair with lace doilies draped over the arms. She was crocheting, but it was evident that her attention was on the strangers and not on her handiwork. She promptly put it down. As she bustled past, she glanced hastily at Freddy. Her mouth pursed into a small smile, as though she had just remembered a funny story but was trying to keep it to herself. Soon she was busy at the sideboard.

To be polite, and to make a point, Price waited for Freddy to sit down first. Unfortunately, they were seated directly opposite the muskrat, who glared unremittingly at the little fairy. Freddy squirmed and looked away.

Price's chair was so small that his knees came practically to his chest. But he rested his hands on the table and smiled at the company. No one would have guessed that he was not perfectly comfortable.

"Now then." The gopher poured them each a tin cupful—Dixie-Cup size—of a clear pink liquid. "Berryade's been chilling in the stream since early this morning. It's as cold as ice." They sipped. It tasted sweet and sharp and very refreshing. Price downed his in one large gulp.

He looked around. It seemed to be a very comfortable home. There was an unlit hearth on one side with a big kettle hanging in it. There were cupboards and a counter for preparing food, a wooden tub, and a couple of buckets for washing. Various dishes and utensils were stacked on the sideboard. The furniture was all square and solid looking, and every piece plainly served some useful function, but he could still detect a feminine touch. There was a vase of wildflowers on the sideboard and a rose-patterned flounce under the counter top. The room had no windows that Price could see, but there were lamps with candles burning in them. But everything was so small, as if it belonged in a child's playhouse.

The gopher sat down next to Price. "Now, about those introductions. My name is Timmins Arbuckle, and over there is my companion, Dot." The she-gopher looked around at them and smiled warmly.

"Opposite you there is Miss Priscilla Smallpatch." The fat muskrat nodded, but her expression remained severe.

"These dwarfs here are Fender and Bray." He motioned first to the larger of the two. "And this black-furred, black-hearted fellow seated on my left is called Bootle." He cuffed the cat playfully on the 'arm.' The animal grinned and chuckled deep in his throat, although it actually sounded more like a wheeze than a chuckle.

Dot placed a dish of juicy apple tart in front of Freddy, and an entire pie (about the size of a saucer) before Price.

"Thanks," he smiled at Dot. "I'm Price Evans and this is my friend, Winifred, but she goes by Freddy." The fairy glanced at him gratefully, clearly relieved that she did not have to speak.

Price had completely forgotten that at that moment O.P. was sleeping in his pocket. Without giving him a thought, he picked up the small wooden spoon next to his dish and scooped up a mouthful of pie. "Mmm. This is delicious," he said to the she-gopher, in a sticky voice. Freddy nodded, too, but only ate a couple of nibbles.

Dot Arbuckle sighed contentedly. "Now, you eat up all that pie, dearie," she coaxed the little fairy. "You want to keep those wings of yours strong and supple so's you can fly all the way to Drumbleton and back." Freddy smiled shyly and took a larger bite.

They talked a bit about the weather and the apple trees. Bootle asked if anyone had spoken to Lambton recently. Bonnie was looking for some yarn to make an afghan. She wanted it ready 'before the wind turned.' Priscilla replied curtly that she hardly thought the sheep would be spinning in the summer. It wouldn't be animal-like. Bootle shrugged loosely and laughed his strange wheezing laugh. He'd been told to ask, that was all. No harm meant.

The two dour-looking dwarfs said nothing. Price was pretty sure they were watching him, but whenever he glanced their way, they quickly averted their eyes.

As soon as they had finished eating, Dot cleared away the dishes. Timmins Arbuckle placed both paws squarely on the table-edge and pushed back his chair.

"So, you found the note left by our friend, Spark. Squirrels are good at hiding things that need to be found. We knew you were a clever lad and could ferret us out." He chuckled. "We knew that King Noble would see to it that you did. Has he told you the reason for bringing you here?"

"No. I haven't spoken to King Noble. He led us part of the way, but then he disappeared, and we had to find you on our own."

"Aye, that sounds like King Noble." Timmins nodded. "He rarely does something for you that he knows you can do for yourself. That's one of the things that makes him such a good king."

"Well?" asked Price. "Why am I here?"

Priscilla Smallpatch suddenly hit both fists squarely on the table. "It's that cat ... that odious cat!" Her voice rose shrilly.

"Now, Priscilla, you let me handle this," interrupted Timmins. "You know how emotional you can get at times like this. It's one of your best qualities, but I think it will only hinder us today. Save it for when we have to convince the others."

Priscilla pulled herself up as tall as her rotund shape would allow, but she grudgingly conceded.

Timmins Arbuckle cleared his throat and looked soberly at the boy. "Before I can tell you about our problem, I think you need to know something about the Land of Tolk."

"Freddy has already told me a bit," said Price.

Timmins nodded. "Good." He looked approvingly at the fairy. "Seems you have already done the job of welcoming our friend to Tolk." He spoke kindly, and Freddy offered him a timid smile. The gopher continued.

"Then perhaps you know that the natural laws that govern your world are not exactly the same as the laws that govern Tolk."

"Well, I know that something inanimate in my world can come to life here. Is that what you mean?"

Timmins looked surprised. "That's part of it," he said, "but that kind of thing is very rare—almost unheard of."

He thoughtfully tugged at a whisker; then went on, "I'm sure you've noticed that in Tolk the animals are intelligent, as people are in your world. We can speak and make things with our paws, and we've learned to read and write. And there are other beings here who don't exist at all in the human world—dwarfs, elves, fairies, giants..." He waved a paw, as if to encompass all of these and more.

"Your world and our world are very closely linked. We're sisters, so to speak. Part of the same family. Your world being the elder sister, having the birthright."

"Birthright? What do you mean?"

Timmins inhaled deeply. "Your world, you see, has humans. And in the hierarchy of living beings, humans are at the top."

Price happened to catch the eye of Fender, glaring at him fiercely. Quickly, the boy refocused on Timmins, who now lowered his voice.

"With a few rare exceptions," he said, "Tolk is completely unknown in the world of humankind. The fact is that we are afraid of men. We fear that if humans found out about us, they would want to take us over."

Price realized that, unfortunately, this was likely true.

"So you see, we have taken a great risk in bringing you here."

"Then why did you?" asked the boy.

Timmins spread his paws flat on the table and thought for a moment. "It's not that we never trust any humans at all. Why, any given man or woman can be as steadfast as an oak, as immovable as a mountain. It's just collectively that we mistrust people, you see." He paused. "Remember that I told you there are beings here who don't exist at all in the world of men, and others of us who are different here, such as the animals? Well, should any one of us leave Tolk and cross the threshold into your world, we instantly become subject to your Earth's natural laws. Animals lose the power of speech. In time they lose their native intelligence and become like the creatures of the Earth. Others—the dwarfs, the giants—must exist in a different form."

"A different form? What do you mean?"

"A dwarf turns into wood, the element from which he sprang. An elf might become a slender tree."

"But..." Price was confused. "Then why don't I change when I come here?" he asked.

"That's a good question. The answer is because, as I said before, your Earth holds the birthright. Humans have always been the dominant creatures. Tolk is like an unconscious arm of the Earth—a branch. We are bound to each other, but in many ways, Tolk is a lesser world. Our scope, our boundaries are limited." He hesitated. "If humans came here, they would only bring corruption, evil, and ... and death. In time, Tolk would cease to be. It would become just a part of your Earth."

"Don't you see?" Dot Arbuckle interrupted, her voice trembling with emotion. "Tolk is a place of innocence.

We are all at peace and happy here. We don't want to lose this happiness!"

"But Tolk must have existed since the beginning of time. What are you so afraid of now?"

There was a shifting of bodies and looks exchanged all around.

"It's that cat, Sinbad," Timmins stated grimly, shaking his head.

"Aye. He has lured away two of our fellows." Fender spoke up now, his voice a deep, ponderous monotone. "Told them a pack of lies about how wonderful it was living amongst humans. Pooh-poohed the old stories that said they couldn't go there and live as dwarfs. He tricked them! Now he tells us that they like it so well they don't want to come back. Lies! All lies. We know what's really happened to them. But there *are* those who believe it."

Instantly the light dawned. Price's eyes opened wide as the truth bore down upon him. "Of course! I know where your friends are."

"Aye."

"They're lawn decorations in Mr. Murphy's garden!"

"Aye."

"That's awful!"

Timmins Arbuckle cleared his throat again.

"That's where you come in, lad," he said. "That's the reason we brought you here."

Part II:
The Rescue

Chapter Eleven:
Doubtful Dwarfs

Price looked in turn at each one seated at the table. Timmins, Bootle, and Priscilla Smallpatch seemed anxious and hopeful at the same time. The two dwarfs looked suspicious and brooding. Freddy watched him closely too, with large, innocent, wondering eyes.

"What do you think *I* can do about it?" he said at last.

"We want you to bring them back to Tolk."

"But how?"

"That we don't know." Timmins spread his paws in a gesture of helplessness. "But there's no way we can rescue them ourselves."

Priscilla's furry chins trembled. "We have no one else to turn to."

Price shifted uneasily. He thought of miserable old Mr. Murphy and realized that he was afraid of him. But he knew that he at least had to try. "I-I'll do what I can," he said.

Timmins and Bootle each expelled a sigh of relief. The two dwarfs, on the other hand, frowned all the more and stared hard at the boy. *They sure don't trust me*, he thought.

Aloud he said, "I don't know how I'll do it, though. I can't just walk into Mr. Murphy's garden and take them."

Timmins was suddenly overflowing with optimism. "Oh, you'll think of a way. King Noble said that if anyone can do it, *you* can. He has great faith in you. And I've never know King Noble to be mistaken." He couldn't have sounded more confident if he'd just told them the sun would still be in the sky when they stepped out of the burrow. But Price wasn't so sure.

"And, of course, you'll have our help all the way." Again Priscilla hit her fists on the table. "If there is anything that we—or for that matter, any one of King Noble's loyal supporters—can do, we will be at your service."

"Aye. And that brings us to another important item of business."

"Thunder and lightning!" Bray's gravelly voice bellowed out for the first time. "He has a rat in his pocket!" The dwarf jumped to his feet. "It must be a spy. One of *them!* I knew it was folly to trust a human. First it's boys, then fairies, and now *spies!*"

Inside Price's pocket, O.P. was going through the usual stretching routine of someone waking up.

"No, no," Price objected. "That's just O.P. He's not a spy."

Still half-asleep, the pinecone man's round head suddenly appeared over the rim of the pocket.

Everyone gaped at the sight of him. Priscilla Smallpatch gasped. O.P. gasped too, and quickly retreated back into his shelter.

"Come on out, O.P. These are friends." Price pulled open the pocket and peered inside. "He's been asleep," he explained to the others. "He's had a hard day."

The small head reappeared. O.P. looked around suspiciously, as if to say, 'What are all of *you* doing here?' Price reached in his hand, lifted him out, and set him on the table. The others gawked in amazement.

"My grandmother made O.P.," he explained. "She gave him to me today. I put him in my pocket, and as soon as I entered Tolk, he came to life. He doesn't know anything about what we've been talking about."

"Well, by my whiskers!" Priscilla's jaw dropped and nestled in her frilly collar.

As a body, they all leaned across the table to get a better look.

Bootle laughed out loud. "He's a piece of a tree come to life," he wheezed. "A tree-mite, that's what he is! Nobody in Tolk's ever seen the likes of him before."

"He's unique, all right, 'one-of-a-kind,'" said Price. He winked at Freddy, and she grinned.

O.P. was very pleased. It was his cue. "And that's more than any of *you* can say! Ha!"

"And glad of it!" intoned Bray.

O.P. glared stonily at the gloomy dwarf. "At least the paint isn't dribbling down the corners of *my* mouth. At least I don't have a lumpy potato for a nose, and hard-boiled eggs for eyes, and cabbage leaves for ears!" Bray's jaw tightened and he clutched the edge of the table in anger.

Price was shocked. "O.P.! That's rude. You'd better get back in the pocket." He reached out a hand, but O.P. drew back.

"No, no. I-I won't do it again."

"All right. But watch your manners."

Price apologized to Bray, knowing that O.P. would not. "Don't mind O.P. It's just his way. He's very proud. And," he added in his friend's defense, "I doubt he liked being called a tree-mite."

The dwarf scowled. But then he leaned back in his chair and his face relaxed. "Aye." He nodded. "I can understand that. I'm a proud one myself." He seemed willing to concede that O.P. was not a spy after all.

"I expect the little fellow is just hungry. Isn't that so?" Dot Arbuckle hurried to the sideboard. "All this talk about potatoes and cabbages and eggs."

O.P.'s face brightened. "Now that you mention it..."

A proportionately large helping of apple pie appeared before him, and even a tiny silver spoon, which Price thought must be some kind of special serving spoon for condiments, such as horseradish. Or maybe Dot kept such utensils on hand for when she entertained mice. O.P. delved into the pie with relish.

"Now, about that other matter." Timmins leaned forward resting his 'arms' on the table. He lowered his voice and said gravely, "It concerns that cat, Sinbad, as he calls himself now." He shook his head. "Now that he cohabits with humans. Before, his name was Flame, and he was a great friend and confidant of King Noble."

"What he means," interjected Priscilla, "is that Sinbad is a traitor. And it's not just that he's turned his back on our king. No! The fact is that *he* now wants to be king. Can you imagine? That overbearing, mangy creature thinking *he* could be our king!" Her voice rose shrilly. "The fact is that he thinks too much of himself by far. He always did. Constantly preening that orange hide and looking down on the rest of us, because of our plain brown coats." Her eyes grew moist with tears.

Timmins gently patted her paw. "Now, Priscilla. Everyone knows you have one of the most beautiful fur coats in all of Tolk. You just let me handle this."

He turned to Price. "Sinbad has been trying to persuade the citizens of Tolk to make him our king. He wants to bring humans into Tolk, says we wouldn't believe the lives that people live. He's been telling us all about motor cars, screens right in your living room that have moving pictures on them, stories about being waited on paw and tail—no more spinning or growing crops. Humans would do all that for us, he says."

"That's ridiculous!" Price was incredulous. "How could anybody believe that?"

"Aye, but there are always those who will believe what they want. And Sinbad is a silver-tongued and sweet-lipped liar; you can be sure of that."

"You're absolutely right. It would be a big mistake to bring humans into Tolk. I hate to be hard on my own kind, but we are used to having our way in everything. It's our nature." Price drummed his fingers on the tabletop as he considered the problem. "So, what do you want me to do about it?"

"Expose him," Timmins said simply. "You're from the world outside. You have credibility."

"But surely the Tolks would believe you and King Noble before they would believe me."

"Most do. But there are some who don't."

"If you can rescue Dori and Smoot, that would be a start," said Fender. Price realized that these must be the names of the two unfortunate dwarfs in Mr. Murphy's garden.

"A start?" Price stared down at his hands for several long minutes. When he raised his eyes, they were filled with resolve. "I'll do whatever I can to help."

Timmins jumped up, grabbed Price's hand, and shook it heartily. "You don't know how grateful we are. And I can say it on behalf of the lot of us."

"Aye, aye."

Price shrugged modestly. "Don't thank me now. I haven't done anything yet."

The afternoon was waning and Price knew that he must be getting home or his mother would begin to worry. They decided that O.P. should stay with Millie Muskin for a while, as her guest, at least until he found his own place in the Land of Tolk. The Muskins, it seemed, were great friends of the Arbuckles and staunch defenders of King Noble.

One thing was certain though: O.P. could never go back home with Price. Never again could he go where he couldn't live and breathe—where he would be completely helpless. *What if something happened to him?* thought Price. *What if he got broken, or lost?* Yes, Tolk would be his permanent home from now on. Price wondered what he would tell his mother, and especially his grandmother.

For the time being, he bid goodbye to the strange little 'tree-mite.' Once outside, O.P. sat astride Bootle's back, clinging tightly to his soft black fur. With a cheery salute, the two set off together.

Timidly, Freddy approached Price. "May I come with you ... to the place where you entered Tolk?"

Price had been deep in thought, but snapped out of it. "Sure." He smiled. "My bike's not far from here. Then we can go fast."

"Bike?" Freddy looked confused. "I-I don't mind if we don't go fast."

"You can fly then. It'll be fun."

The fairy shrugged. "All right." And they set off walking, side by side.

Freddy glanced up at Price. "I ... Something's happened," she said. She seemed to be searching her mind. "I don't understand."

"Happened? What d'you mean?"

"At the meeting, I sat just listening and watching. I never said a word. But I felt a ... a feeling growing inside me."

Price wrinkled his nose. "Were you scared or something?"

"No!" Freddy scoffed. "Of course not. Fear is something we rarely experience here. Tolk is such a safe place to be."

Price grinned. "Yeah, I forgot. But then I'm just an 'ignorant human boy,'" he said, repeating O.P.'s earlier remark. The fairy giggled.

They walked in silence for a moment. Then Freddy went on, "It started when you said that I could be trusted. No one has ever said anything like that about me before." She looked curiously at Price.

"Well, it's true, isn't it?"

"That's the surprising thing. As soon as you said it, I realized that it *was* true. I just knew it! But," she paused again, "there's something else."

She looked straight ahead, lifting her chin. "By the end of the meeting, an idea was forming in my mind."

"What idea?"

"*I* think I can do much more than just be trustworthy."

"What d'you mean?"

"I don't know," Freddy said vaguely. "I don't know..." She glanced sidelong at Price. "Do *you* notice anything different about me?" she asked quietly.

"Um..." Price squinted at her. He shook his head.

"In the meeting," Freddy said. "I could *feel* my heart beating. And the skin on my arms..." she held out her arms, "was prickling!" She looked up at Price in alarm. "It was so strange! Nothing like this has ever happened to me before!"

Price had no idea how to explain these reactions.

Freddy dropped her arms. They continued on in silence, each lost in their own thoughts.

At last Freddy said, "If you chose to stay in Tolk, you would never grow old ... you would never die. You could be happy here." She said this carefully, as though the words were important, but she herself wasn't sure why.

Price shook his head. "I could never do that."

"But why not?"

"Well, because of my family, my mom and dad and my grandma."

"Your family? They don't even know about Tolk. What have they got to do with it?"

"I don't know. They're my family, and they love me, I guess." He searched the fairy's face, hoping she would understand without further explanation. But the large, slanted eyes stared right back at him. Price looked away. "Don't you see?"

Freddy was silent. As far as Price could tell, she didn't see at all.

"When a new fairy is born," she said at last, "it comes out of the center of a flower and is hardly bigger than a starling."

"Then don't you belong to anybody at all?" asked Price.

"Yes ... in a way. There are three fairy clans in Tolk," she explained, "the Fairchilds, the Fairborns, and the Fairbes, depending on where you were born. I am a Fairchild. That is my clan." Freddy was silent as she contemplated this for a few seconds.

"The place where we live is called Shadowfir," she went on. "It's a great ancient pine forest filled with dark, brooding shadows—even in daylight. You can be in there for days without ever being seen. But," she said, her face lighting up, "there's a beautiful glen in the center. In summer it's always bright with wildflowers and green grass. That's where we go to dance."

"Really? Wow, I wish I could see that. It must be awesome."

"Oh yes, it is. But fairies are very shy. We only dance at night under the moon."

They were silent again as Price tried to visualize this—hundreds of pale, winged fairies dancing in the moonlight. "Do you think I could come and watch sometime? Would the fairies let me?"

"Oh yes, you could!" Freddy was ecstatic. "The fairies wouldn't mind, if I prepared them first. We're shy folk, but very trusting." Her face fell. "Some see that as a failing."

Price remembered how Priscilla Smallpatch and the dwarfs had reacted to Freddy's presence at the meeting. "I don't see that as a bad thing," he said kindly. "I think it's a good way to be. Only you have to be careful who you trust; that's all."

"But how can you tell?"

Price squirmed. Why was this girl always asking such difficult questions? "Just ... look in the person's eyes. You'll know. Hey, there's my bike!"

He was glad to change the subject. He could see the bicycle a few yards away, still leaning against the tree where he'd left it. All else was forgotten, as Freddy stared in amazement at the two-wheeled vehicle. He unlocked the bicycle chain and stowed it in his backpack.

"Does it really work?" she asked as Price mounted. "Does it fly?"

Price laughed. "No, it can't fly. But it's a lot faster than walking. Still, through all that grass, it's going to be tough slogging." He pulled his baseball cap out of his backpack and put it on. The next minute, he was rolling along steadily across the meadow, following the sliver of a trail he'd cut earlier that day. Freddy launched gracefully into the air and flew alongside him, her wings humming like wires in the wind.

Price wanted to show Freddy that his bicycle could 'fly.' With cheerful determination, he channeled all the energy he could muster into riding as hard and fast as he could. About half an hour later, they arrived at the grove of trees that hid the stone wall.

"This is it." The face under his visor was damp and flushed, and he was panting. He grinned.

"So ... this is the place." Freddy's voice was hushed, almost reverent. She peered into the bushes but wouldn't go any farther. "So this is a gateway into another world," she breathed.

Price removed the yellow cord he had tied to the bush, and stuffed it into his pocket.

"See you soon, Freddy." With one backward glance, and a quick wave of the hand, he strode toward the wall, guiding his bicycle.

"When?" Freddy called after him, but he was gone.

A second later, the fairy was gone too.

Chapter Twelve:
An Understanding
Grandmother

Price wheeled his bicycle into the garage and parked it for the night. He could hear voices coming from the open kitchen window as he approached the back door.

"Did you remember to pack the gift for your Aunt Pat?" his mother was asking.

"Mm-hm," his dad responded, with something in his mouth.

Price hoped that no one would bring up the subject of the pinecone man, but he had no other option than to pass through the kitchen.

"Hi, Mom. Hi, Dad." They were standing at the counter, preparing dinner.

"Price. You're home. Good!" His mother smiled warmly. "You've had a long day."

"Yup."

"Hi, Price." His dad glanced at him and smiled. "So..." he returned to the task at hand, "you want me to chop up this celery? What size pieces?" His dad's limited culinary skills were legendary.

"Oh, I don't care," Mother replied. "Anything that fits in the mouth."

Price sidled by as quickly as possible and slipped upstairs to his bedroom. It was lucky his parents were so preoccupied with their impending trip. They were leaving around four o'clock the next morning to catch an early flight. He heard his mother call after him that supper would be ready in fifteen minutes.

"Okay," he called back.

He shut his bedroom door and stood there, wondering what to do next. Then, pulling a clean sheet of paper from his desk drawer, he sat down to begin a sketch. One of the things he liked best about drawing was that he could think about other things while he did it. While one part of the brain was occupied with the eyes, the hand, and the pencil, another part could be thinking about problems. The problem on his mind right now, of course, was how he was going to get those dwarfs safely out of Mr. Murphy's backyard and into Tolk without getting caught.

The pencil began to round out the form of Javelin Man, a huge muscular hero who stood more than eight feet tall and weighed about three hundred pounds. He had horns like a goat's and wore nothing but a loincloth and a fearsome expression. His teeth were long and sharp, like a tiger's, and saliva foamed at the corners of his mouth. The enchanted javelin (a weapon that had been carved out of the last of the ancient gargantuan ironwood trees, by the village shaman, and was endowed with supernatural powers) was poised to strike a loathsome cat-like creature...

Sinbad! Price thought miserably. He put down the pencil. *I'm getting nowhere with this problem.* Javelin Man wasn't helping at all.

There was a light tap at the door.

"Open," called Price.

Grandmother's wrinkled face peered into the room. "May I come in?"

"Sure." The truth was that Price welcomed the interruption. It meant that for the time being he wouldn't have to think.

"I thought I heard you come up the stairs. My, what have we here? Now this is a very ferocious-looking character." Her eyes lingered over the sketch. That was one of the nicest things about Grandmother: She was rarely in a hurry—at least where he was concerned. "Very skillful, Price. Very skillfully done, indeed. You're developing into quite an artist."

"Thanks."

He was glad that she didn't badger him with questions like, 'Why did Javelin Man have horns?' or 'Why was he going to kill the cat?' He wouldn't have known what to say. It was just the way these things were done.

Grandmother pulled up a chair. "Now, my notion of a hero is a bit different from yours." She eased herself down. "My hero at the moment is a small bald man named Mr. Wray. His face looks something like Wax Man who stayed out too long in the sun. But ever since your grandpa died, he has shoveled my walks in the winter and swept up the leaves every autumn. You see how your point of view changes, if you happen to be old and frail." She chuckled.

Price grinned. "You may be old, but you're not frail."

Grandmother did not reply, and Price noticed that she did look frailer than he remembered. Her gray eyes crinkled into a smile—those quirky eyes, as O.P. had described them. They began to browse the room, searching the shelves where Price's proud collection of superhero action figures was displayed.

"Now, what has happened to that insolent little man that I made?"

Price swallowed and looked down at Javelin Man. He began to fidget with his pencil. Grandmother watched him expectantly.

"He's gone," said Price.

"Gone? You mean you lost him?"

"Not exactly."

No one spoke for a couple of minutes, while Grandmother waited for the inevitable explanation. But none came. At last Price looked over at her.

"Grandma, I know you were adopted when you were a kid, but what happened before that? Where were you born?"

The old woman pursed her lips. "Odd that you should mention that. I've been thinking a lot about it myself lately. I've come nearly full circle, you see, and strange as it may seem, as you approach the end, you find yourself so much nearer to the beginning. But the fact is, I can't remember anything about that time of my life. I've searched my mind mightily for some faint recollection, but there is nothing. I suppose I must have buried the memories because they were too painful to deal with. I can only recall that I was unhappy, and that I wanted something more than what I had. I can remember nothing at all of my real parents. But that has never mattered to me. My adoptive parents were the best that anyone could have."

She leaned back in the chair and smiled. "Sometimes, though, I dream that I'm a child again, flying, soaring over forests and lakes like a bird, and it seems so real. Ha! Imagine that. Flying! I understand flying dreams are common and have some deep meaning, but I'm sure I don't know what it is."

"Do you remember your name—the name you had before?"

"Oh yes. Now *that* I do remember. My last name was Fairborn. Yes ... Felicity Fairborn. Nice name, don't you think?"

Price nodded dumbly. *Could it be? My own grandmother?*

"Grandma, d-do you believe in fairies?"

"Fairies? You mean as in the Tooth Fairy or the Sandman?"

"No, I mean, like ... fairies. For real."

Grandmother looked at him oddly. "As a child, I did believe in fairies. More than most children do. But ... what made you think of it? Don't tell me you're interested in fairies, Price? How strange are the ties that bind us! But I'm afraid I haven't given it any thought for many years. Reality managed to creep in and crowd out the childhood fancies, you see."

Price bit his lower lip. Suddenly his brown eyes were troubled. "Grandma, about the pinecone man..." He stopped and looked at her, his eyes begging for understanding.

Grandmother touched his arm. "Didn't you like him, Price?" Her voice was soft and apologetic. "I know he wasn't like any of these." She glanced up at Price's collection of muscled figurines. "But he seemed so wonderful to me. Oh, I forget sometimes what a pitiful old woman I am."

"Oh no, Grandma! I like him a lot. Really a lot. He's ... I ... I've left him with someone ... someone who *really* likes him and ... who will take good care of him."

Grandmother stared at the boy. "Left him with someone?" He nodded.

"Well." She blinked a couple of times, trying to take this in. Then all at once she smiled sweetly and gave him a side-long look. "A-a-h. I think I begin to see. Is this person by any chance a girl?"

Price crossed his fingers under the desk. "Y-e-es ... it is." Millie Muskin was female after all, although not exactly a girl. When he couldn't look his grandmother in the eye, she assumed he was being bashful.

"Well then, I see that quite an honor has been bestowed upon my lowly creation." She leaned forward and whispered conspiratorially, "Now, Price, you have my word that I will not tell a soul. This will be a secret, just between you and me."

Price felt a great wave of relief wash over him. "Thanks, Grandma. Thanks for understanding."

Chapter Thirteen: The Bonfire

There was a small clearing in the Land of Tolk—a secluded, hidden place carved out of a rocky cliff on one side and surrounded by woods on the other. On this night, there was a huge bonfire roaring in its center. Grotesque pennants of flame billowed up, unfurling and then collapsing in fountains of sparks. All around, eerie shadows writhed in and out of the trees and engaged in a macabre dance on the rock face. Crowded around the fire in a half-circle, faces glowing hotly, was a large assembly of dwarfs, bears, giants, and numerous small animals. There was even a small party of elves, which was very unusual since elves were normally extremely shy and reclusive. It was a warm, starry night, and torches would have provided sufficient light, but Sinbad understood well the hypnotic effect of a bonfire.

He stood on a rise, just above the flames and in front of the rocky cliff, his coat a blaze of orange and his eyes glittering. He had chosen this spot carefully. The cliff wall behind him ensured that no one could come up unexpectedly from the rear. And every creature present could clearly see his face and hear his voice. But most important, he himself could look directly into every eye. And all eyes were now trained upon him expectantly. His large feline shadow paced back and forth on the rock face behind him.

"My dear friends," began the honeyed voice, "so many have come tonight; I am deeply honored and deeply touched. I thank you all." He paused. "Now, I have tales to tell from the world of humankind that are sure to outstrip your wildest imaginings—things I've seen with my own eyes and heard with my own ears. And I've brought treasures, gifts with magical powers—powers that could be yours if you wanted them. Yes, yours! Without ever leaving your beloved Tolk and without having to surrender your immortal condition. Watch and listen!"

One of Sinbad's favorite pastimes was to stroll up and down the streets of Clareburn, sneak onto people's property, and carry things off—things like small tools, knives, and scissors, and anything made of plastic or metal. He even made off with magazines, articles of clothing, jewelry, and children's toys. He particularly liked things with shock-appeal. Today had been an especially good day.

He rose up on his hind legs, and with a front paw, held up a black and supple leather strap. It was so long that most of it was looped around his foreleg like a lasso. In Tolk, nothing was made of leather since leather comes from the hides of animals (although Sinbad was careful not to mention that). The audience looked with interest at the curiosity. Now and then, the flickering firelight glinted off its flat, polished surface. It seemed alternately to disappear and reappear, as if under a strobe light.

"Why, it's just a piece of rope," shouted a heckler.

"Aye."

"Maybe it's one of those monster snakes he told us about," quailed a high-pitched mousy voice.

"O-o-o-o." A nervous tremor ran through the crowd. The only snakes in Tolk were the small, harmless garden variety.

"A snake?" cried Sinbad. "Never!" He whipped one end of the strap sharply against the ground at his feet. "Why I am here to protect you from such despicable creatures as snakes ... creatures that devour mice!" He turned and pointed a claw directly at a lady mouse sitting in the front row.

"And squirrels!" He swung round and looked Chetly Squirrel straight in the eye. Chetly shrank back. "And other small rodents!" Sinbad did not mention that he himself had developed a taste for rodents—a taste that, regretfully, he could not indulge in Tolk.

(The fact was, when the predatory instinct had first gripped Sinbad, he had been alarmed. And after the kill he had felt guilty and remorseful. But then he'd thought about it. Earth mice, after all, weren't exactly the same as the mice from Tolk. Earth mice, he'd learned, were primitive and pea-brained. He had long since gotten used to the idea.)

Now he raised his eyes heavenward. "It's only a matter of time, my friends, before such terrible creatures find their way into Tolk. Only a matter of time. How fortunate that I have found this out while it can still be prevented."

The yellow orbs narrowed ominously. "Lions!" he cried. "Cats as big as boulders, with jaws that can crush bones in a single bite. With teeth as long as Baldur's toes." Baldur, a tall stringbean of a giant, gawked at his large feet in horror and then quickly sat down on them.

"Ferocious bears with long, sharp claws, like scythes— scythes that harvest living beings instead of corn." Rolla-Paula, a fat brown bear, whimpered in fear.

"Vicious wild dogs called wolves. *Predators!* In the world outside, they rule over the smaller animals, the *lesser* beasts, who live in constant fear for their lives." He paused. "Instruments of *death* are what they are! Yes, death."

His voice fell to an intense whisper and an expectant hush fell over the crowd. "How long will it be, my friends, before these predators find their way here?"

A dwarf jumped angrily to his feet. It was Fender. "That's all lies, Sinbad! Lies! You know as sure as the moon shines that beasts of that sort are barred from Tolk!"

Sinbad did not respond at once. He began to pace again, shaking his head, grinning and cackling to himself as though he couldn't believe that anyone could be so naive and stupid. He stared at Fender for a few seconds, and then sat down. With deliberate patience, he examined his claws.

In fact, Sinbad knew that such ferocious wild animals could not exist in Tolk, but he'd learned early on that scare tactics could be put to good use. And the Tolks, ignorant as they were, had a kind of morbid curiosity about such things. They were easily alarmed.

"And who told you that, stump-man?" the cat went on. "Surely not that dumb brute of a dog you call king."

A gasp rose from the crowd. How could anyone dare to make such a slanderous remark against their king?

But Sinbad only sighed deeply, as though mustering the greatest forbearance.

"It would take only one, just *one* portal being discovered, by accident, or..." The cat paused, staring into the crowd. "Or by design."

A whisper ran through the assembly.

"And whom can we trust after all?" he said. "If a portal were discovered, that would be the beginning of the end. You see, one of the chief differences between King Noble and myself is that I have actually seen these creatures with my own eyes. *I* know what I'm talking about."

(Actually, Sinbad got most of his information from TV and the Internet. Mastering the remote and the mouse had been easy. Mr. Murphy was not aware that, late at night or when left alone in the house, his 'pet' would be watching television or scouring the Internet for hours.)

"King Noble doesn't need to live in the world to know things," said Fender. "He knows because he is wise."

"Hmm." Sinbad scratched behind his ear and yawned. He patted the open cavity indifferently. "And what kind of knowledge is that—that knows without any evidence or experience? Is it simply absorbed into the canine brain? Like muddy water seeping into a well after a rainstorm?" He looked questioningly around the group. "Is this how *we* come to *know* things, my friends? Or could it be fabrication? Or even deceit?"

Fender opened his mouth to protest. "But, you ... it's..." He looked confused. After all, defending King Noble should be as easy as eating a mushroom pie.

Sinbad seized the advantage. He glared at the fumbling dwarf. "Hmm? No convincing rebuttal from our friend, Mr. Squat-Pants?"

Fender leapt up in a fury and rushed at the cat. "Why you mis'rable pumped-up, pumpkin head!"

Sinbad jumped lightly onto a small ledge protruding from the rock face. He looked down at the scrambling dwarf.

"Tut, tut. Such a temper now. We can't have that, can we? This is a peaceful gathering, after all."

"Peaceful, my sun slicker!" shot back the dwarf, using a common expression referring to his bald head. "This is treason! And you know it."

"Duff!" Sinbad called to the largest of the giants present. "Duff! Remove this person immediately. He is disturbing the peace. Really, if you don't have anything reasonable to say, you shouldn't say anything at all. Go back to that beetle-headed hound friend of yours and leave the talking to someone who knows what he's talking about."

A great oafish giant, at least fifteen-feet tall, shuffled forward. His hair was as red as rust and sprouted from a fat freckled brow like an unruly patch of quack grass. With a hand the size of a briefcase, he grabbed the scrabbling dwarf by the back of his shirt. He grinned toothily at the cat. "Where do you want me to put him, Sire?"

"*Sire?*" Fender could hardly believe his ears.

Sinbad waved a paw in dismissal. "Just take him away ... far away. Somewhere that he can't find his way back from in a hurry."

"Right, Sire. Glad to oblige. Come along now, you little rapscallion rebel."

"*Rebel? Me?*" Fender was horrified. "Sinbad's the rebel, you blunder-brain!"

"Hey! Watch who you is calling names."

"I won't forget this, cat!" Fender shook a fist at Sinbad. "You'll pay! Just you wait. I'll get my own back." With great lumbering strides, the giant and Fender disappeared into the surrounding woods.

All heads swiveled after them. The crowd was stupefied. In all the long history of Tolk, they had never before seen the likes of this: insults slung like stones, a giant obeying the command of a cat, and worst of all, one of their fellows bodily removed from a public gathering. They could only gape in stunned silence, even after the two figures had been engulfed in darkness.

Then they heard a loud whirring sound, like hundreds of bees descending on them in a swarm. A murmur of confusion buzzed through the crowd until they located the source. It was Sinbad. He was spinning the long strap over his head at high speed. It hummed like a live wire. He pulled back on it sharply. CRACK! The sound reverberated off the rock face and up into the still black sky. He spun it again, and then whipped it back suddenly. CRACK!

"O-o-oh," the crowd sighed in one voice.

"Ah-ha!" Whiz ... CRACK! "You see what I can do? Behold the power of Sinbad! Sinbad, the Great Flaming Cat! Sinbad, the Royal Feline! Ah-ha!" Whiz ... CRACK! "Isn't it marvelous?"

He stopped, and then shut his eyes and drew in a long breath. He was panting slightly.

"I have seen whips like this used to force animals into submission—slavery! Should such power come to Tolk, should it fall into the wrong hands, what would happen then? Who would protect you? Ah." He seemed suddenly overcome with sorrow. "I can hardly bear the thought of it."

The entire assembly stared in mute wonder at the grieving cat. His lower lip was trembling and a real tear slid down his nose. He wiped it away ceremoniously with the back of his paw.

A small, earnest voice piped up. "What 'wrong hands' do you mean, Sire?" It was Meepy. He was sitting in the front row, black eyes shining and alert.

Sinbad promptly recovered from his anguish. "Ah now, my young friend, that's a good question. And you are very clever to think of it." Meepy sat up taller and watched the cat eagerly, hopefully.

Sinbad sat back on his haunches and looked soberly out over the crowd. His voice was hushed, but so intense that it carried to the farthermost edge of the clearing.

"Not everyone, you know, is as honest and straightforward as you or me. It pains me to tell you that there are those amongst us who are keeping *secrets!*"

"Who?" Barlow Bear's deep voice sounded skeptical.

"Yes, who?"

"Ah, now, I cannot be naming names. But..." His voice dropped lower yet. "There is that *human* creature." Then he spoke more loudly again. "That ... *boy*. What *has* he been up to, prowling around Tolk? Now I ask you."

"Boy!"

"What boy?"

"Oh, just some 'acquaintance' of King Noble. A human. Of course, there are humans and then there are humans. Some can be trusted and some cannot."

"A *boy*?"

"A *human*?"

"Here in Tolk?"

It was unheard of.

"Well, I say if there *is* a boy and King Noble brought him here, then we know he *can* be trusted!" declared Mertyl, a large brown bear.

"Oh ... apparently our friend Mertyl has already met the lad. Is that so, Mertyl?"

Mertyl frowned. "King Noble's good opinion is good enough for me!"

"I see." Sinbad stroked his chin whiskers. "I see that you acquire knowledge in the same way that the great King Noble himself does, not to mention that bad-tempered dwarf who left us in such a hurry this evening. It's the same method, I think, that you use to capture rainbows or elf song. With a sort of invisible net. Isn't that so? Hmm?"

"Sinbad, that's ridiculous!" Mertyl spluttered angrily.

"Ridiculous? Did you hear that, everyone? Mertyl, the brown bear, has just admitted that forming opinions based on nothing more than hearsay is ridiculous. Remember now, that *was* your own word for it. Do you agree or don't you?"

"Yes, of course, but..."

"There you have it my friends!" Sinbad again raised the strap high into the air and spun it rapidly. Whiz ... CRACK! Then he called out in a loud voice, "It just so happens, my fellow Tolks, that *I* had a chat with the boy this afternoon!"

Every pair of eyes was suddenly riveted on the cat. He had spoken to the boy, this unknown interloper? Open-mouthed and staring, all were keenly anticipating what he would divulge next.

But Sinbad took his time. He studied his claws again for a moment; then he looked directly out over the crowd.

"The boy is a liar!" he said at last. "He told me flat out that he had never spoken to King Noble. Never. But what *he* didn't know is that I saw him and that dog have a conversation this morning. Saw them with my own eyes! Now..." He paused again. "Why do you suppose he would lie to me?"

Of course, no one had any idea.

"I'll tell you why. Because he is hiding something, that's why. Why else? Oh, you must shun this deceitful human boy.

"And so, my friends, you learn the *truth* about the kind of monarch who rules in the Land of Tolk. Our own king associating with a human boy who is a liar. And to what end, I ask? Why? *Why* should he deign to bring a human into Tolk? Do any of *you* know the reason?"

The Tolks stole uneasy glances at one another. Many were shaking their heads. All eyes refocused on the cat.

"No? Can any of you explain *why* no one knows what the boy was doing here?"

Again many heads shook 'no.'

The cat lowered his voice to an intense whisper. "Then it must be a *s-s-secret!*" he hissed.

Sinbad began to pace again, as though deep in thought, giving the audience some time to mull this over.

The bonfire had been gradually diminishing and the feline shadow, slinking back and forth across the rock face behind, had grown proportionately larger.

"That is not to say that *all* humans are deceitful. Oh, no-no. That is not so. Humans, I have learned, are of two kinds. Simply put, there are those who adore me and those who don't."

(Next to the time spent with Frank Murphy, Sinbad's most regular haunt was the local mall. It all began one day when a small group of girls from the junior high school discovered him snuffing around outside the entrance. One of the girls had picked him up, cooing over him as she stroked his brassy coat. The others gathered around, oohing and ahhing, and naturally, Sinbad had basked in all of this attention.

He hardly objected when the first girl placed him gently into her backpack, making sure that his head and front paws protruded from the top. It wasn't a position of dignity, exactly—the girls commented on how 'cute' he looked— but it *was* a way to gain entrance to the mall, a privilege he would enjoy many times.

Once inside, the girls often made small cash purchases, and it was from this perspective that Sinbad had acquired his interesting take on money. He soon noticed people getting bills by inserting small plastic cards into the ATM machines, and then using either these bills or the same cards in exchange for the things they wanted. Being somewhat familiar with the computer, he imagined that the cashiers were simply tracking the flow of merchandise on some massive site on the Internet. *How inventive these humans are!* he marveled. *How clever. To think, they have devised such a cunning way to manage the distribution of all of these goods!* After all, how else would they know what and how much to stock? The idea that people might actually have to earn the money never entered his mind.

With each visit, they made their way through the various shops, and it wasn't long before Sinbad had won the admiration of a number of the salesclerks, even the cleaning staff. The two women who kept the craft shop fawned over his gorgeous coat. The shoe lady and the convenience store clerk were charmed by his shamelessly arrogant poise. The fat, smiling owner of the Meat Shoppe liked to slip him a sardine from time to time. In fact, the cat had become a sort of mascot. Even Security turned a blind eye to his presence. Pretty soon Sinbad was coming and going on his own, whenever he felt like it.)

"In the outside world," the cat went on now, "there are humans who simply dote on me. Tch, if you only knew how wonderful it is. There's one particularly kind and generous man who waits upon me daily. Ah ... Mr. Frank Murphy. He feeds me ... oh, the food that he feeds me, and the quantity, you cannot even begin to imagine!

"He has a tremendous garden. Beans, peas, carrots sprouting as long as my tail, squash the size of Duff's head, juicy strawberries, and raspberries, big as plums. And corn as pale and plump as the Sowbe's little piggies. And the cream ... oh, the cream!" He shut his eyes and began to purr magnificently. "As fresh and cool as dew on the grass at dawn. He brings it to me, this man, every afternoon, in my own dish, when I awaken in my room where I have been sleeping on silken cushions. Oh, it is such a life of ease and plenty."

Then, with a doleful look, he cast his eyes down. "How sad it is that you must only just imagine it."

"Aye, Sinbad!" called a suspicious voice. "And what do you have to do to *deserve* all this luxury?"

"Do? What do I have to *do*?" The cat laughed his brittle, dry laugh. "I *do* nothing at all. Humans adore cats: There's the truth of it. Most humans, that is. The good ones. Actually, they are fond of nearly all animals—with the exception, of course, of dogs. Humans have very little use for dogs."

The foundation for this belief was the dog that lived just down the street. Sinbad had noticed that the animal was sometimes kept in a kennel where he was given bones to chew on and mere water to drink. Why, the poor dumb animal had to fetch and obey at the slightest command from its master—and even seemed to enjoy it. Sinbad had come to see this as a very fitting life for a dog.

"Uh, by the way, are there any dogs here this evening?" he asked.

"No," someone answered. "The dogs all hate you, Sinbad. Every last one of them is loyal to King Noble. They refuse to come anymore. That's the way dogs are."

"Yes, I thought so. You know, the trouble with dogs is that they are far too blundering and inept. They're not shrewd, not lithe and graceful, like a cat." With that he arched his supple back and stretched. "And one dog in particular that we all know—I won't mention any names—is about as competent as a cricket that's lost his fiddlestick. He's no longer fit to lead a bear to a beehive. The merest hint of any improvement to our present way of life and he balks, like a dwarf dodging a dig, when all the time there's treasure, my friends, *treasure*. Treasure so immense we couldn't put it all into Wildwood Canyon!"

In the beginning, Sinbad had shared his dreams and schemes with King Noble, friend to friend. It was inevitable that a rift would follow as that 'incompetent' dog just could *not* see the folly of his ways.

"Did you know that humans actually build large houses for cows and sheep and horses and goats, and even the pigs?" he went on.

"No-o-o." A murmur of disbelief rippled through the crowd.

"Really. It's as true as I'm standing here and speaking to you at this moment. Warm, comfortable houses. They're called 'barns' and they're nothing like those primitive huts the giants live in or the thatched cottages of the dwarfs. These are made from metal or smooth, flat boards. There is fresh straw to lie on every day, all amenities provided. Some animals even get brushed and groomed from time to time."

"I still say you must have to *do* something—give the humans something back. Why would they wait on us for nothing?" It was that same suspicious voice again.

Sinbad sat down and glared angrily out over the crowd.

"Someone here doesn't listen very well. The truth is that humans revere animals—and the likes of everyone assembled here tonight. There are kings, you know, who try to keep their subjects down, in the dark. It makes them feel superior. I won't mention any names." The cat half shut his yellow eyes.

"Now, perhaps some of you recall our good friends, Dori and Smoot? Why, only last week I invited them to come with me into the outside world. They were skeptical, too. But now I find myself in an embarrassing position. Heh-heh. I'm afraid I must convey my sincerest regrets to their kin and friends. The fact is, I just can't persuade them to come back. They're enjoying their new life so much that they don't want to leave!"

"You mean they wasn't changed into stumps or something?" This question came from Duff, who had just returned from accomplishing his errand.

The cat chortled. "No, no. Such an idea! Just an old puppy's tale."

"That's a lie, Sinbad!" This from Spark, the black squirrel. "I know. I was there myself today. I saw them, solid wood, propped up for all to see, put on display by your 'kind' Mr. Murphy, on his very own property!"

Sinbad stood stock-still. Only the tip of his tail twitched slightly. A hush fell over the assembly.

(Now, the truth was that Sinbad's luring of the dwarfs out of Tolk had been a serious blunder. It had all begun one afternoon when he was at the mall visiting Joe Kanutz, the barber, hoping for a dish of cream. At first he'd thought the person sitting in the barber's chair was a child. It wasn't until he heard him speak that Sinbad realized it was actually a man—a very small man just over a yard tall, one of the little people. Sinbad could hardly believe his eyes. Then, as luck would have it, the very next day he was watching a popular talk show on TV when the host happened to interview two dwarfs. And later that same week, he'd seen MGM's 1939 version of *The Wizard of Oz*. Why, apparently there were hundreds of dwarfs existing in the human world, living perfectly normal lives!

You'd think he would have noticed some striking differences between the dwarfs from Tolk and human dwarfs and little people. But he didn't notice, and all of this had gotten Sinbad to thinking. You can imagine his state of shock and horror when Dori and Smoot stiffened into wooden dwarf-like logs. Coward that he was, Sinbad had immediately fled the scene. Later, when Mr. Murphy stumbled on them, he'd been so charmed by the figures, actually ecstatic with happiness, that he'd promptly put them in his garden. Now it had become absolutely crucial to Sinbad to keep them there, at least for the time being—not only to please Mr.

Murphy, but also to save face. After all, if Dori and Smoot were to return to Tolk, what would they say about him to the others?)

"Ah, so you saw them, did you? Hm, there seems to be something amiss here." Innocently, the cat cocked his head to one side. "For I saw them myself today, spoke to them, in fact. They were alive and well, and enjoying themselves immensely. In fact, Dori asked me to pass on a message to Dileen. He says not to worry about the hole in the thatch on their miserable hovel. Soon he will be coming back to build her a real house. Uh, by the way, has anyone seen Dileen here this evening?" he asked pleasantly. "Dileen Toadbry, are you present?"

A deep, trembling voice came from somewhere near the back. "Aye, I'm here." A short, round dwarf-lady, wearing a red-and-white polka-dotted kerchief over thick dark curls, rose unsteadily to her feet. She had large, anxious eyes and nervously licked her big lips.

"Now, please, Dileen, won't you ... help me out of this predicament here? It seems my word is being called to task. But, has Dori been concerned at all about the sad state of your thatched hovel? Has not the roof been leaking?"

Dileen glanced about nervously. "Yes, it's true," she said. "Dori promised to mend it last half-moon. Before he went..." Her voice failed and she began to furiously fight back tears.

"Now, now. You mustn't cry, my dear. Dori is well. I'm sure he'll be coming home soon. He sends his love, says not to worry. He is having such a marvelous time."

"No! No! It's not true. Dori would never leave me all alone. It must be a lie!"

"There-there, now. It's only that you cannot imagine such bliss. It's like—"

"No, Sinbad. That won't do!" It was Spark again. "I say that Dori spoke to you about the broken thatch *before* you lured him to his fate. I say that you are—"

"*You* say. You! I am straight and plain about my dealings in the outside world. What about you? Just exactly what were you doing there, poking about in death's domain? Hm? And who showed you the portal? Was it King Noble? And *why?*"

"Well, for one thing, I went to see for myself the fate of our two dwarfs—"

"For *one* thing? Did you hear that, folks? For *one* thing. Really? And what *other* reasons did you have for trespassing on human territory? Tell me."

Spark hesitated. "I'm sorry, but I'm not at liberty to say."

"You're not? Well then..." Sinbad glowered down at the squirrel. "I guess *you* must be in on the *secret!* Isn't that so?"

Spark did not reply.

Sinbad chuckled dryly. "And what about that lying boy? I don't suppose you've had any dealings with him?"

"I have seen the boy, though I've never spoken to him."

"Do you deny that he is a liar?"

"As far as I know he is not a liar."

"He lied to me."

This, Spark could not readily refute, so he said nothing.

Then Sinbad spoke very softly and slowly, testing the weight of each word. "I think that you, too, are a liar."

"No!" cried Spark, jumping to his feet. But no one heard him, for at that same instant Sinbad had leapt up, too. Suddenly there was a loud hissing from the bonfire and a cloud of smoke ascended skyward.

"Ah-ha!" Under his arm the cat sported a formidable looking water gun, the kind with a big plastic barrel and a pump. Swish ... HISSSS! He directed a second stream of water into the fire. Again, smoke billowed up.

Suddenly he turned and shot a jet of water into the crowd. It hit Spark right on the nose. Startled, the squirrel spluttered noisily. Then, dazed and frightened, he fled into the woods.

"Ha, ha, ha!" Sinbad chortled gleefully. "It's only water! Water! Ha, ha, ha!" He continued to laugh with such genuine hilarity that soon others had joined in. Before long much of the crowd was roaring. "Only water!" they shouted joyfully.

Wiping tears from his eyes, Sinbad raised a paw for silence.

"Ah, my friends. You see this." He held up the gun. "It's called a water pistol. Humans use a somewhat different version to keep at bay those ferocious, wild animals I told you about." He shot one more stream into the crowd, at a couple of beavers. They wriggled in delight, lapping at the water with their tongues. Everyone laughed again.

"Ha, that was a great joke." Sinbad sighed and resumed his discourse good-naturedly. "Now, tell me, Buckley, you look like a clever fellow. Beavers are, of course. Have you ever considered speaking directly to your friend, Frip, here, five miles downstream, without even leaving the comfort of your dam?"

"Well now, I can't say as I have." Buckley looked up inquiringly.

"Do you think you might like to do that?"

"I expect it could come in useful on occasion."

"Well then, let me tell you about *this!*" He held up a small, flat, black, plastic object. "It's called a cell phone." He'd stolen it from a lady who'd fallen asleep outdoors in her lounge chair with the phone on the table beside her. With a toenail, Sinbad punched in some numbers and set it on speaker-phone. Everyone listened, enthralled. The machine began to buzz intermittently. Then there was a click.

"Hello?" the telephone spoke.

Everyone gasped in amazement.

"Hello there," the cat sang out jovially. "Is this Frank Murphy?"

Grinning, Sinbad pointed the instrument at the crowd for all to hear.

"Yes, this is Frank. Who is this? Hello? Are you there?"

"And how are you this evening, Frank?"

"Say, who is this, anyway? Are you aware that it's almost eleven o'clock?"

"This is Sinbad, Frank. I'm just letting you know that I won't be home 'til morning, so please, don't wait up for me."

"What? Why, of all th..." There was a click. Then silence.

"Ha-ha!" Sinbad crowed, slapping his cat 'knee.'

No one there had noticed Meepy slip silently away and disappear into the surrounding darkness. And no one was aware that lying flat upon the crest of the rocky cliff high above them, watching everything, was King Noble himself. The canine brow was furrowed, as though deep in thought. But he did nothing to interfere.

Chapter Fourteen: Price has a Plan

At the same time these events were unfolding in Tolk, Price was lying awake in bed staring blankly at a pale patch of window light reflected on the closet door. Gradually, a plan had begun to take shape in his mind. To begin with, he realized he would have to make the rescue at night, when Mr. Murphy and Grandmother were asleep. Even if Mr. Murphy happened to be gone during the day, it would be too risky to attempt it then. If he tried and failed, it would be game over for the dwarfs—*and* land him in a heap of trouble.

Of course, now that Sinbad knew that Price had been to Tolk, there was no question he would have guessed the reason why. The boy shut his eyes tightly. Sinbad would also realize that the rescue had to happen at night. That would put him on his guard. He would make sure that Mr. Murphy let him outside by sunset each evening. Those dwarfs would be watched every minute. And everybody knows that a cat can make enough irksome noise to wake the dead.

Anyway, Price thought smugly, *now that he has to hang around here all night, it'll at least put a stop to his troublemaking.* He flipped onto his back.

Somehow Sinbad would have to be distracted. The boy's eyes shifted from point to point around the room, seeing nothing. In his mind, however, he plainly saw Mr. Murphy's garden. He could picture the dwarfs standing rigid under the boughs of the poplar tree, dark and shadowy in the moonlight. He could even hear the fountain and the water-fall gurgling softly, and could vaguely make out the gently nodding heads of the hundreds of flowers—no longer shining with color, but muted and gray. *Yes, the flowers. They could be useful,* he thought, and rolled back onto his side.

Somehow he'd have to trick the cat into raising a ruckus on a false alarm. Then the old man would be forced to take him in the house. That would leave the coast clear. But how could he do it? *What about some of the smaller animals?* he wondered. *Could they help out?* Once more Price's eyes began to rove. At last a satisfied smile crept over his face. He clucked softly under his breath. "Yes!" he whispered. Rolling over, he nestled into his pillow, shut his eyes, and went to sleep.

The next morning Price skipped blithely down the stairs whistling "The Cat Came Back." (Cats were still playing prominently on his mind.) Grandmother was sitting at the kitchen table reading the newspaper and eating toast. His parents hadn't wakened him when they'd left for the airport early that morning. They'd said their goodbyes the night before, and he'd received all of the necessary admonitions about how to behave in their absence, such as listen to your grandmother, eat what she cooks, help with the dishes, don't wear the same pair of shorts and T-shirt for the entire month, and so on. He felt a bit lonely knowing that he wouldn't see his parents for such a long time, but on the bright side, he realized it would make visits into

Tolk easier to arrange and execute. Unlike his mom and dad, his grandma had absolute confidence that the universe was unfolding exactly as it should. She didn't worry about things.

"Good morning, Price!" she chirruped. Grandmother never made him breakfast or even suggested that he eat any. She left that strictly up to him. He popped some bread into the toaster.

"Morning, Grandma."

"You're up late. Didn't you sleep well?"

"Mm. Okay, I guess." He was glad that his back was turned.

"I see it's going to be a hot one again today," said Grandmother. "Still, I refuse to complain. Winters are long enough." She pulled her glasses down to the end of her nose and looked at him over the top of the newspaper. "Your mother asked me to take you into town to get some new shoes and pants for school. And there's a list of supplies— notebooks, pencils, and the like. Shall we do that today and get it over with?"

For a few seconds Price didn't move. But then he quickly swallowed his disappointment. "Sure," he answered carelessly. Apparently he would not be venturing into Tolk today.

"Good!" Grandmother took a sip of orange juice. "And as long as we're in town, I'll treat you to lunch. How does that sound?"

Price didn't get into Tolk the next day either. Grandmother had a headache. Their shopping excursion in the heat the day before had been too much for her. She spent most of the day in a darkened room with an ice pack. He didn't like to leave her alone, so he stayed close by and brought her cheese and crackers and vegetable soup he'd prepared from a can.

But the following day she was up before he was. Early in the morning, he found her sitting in the den crocheting and watching an old black-and-white movie on television. Her hands worked feverishly—like two busy five-legged spiders. Price sat down on the arm of the sofa.

"Can I go to the park today, Grandma?"

She looked up at him. "I don't see why not. By the way, thank you for taking such good care of me yesterday."

Price smiled bashfully. "How're you feeling?"

"Fine, thanks to you."

"Is it okay if I pack a lunch? I'll be home for supper."

"You may, of course. Will you be seeing your friend?" Grandmother winked slyly.

"I hope so." He was already halfway to the door.

"Then you'd better pack enough for two."

Outdoors, Price climbed onto a lawn chair and peered over the wall into Mr. Murphy's garden. He could hear dishes clattering through the open kitchen window, but no person or cat was in sight.

It was then that he noticed the black motion-detector light high up over the door.

Of course! He slapped his forehead with his palm. Nowadays, nearly all backyards had lights with motion detectors. How could he have missed such an important detail? And for his plan to work, he knew, there could be no light on the scene brighter than an ordinary flashlight. Somehow, it would have to be deactivated. But how?

With that on his mind, he jumped back down and headed to the garage to get his bicycle. The animals wouldn't trigger it, he realized: they were too low to the ground. But as soon as Mr. Murphy stepped outside, he'd see everything. Those LED lights were glaring. He'd have to figure something out.

Price had reached the poplar tree by this time. He was glad that it blocked any view of their gate from the old man's house; he knew that he could slip through without being seen. But, to his dismay, when he pulled on the latch, it didn't budge.

Oh no! he thought. *Another problem.* He was sure that Mr. Murphy must have discovered the open padlock. Frustrated, he reached a hand over the top of the gate and gave the lock a belligerent tug. To his surprise, it opened immediately. *How about that!* he thought. Someone must have rigged it so that it looked locked, but wasn't. *Someone,* he smiled to himself, *with small, bony claws.*

Once in the space, he carefully re-closed the tampered padlock. He let out a long sigh of relief, grateful that he was not alone on this mission.

Soon he was speeding through the tall grass with fresh morning air whipping against his face. He decided to head straight to Number 12, Riverbend.

Half an hour later, after he'd chained his bicycle to the same tree as before, he squeezed under the bushes and made his way through the hidden tunnel. He was just about to knock on the small wooden door when he spied a note.

P.E.

We're not home. Ask Millie for directions.

T.A.

As soon as he'd read it, he crumpled the note and stuffed it into his shorts' pocket. *Never leave behind any incriminating evidence*, he thought with a smile.

There was such a tittering and squawking coming from behind the Muskin door that Price wondered if something was wrong. He hesitated before knocking.

"Is anybody there?" he called.

The squawking stopped immediately and a few seconds later the door was opened by O.P. The small round face lit up with pleasure. "It's you!" he exclaimed, but then abruptly caught himself. "Is anybody here!" he scolded. "I should think that would be obvious. Unless you've got buds in your ears."

Price grinned. "Hi, O.P. Nice to see you, too. I can tell you've made yourself right at home. Is Millie around?"

"Nope."

"Well, I'm supposed to ask her for directions."

"Again? Are you *always* lost?"

Price laughed. "No more than usual, I guess."

Meepy appeared in the doorway next to O.P. He was wiping a tear from his eye and blew his nose forcefully into a handkerchief about the size of a playing card. It sounded like one of those tin horns you buy at the Dollar Store and blow on New Year's Eve.

"Are you okay?" asked Price.

"As right as watercress and acorn gravy," the mouse replied, draping an arm across O.P.'s shoulder. Then he began to giggle.

Price rolled his eyes. "So, you guys are pals now?"

"It's like this..." explained O.P. "We've discovered that we have two essential things in common. One is that we're roughly the same size, and that's an important consideration when you're only eight inches tall. And the second is that we are firmly united in our contempt for that scurvy cat." O.P. scowled. "I met him yesterday for the first time. D'you know what he called me?"

"No. What?"

"He called *me* a knothead! Me!"

Price quickly coughed into his hand, so that he wouldn't laugh.

"But that's not the only reason I don't like him. He's also a troublemaker and a liar."

"I agree." Price nodded sagely. "Anyway ... where's Millie?" he asked.

Meepy looked up at him through bleary eyes. "Tee-hee-hee." He swabbed a cheek with the back of his paw. "She and Tommy are at the meeting. If you came by, I was supposed to take you there."

"A meeting? Okay. Well, here I am."

"Yes. Tee-hee-hee. Say, have you seen O.P.'s impersonation of Sinbad combing his fur? Ha, ha!" In a fit of mirth, he plunked himself down on the threshold.

Price glanced suspiciously at the pinecone man, who (suddenly overcome with modesty) bowed his head and turned slightly away. "Can't say as I have," Price replied.

"It's really nothing much," muttered O.P. with the abject humility of a monk in sackcloth and ashes. Then his face brightened. "Watch this!"

With painted nose in the air, strutting grandly in a circle, he proceeded to glide an invisible comb through long, invisible strands of fur with such exaggerated vanity that it really was pretty amusing. Especially when the comb caught on an imaginary snarl.

The meeting was taking place within the shelter of a small wood. From the outside, it was impossible to see that the trees enclosed a grassy clearing. Meepy led them past the sentinel—a speckled brown hare. Like the entrance, the hare was invisible—until they heard him speak. Price jumped at the sound of an unfamiliar voice.

"The long-beards are having their say. Tch. Grim tidings these, grim tidings."

Meepy acknowledged the hare with a casual salute.

"Does he mean the dwarfs?" asked Price as they crept into the covey.

The mouse nodded.

King Noble reclined in the center of a group of beings and animals seated on the grass. He looked like a sphinx with his magnificent head erect and front paws stretched out before him. A dwarf whom Price did not recognize was addressing him. At that moment, the king's attention was focused entirely on the dwarf.

Price looked out over the crowd. He spied Timmins and Dot Arbuckle, Bootle, Spark the squirrel, Fender and Bray, Priscilla, and Millie Muskin. Millie was seated primly next to a male mouse dressed in trousers and suspenders. There were many others whom he had never seen before, creatures of different shapes and sizes, including (he noted with some trepidation) three enormous people as large as trucks—two giants and a giantess. Then he saw a small group of tiny people, all dressed in green, huddled together in a corner. They were as slender as willows and he guessed that, when standing, each would be no more than eighteen inches high. They had sweet pixie faces with large eyes and pointed ears. Price stared at them in wonder for several minutes. *Elves*, he thought in awe.

Near the back, Freddy sat cross-legged with three other fairies, each remarkably beautiful. One had cranberry-red hair cascading over her shoulders in long, loose coils. The second's straight blonde hair flowed down her back like a shining river. The third was a boy fairy with thick black curls and flawless brown skin, as smooth as a stone that has been tumbled about and worn for hundreds of years.

When Freddy caught sight of Price, her eyes fluttered wide open and shone like two stars. A smile as bright as daybreak flooded her face.

Price smiled back and nodded. The three other fairies turned and looked at him curiously with three pairs of large, slanted, unfathomable eyes—sea-green, sapphire-blue, and black.

"There is *some* good news," the dwarf was saying. "There are the birds, of course. They're all loyal. Every claw and feather, every beak and talon, right to the last wisp of down."

"That doesn't surprise me. Birds are of such free and independent spirit. There is little that Sinbad could tempt them with." It was the first time Price had heard King Noble's deep, mellow voice.

"Aye. But many more have gone over to his side, Sire. Many more: Ipscon and his kin, and the two beavers, Buckley and Frip. And Monscottle, the otter, he's gone over, too. His kin will no longer let him pass through the door."

King Noble's dark eyes looked steadily at the dwarf. "Go on," he said.

"Even Maebry, Sire." The dwarf shook his head in disbelief.

"Maebry?" It seemed King Noble could hardly believe it himself.

"Aye, Sire. Maebry and about six of her elf kin: Twinkles, Willowwood, Winderbry, Berrybrown and ... and some others. I can't recall all their names."

"But why? Elves don't normally keep company with the likes of Sinbad. What could he possibly say to the elves that would interest them?"

"Ah, but that's not the problem, Sire. I was speaking to Eidelbry about it yesterday. He tells me that, ever since you forbade Maebry and her friends to take strawb'ries from Lynwood's garden, she's been seething resentful. She's taken offense, you see, Sire. And you know how touchy elves can be."

"So that's it." King Noble growled softly and shut his eyes. "Such a foolish little wood nymph. I will have to speak to her myself."

"But that's not the worst of it," continued the dwarf, lowering his voice. "I hear as some have begun to collect implements such as rocks, staffs, sharp sticks, kettles, and pans. Storing them in a cave somewhere, so they say. I haven't as yet discovered where."

King Noble frowned deeply. "This is bad news," he said. "Very bad news."

The dwarf squirmed uncomfortably, as though he could hardly bear to impart the next bad news. He blew out a puff of air and looked out over the treetops. "It has even been reported..." He pursed his lips and looked down at his feet.

King Noble coaxed him gently. "Don't be afraid, Mobbly. Go on."

"It has been reported," Mobbly began again, this time looking the king directly in the eye, "that last night there was a scuffle. Bran and one of the larger bears exchanged blows."

Whispered exclamations of surprise and shock rippled through the company.

"Bran, is this true?" King Noble's regal head swung round and his eyes singled out one of the giants.

Bran rose reluctantly to his feet. The great hulking giant-man hung his head. "Yes, it's true." Despite the meek demeanor, his voice rolled like distant thunder. "But, but..." He compressed his big lips and blinked rapidly, trying to harness his emotions. "Sire, he called you a tongue-lolling, slobbering idiot! I just couldn't bear it! And ... and then," the giant swallowed, "he up and bonked me on the snorer!"

To everyone's surprise, King Noble laughed. It was a deep, bass, throaty chuckle. "Did you get the better of him, Bran?"

"That I did, Sire."

"And what was his condition after the fact?"

"Oh, Sire," Bran was breathing hard. "He was weeping like a fairy caught out in the rain. His one eye swelled up like a ripe tomato!"

"And did you leave him in that state?"

"Oh, no, Sire! Mertyl and me took him home and made a poultice—chopped up cucumber and horseradish, with a dash of salt—Mertyl's own recipe."

King Noble grimaced, and then laughed again. "You have done well, Bran. You are truly an honorable giant. You have recognized the real enemy and have done more good for our cause than you know. After all, our principles are of little value if we cannot defend them, or each other, in a moment of truth. But remember: *Never* needlessly provoke your adversary and *never* go looking for trouble."

"But how can we tell, Sire?" asked Mobbly. "You have always said, in such a case, to turn front to back."

"Oh Mobbly, there has never before been a time like this in all the history of Tolk." The great dog's eyes glowered darkly under a heavy brow. "You will know how to act when your sense of justice is tempered with mercy. As our friend Bran here has demonstrated so well."

Then, all at once, King Noble looked directly at Price. "But listen, my friends! Here is someone who has come to help us. Price, please come forward and share with us what you have to say? We have been waiting for you."

Chapter Fifteen:
Setting the Plan in Motion

Sensing all eyes on him, Price stepped awkwardly into the clearing and stood before King Noble.

The dog rose and looked out over the assembly. "Fellow Tolks," he announced, "I now present to you Price Evans, a goodly human boy who has come to help us." He turned to Price. "We are eager to hear what you have to say." He signaled with a nod that he should begin. The king then resumed his sphinx pose on the grass.

Price cleared his throat. "I have a plan for rescuing the dwarfs," he said, speaking loudly enough for all to hear. "I'll need some of the small animals to help, those that are the swiftest and sharpest." He turned to King Noble. "It could be very dangerous."

"Let's hear what you have to say," said the king, "and then we'll decide."

Price drew in a long breath.

"The rescue," he began, "has to happen at night, when it's dark and all the humans are in bed asleep." He made a quick decision not to say anything about the backdoor light. He had an idea about that and would deal with it later.

"I can set up a rig in the poplar tree for hoisting up the dwarfs. I'll need..." he thought for a second, "about five yards of strong, dark-colored twine. The only kind we have at home is yellow." Again, he looked questioningly at King Noble.

"That can be arranged," the dog replied.

Price nodded, then continued, "Sinbad knows I've been to Tolk, and he's bound to have guessed why. He'll be like a pirate guarding his treasure. Every night, he'll make sure to be outside at sunset. He won't let those dwarfs out of his sight for a second.

"So, what we have to do is trick Sinbad into rousing Mr. Murphy on a false alarm. Uh ... Mr. Murphy—that's Sinbad's human master," Price explained. "Everybody knows that when cats get riled they can make a lot of noise. Where I live, people aren't allowed to let their pets—uh, animals—make a big disturbance at night. So if the noise gets too loud, Mr. Murphy will have to take Sinbad inside the house. Then the coast will be clear and we can make the rescue."

King Noble lifted his dog brow. "I see what you're getting at," he said, "but how do you propose we trick Sinbad?"

"Mr. Murphy is an award-winning gardener," Price explained. "He has the most beautiful garden in town. It's his pride and joy. So, this is my plan: On the night of the rescue, around midnight, some of the smaller animals and birds will sneak into the garden and hide all over the place without Sinbad seeing them." Again Price turned to the king. "Can they do that?"

"Oh yes," the dog chuckled. "Many of us have been out-witting Sinbad for months."

"Good." Price continued, "Later, when everything is quiet, at a signal all the animals will start wrecking the garden, all at the same time. You know, digging things up, eating the vegetables, trampling on the plants, things like that."

King Noble nodded his understanding.

"If Sinbad just let it happen, if he didn't try and stop it, Mr. Murphy'd be furious. He might even think Sinbad was responsible. He only keeps him around because he's ... useful in some way." Price looked down at his feet. He didn't want to reveal, at least not just then, that Sinbad was a mouser. He looked up again.

"So we have to bait Sinbad and confuse him, so he'll wake up Mr. Murphy. Then as soon as the old man comes on the scene, everything has to go still again. Everybody has to disappear into hiding in a flash. In the dark, Mr. Murphy won't be able to see anybody or any of the damage. Then, when Sinbad is gone, I can raise the dwarfs and..." Price paused. "And that's it."

King Noble was silent for a moment as he considered this scheme. "Yes, I think this is a good plan. It needs some development, but I believe it will work."

Price let out a long breath, relieved that the king agreed with his proposal. But then, suddenly, he tensed. "There is one hitch. Someone could get hurt, or even... It's different there than it is here in Tolk."

"Yes, I know," King Noble said softly. He stared at the ground for a few seconds. "I believe I can deal with that problem."

The dog rose to his feet. "You have heard the proposal," he said in a loud voice. "I think, with some careful preparation, it will work. Do we accept this plan to rescue our friends, or not?"

Heads came together as they consulted amongst themselves in whispers.

"Aye!" someone called. "I guess we don't have much choice."

"Yes, yes!"

"Aye!"

Every hand, wing, or paw was raised in agreement.

"You do understand that there is a risk involved—a risk to your lives?"

Another chorus of 'ayes' followed this pronouncement.

"Good. Now, who will be responsible for recruiting and training the volunteers?"

Meepy leapt to his feet. "I will, Sire."

King Noble nodded approvingly. "Very well, Meepy. You will be the captain, and Price will be your advisor. Come along with me, both of you, and we'll work out some of the details."

He turned to the others. "The rest of you can go now. But be ready at a moment's notice. And ... be wary." The dog's voice suddenly took on a deeper, more penetrating edge. "Be wary, I say! Every tongue must be bound to secrecy. I do not say merely to trust no one, I say, *do not even trust yourselves!*" It sounded like a judgment and a warning rolled into one. "A single thoughtless, stray remark could make one of *you* the enemy. Remember: This is no game we're playing. Dori and Smoot are depending on us for their lives. This may be our only chance to rescue them.

"Be off, then. But be cautious and be prepared. We shall meet again soon."

He led Price and Meepy aside, into the bushes. It was not the same place where they had first entered the clearing earlier; it was another invisible passage. In an instant, they were out of sight.

Quietly then, some going singly and some in pairs, the others began to slip away. The three exquisite fairies flitted off hand-in-hand. They did not fly high up over the woods as one might expect; instead, they threaded deftly in and out amongst the tree-trunks, beneath the branches, where they could not easily be seen. Even the giants hardly made a sound as they lumbered away, one by one, each in a different direction. Even they moved so stealthily that their passing was scarcely noticed, like the shadows of clouds gliding across the ground. The smaller animals scuttled off without the rustle of a leaf or the snap of a twig to give them away. Ten minutes later, the only person remaining, sitting all by herself in the middle of the clearing and looking very lonely and dejected, was Freddy.

Chapter Sixteen:
The Trouble with Freddy

More than half an hour later, Freddy still had not moved from where she'd been sitting at the meeting. Her large, gray eyes had grown sullen.

"That boy!" she muttered. "He didn't even speak to me. I thought he was my friend!" Angry, she clenched both small fists. "Ooooo!" Jumping up, she did a little tantrum dance with her feet. "Well, I don't care!" But if she could have seen her pouting face, she would not have been so sure. Then suddenly she deflated. A tear rolled down her cheek. "It's just that I thought that he—that *they* might need me."

Sniffing loudly, Freddy didn't hear the voices approaching until King Noble and Price were nearly upon her. They'd been only a few yards away the entire time, couched in the depths of an invisible leaf-bound hideaway. She quickly dabbed at her face with the palms of her hands. There was no time to fly off, but she managed (or so she thought) a look of pretend indifference. The dog and the boy, however, were so absorbed in conversation that they didn't notice the fairy doing her best to ignore them.

"I'm glad you thought of the backdoor light," King Noble was saying. "Yes, Spark can help you with that. He can easily scale the brick wall of the house."

"All he has to do it put black tape over the motion detector part," said Price. "The fixture's black so no one'll be able to see the tape. And no one will know it's not working until after dark. Mr. Murphy should be in the house by then."

King Noble nodded his approval. "Good thinking, Price."

"I'll cut up the tape," the boy went on, "and get it to you as soon as I can."

The dog nodded again. "You'll find a length of twine by the gate early tomorrow morning," he said. "You'd better get to it ahead of the old man."

"Okay," said Price. Then, frowning, he dug at the ground with the toe of a sneaker.

King Noble nudged him with his nose. "What's wrong?" he asked.

"What if something does happen to any of those animals? You know, Sinbad would stop at nothing."

"I'm aware of that, but don't worry. I won't let any harm come to even one of them. You'll have to trust me, Price. Do you?"

The boy looked steadily into the king's dark, kind eyes. "Yes, I do trust you. But how—?"

"Then there's nothing more to say, and I have many things to do. I must leave you for now. But we will all be anxiously awaiting further word."

As the dog turned to leave, he caught sight of Freddy, still sulking in the middle of the clearing, looking for all the world like a lost and fractious child.

"Winifred!" King Noble trotted over to her. "I thought I smelled a fairy. I noticed Elaine and Sylvia and Roland here today. Thank you for bringing them."

Freddy's mouth twisted indifferently. "If you must know, at first they refused to come," she said. "They didn't want to be drawn into a matter that is clearly the concern of the dwarfs."

"Then I'm glad you pressed them into joining us."

The fairy glanced down at her feet; then, with troubled eyes, looked up again at King Noble. "At the time, I felt such a sense of urgency. But now ... what difference did it make if fairies came to the meeting? It all seems so pointless!"

"Oh, I assure you, it makes a great difference. After all, they raised their hands along with the others. That was significant. Believe me Freddy, there's much more at stake here than the fate of two dwarfs. And you have much work to do yet."

Freddy stared.

King Noble smiled at her obvious confusion. "You'll understand soon enough," he said. "Now I have to leave you two. I'm sure there are things you want to talk about. And I, myself, have many promises to keep." As he bounded off, he called back. "We'll meet again soon!"

Price turned to Freddy and grinned.

But the fairy indignantly folded her arms. "Things to talk about!" she repeated. "I have no idea what he means. I have nothing at all to say to you."

Price was surprised. "What d'you mean? I thought we were friends."

"Oh, *are* we?" she said, looking the other way. But the trusting little fairy just couldn't keep it up. All at once, the bravado crumbled. "Yes..." she said in a small voice. "I thought we were friends, too. But then I began to wonder—"

"Why? Don't you want to be my friend?"

"Maybe ... maybe *you* don't want to be *my* friend." Freddy suddenly clapped a hand over her mouth. "Ooh..." she moaned. "It's as if I'm in a play and someone else has taken over my lines!"

Price was baffled. "What're you talking about?"

Freddy turned away. "It's just that these days so many Tolks are saying bad things about King Noble. Good King Noble. How could they!" She looked at Price in disbelief. "And ... and now you're so important. Everyone is counting on you. But *me* ... I'm nothing but a fairy."

Price stared at her vacantly. Then the light dawned. "Oh, so that's it!" He laughed. "Freddy, you're not just *any* fairy; you're the nicest fairy I know. Well ... so what if you're the only fairy I know. You're my friend. Come on!" Then, as if she were a small child, he reached down for her hand. But Freddy pulled away.

Price sighed. "Let's go find O.P." he suggested. "He's always good for some fun. And I've got my bike. Maybe you could show me around. Do you think we could see that town where the giants live? What's it called?" They started walking together toward the edge of the clearing.

"Drumbleton."

"Right. Maybe we could just look down at it from the top of a hill or something. Do you really think it's safe?"

"Every place in Tolk is safe. At least it used to be."

"But what if I fell off a cliff or something? What would happen to me?"

"That would be a very dumb thing to do!"

"I said, 'What if?'"

"What do you think would happen? You'd be banged up and probably sore for quite a while."

"Well, what if I had a knife and it slipped and cut off my finger?" He held up a token digit to illustrate his point. "Then what would happen?"

"Now I don't know what *you're* talking about." Freddy laughed at the ridiculous notion. "That's impossible!"

And so it was, in only one moment, all of the anxious thoughts and nagging doubts had been dispelled and forgotten.

Chapter Seventeen:
Sinbad has a Bad Day

The next morning, Price awoke at dawn. He was still weary after yesterday's adventures. He and Freddy and O.P. had trekked for miles across the countryside of Tolk. They'd gone to Drumbleton and watched the giants' comings and goings from the top of a bluff (even though Freddy had assured Price that it was perfectly safe to visit them in person). Later, Freddy had taken them up into her wonderful tree house. The fairies were weavers and lived in tree-dwellings with silken walls and roofs, like tents. But what a climb! Now Price had to summon his stiff muscles into action and get to that rope before Sinbad or Mr. Murphy found it. He dragged himself out of bed and quickly got dressed.

Outside, Sinbad was sitting on the west wall. Price realized that he must have been there all night keeping watch over the dwarfs. For a couple of seconds, their eyes locked in mutual mistrust. Then, ignoring him, Price headed to the gate. The yellow eyes followed him closely. Sinbad suddenly jumped down to the other side of the wall and out of sight.

A long coil of dark-green twine was waiting in the space just as King Noble had promised. But slick as greased glass, the cat got to it first. With a swift shifting motion, he began looping the coils over his shoulder—a bizarre sight, indeed, for any human used to the common house-cat. But of course, this was no ordinary cat.

"Unhand the rope, Sinbad."

Without batting an eye, the cat went right on looping. Price reached down to grab the rope, but Sinbad hissed, unveiling his dagger claws. The boy drew back.

"If you scratch me or bite me, you know, Mr. Murphy will have to 'put you down.' D'you know what that means?" Price made a slicing motion across his throat. "That's the way it is in this world, Sinbad. Cats can't attack kids. It's the law. And here—people rule."

The cat hesitated, but then stubbornly continued raveling the coils of rope.

Price steeled himself, grabbed the rope, and yanked. There was no question that the boy was bigger and stronger. Reluctantly Sinbad surrendered his booty. He slunk away, but not before casting back a lingering, malignant glare. Though he could say nothing, his meaning was clear.

Price took the rope into the house. Then he brought his toolbox up from the cellar and grabbed yesterday's newspaper from the kitchen table. He hurried upstairs to his room and quietly shut the door.

The first thing he did was pull out his roll of black electrical tape, which he used sometimes in his art—if he wanted to put a black border around a drawing to set it off, for example. He cut several strips of the tape, each about four-inches long, and stuck them, side-by-side, onto a piece of waxed paper. He folded the paper, along the long edges of the tape, into a neat rectangle, about the size and shape of a giant stick of gum.

Then he hurried downstairs to the den where the family computer was set up. Once logged onto the Internet, he Googled 'outdoor motion-detector lights.' Finding a good, clear image of a fixture that was similar to Mr. Murphy's, he printed it off. With a pen, he circled and labeled the area that had to be taped. Then he cut the page down to a more workable size—for a squirrel that is.

The job would have to be done sometime on the same day they made the rescue, when the coast was clear. He would pass the tape and the diagram on to Spark, as soon as it could be arranged.

Next, the pulley, he thought, running back upstairs to his bedroom.

Price had two skateboards under his bed. One was his—the one he had diligently saved birthday money and allowances to buy. The other was broken, but an older boy had given it to him in a rare moment of generosity, so he'd decided to keep it. (After all, you never knew when something might come in handy.) He pulled out the broken skateboard, and rummaging through the toolbox, found the appropriate screwdriver.

With the screwdriver, he carefully removed one set of wheels, complete with the metal apparatus that supported them on the skateboard. He gave one of the wheels a few drops of oil and spun it several times to make sure it ran smoothly. It hummed—no wobbles or glitches—almost musically. He took a yellow colored pencil, and after measuring carefully, drew a line down the center of the wheel. Spreading some newspaper on the floor, he flopped down on his knees, and with his sharp penknife, began whittling out a notch along the line. It was slow going, because the plastic was very hard. Intermittently he would stop and smooth it with sandpaper.

It took more than an hour to carve out a reasonably straight groove all the way around, just the right width and depth to fit the green rope. He planned to use only one pulley, so he ignored the second wheel.

Next, he assembled all of the items he would need. There were the four screws from the skateboard, the screwdriver, his grandfather's old-fashioned hand drill (with the correct size of bit), two sharp pencils (in case one broke), the rope, and of course, his penknife. He made a slipknot and a loop on one end of the rope. Then he put everything but the rope into a plastic bread bag and set them by the bedroom door.

Then he opened a dresser drawer and began rummaging through his clothes. He pulled out his black jeans, a black pullover with long sleeves, and some black socks. The only black shoes he owned were the dress shoes he wore to church. *They'll have to do*, he thought. At least they had rubber soles. He folded the clothes and set them neatly on the end of his bed, with the shoes to one side.

Buried in a back corner of his top dresser drawer, he located the brown Halloween make-up he'd used two years ago—all that remained of his escapade as a werewolf. He set the tube of make-up on top of the black clothes, none of which he would need until the fateful night.

Then he stood back and thought. Had he forgotten anything? Just the wagon. He had to make sure that his wagon was handy. And the rock. He intended to tie a rock to the rope as a tester. But he couldn't think of anything else. Now he had only to wait—wait until the middle of the afternoon, when the heat would drive Mr. Murphy and Sinbad indoors.

Price passed the time reading comics and playing *UNO* with his grandmother. She noticed, with a kind of detached interest, that while he had one eye on the cards, his other was plainly on the clock. By 2:00 p.m., his impatience was clearly escalating.

"I'm going outside, Grandma. I'll be in the yard, okay?"

"Of course." Grandmother leaned back in her chair and rubbed her eyes. "As a matter of fact, I'm a little tired. I think I'll go upstairs and take a nap." She yawned.

Price tried not to hurry too conspicuously, but breathed a sigh of relief when he was finally ready and stepped out the back door. He had fastened the plastic bag to a belt loop on his shorts, and the rope was coiled around his arm. He'd tied a knobby rock, about the size of a baseball, to one end of it.

He took a peek over the wall. No Mr. Murphy and no cat. Quickly and quietly, he climbed into the big tree and inched himself out along one of the stout boughs to get a better look. There was no sign of anyone in any part of the garden.

Just above him, he located the large limb that grew over the exact place where the dwarfs were standing. Grabbing hold of it, he braced his feet against the main trunk and pulled himself up. The bark felt rough against his bare legs as he scrambled onto the bough. A little shakily, he stood up, clinging to some leafy twigs. Step-together, step-together, he made his way along, clutching at the branches around him for balance. His heart was beating fast, and even in the heat of the day, his hands felt clammy. Every so often, he would check Mr. Murphy's back door. Then, shakily, he knelt down, pushed aside a tangle of leaves, and peered below. He was now directly over the dwarfs. Carefully, he straddled the limb.

Using the rock dangling from the rope as a plumb bob, he found the best spot to attach his pulley. Fetching his knife from the bag, he cut a slit in the limb to mark the spot. Then he raised the line. Next he began carving away some of the bark, to make a smooth, flat surface to attach the pulley. With great care, he put all the shavings and woodchips into the plastic bag—he didn't want any incriminating evidence dropping down onto Mr. Murphy's manicured lawn. He set the pulley temporarily in place and marked the position of the screw holes with the pencil. Then, holding the drill perpendicular to the branch, he cranked the handle. It whirred softly, but that couldn't be helped; it only meant that he would have to hurry.

To Price's dismay, each time he pulled the drill bit out of the wood, sawdust sprinkled down, landing right on the dark, domed head of one of the dwarfs, like flakes of dwarf dandruff. Price grimaced. He wished a breeze would spring up and blow the sawdust off, but the air was as still as death. The best he could hope for was that no one would notice, and if someone *did* notice, that they wouldn't look up into the tree and discover the source.

Price set the pulley back in place. With screwdriver and screws, he attached it tightly to the limb in the same way that it had been attached to his skateboard—only in this case, it stuck out to the side. Finally, he ran the twine into the groove he'd carved and lowered the stone to test it. It fell directly over the head of the dwarf. Satisfied, Price retrieved the stone. It was exactly as he'd planned.

He had just begun collecting his things when he saw a robin watching him from a nearby branch. He noted that she was larger than the robins that nested in the area—and bolder. She cocked her head to one side and watched him closely, seemingly without fear.

Price realized that she must be from Tolk and that King Noble had sent her to help him.

"There's sawdust on one of the dwarfs," he whispered, pointing down.

The words were not even out of his mouth when Mr. Murphy's back door swung open. Out stepped Sinbad. Price froze. The cat yawned, stretched, and without the least concern, strolled into the sunshine. He sauntered over to the wall, and with a bound, leapt to the top. He looked carefully around Price's yard. Satisfied that no one was there, he dropped back down again. It didn't occur to him to look up in the tree or check on the dwarfs. Instead he ambled over to the patio, which at this time of day was nicely shaded by the house. Then, stretching out full-length on the cool concrete floor, he shut his eyes.

Slowly Price inched his way back along the bough to his own side of the wall. Hiding behind some foliage, he watched as the robin swooped down, and with a wingtip, brushed away the sawdust.

Instantly Sinbad was alert. He craned suspiciously after the bird as she soared off into the blue sky. At once the cat trotted over to the dwarfs. The yellow eyes narrowed almost to nothing as he carefully checked them over. He circled them twice, but couldn't find anything amiss. The next moment he had jumped up on the wall, and for the second time, surveyed Price's backyard, his tail twitching in irritation. Then he saw Price crouched in the tree.

Neither boy nor cat moved. Price was wishing he'd stashed the tools in something more covert than a plastic bread bag, but there was nothing he could do about it now. And since Sinbad had seen him, there was no point in hanging around. Clutching his hand to the bag, he jumped down to the ground. He watched as the cat bounded up into the tree and began to creep along one of the boughs. Soon he was lost from sight in the greenery.

Price knew that Sinbad would find the pulley. Still, he was pretty sure that he couldn't budge it. And he was right. At that moment the cat was batting at it uselessly with a paw. He gnawed a bit at the wheel, but it was much too hard and tasted terrible. He spat.

Lingering uncertainly near the back door, Price realized that the cat would try everything possible to bring it to Mr. Murphy's attention. Would he succeed? Only time would tell.

Hurrying up to his room, Price took a scrap of paper from his desk drawer, and in small printed letters, wrote a brief message:

Sinbad found the pulley. We must act tonight. I will be by the wall at sunset. Be ready.

P.E.

P.S. I've attached the black tape and a picture for Spark. See that he gets it right away. King Noble can explain.

He wrapped the two pieces of paper together and secured them with scotch tape. Glancing out the window, he spied the robin sitting on the nethermost, tip-top branch of the poplar tree, apparently still keeping watch. *Good*, he thought, as he opened the window and partly lifted out the screen. Softly, he whistled to the bird. The robin had seen him as soon as he'd appeared at the window, and glided down from her perch, landing adroitly on the ledge.

Price handed her the message. "Take this to King Noble. Right away!"

The robin clasped the paper in her claws, and with a flap of her wings, was gone.

Just at that moment, Sinbad had resumed his post on the top of the wall. He spotted the robin as she swooped down and around the tree trunk, into the space. Like a streak of orange fire, he was after her.

Back in Tolk, the robin caught sight of Sinbad far below her. He was charging through the grass at a tremendous speed, trying to stay on her course. The robin, unwilling to risk dropping the precious cargo, coasted through the air, wings outspread. She tucked up her feet, with the message, into the downy feathers of her underside, and called out loudly three times. In a matter of seconds, a dozen other robins had joined her in the air. They flocked together, and then scattered in all directions.

Sinbad stopped. It was impossible to tell which bird was carrying the message. His pursuit had ended. He collapsed in the grass.

As soon as he got his breath back, the cat set off on his way home. He padded along slowly, deep in thought. He knew that tonight would be the night. And if Mr. Murphy caught Price in the act, the boy would likely never have another opportunity—tonight would be his one chance to rescue the dwarfs. Sinbad must see to it that Price was caught.

About an hour later, the cat was back again. Mr. Murphy was now outside, puttering amongst his famous lilies. Sinbad climbed into the poplar tree and sat down by the pulley. He began meowing repeatedly, keeping his eyes fixed on the old man.

"Mee-ow-eer-r, mee-ow-eer-r!" he crooned. It sounded almost like "Me over here. Me over here." Mr. Murphy looked up.

"If you think I'm gonna come an' get you out of that tree, you've got another 'think' coming." He chuckled over his clever pun, and then got down on his hands and knees to inspect the soil for weeds. "Nothin' but a conniving old faker." He cackled softly to himself.

But Sinbad kept right on caterwauling. Unperturbed, the old man ignored him, and was soon caught up in digging around the roots of a rose bush.

With an exasperated 'harrumph' and a couple of mute roars (the kind cats make when they know they've been outwitted), Sinbad gave it up.

This has not been a good day, he admitted grudgingly. *Nothing has gone my way.* The fur along his back prickled in annoyance as he stalked back along the bough. *Mark my words, tonight will be a different story.*

Chapter Eighteen:
A Journey into
Tolk at Night

At about 9:15, Price said goodnight to Grandmother, who was settled comfortably on the sofa in the den, knitting something very tiny.

She smiled up at him. "You're going to bed early."

"Mm. Kind of tired," he mumbled.

"Me, too," she said. "I'll be following you shortly. I just want to finish this bootie."

Upstairs in his room, Price quickly dressed in the black jeans and pullover, the black socks, and his good shoes. He put the coil of rope, the Halloween makeup, and a small black bag with the screwdriver and a flashlight into his backpack. Then he sat on the end of his bed in the fading light and waited.

He smiled to himself, recalling how he'd gone out after supper to check on the backdoor light situation, just in time to see Spark and another squirrel skittering across the top of the west wall, on their way into Tolk.

"Hey!" he'd called after them. The two had stopped in their tracks. Spark, looking back, had given him a quick salute before they'd both disappeared behind the poplar tree. That said it all. The job was done. Even now, Price could sense the relief.

Just then he heard Grandmother's slippered feet shuffling up the stairs. She made the inevitable trip to the bathroom, which was next to Price's bedroom. He could hear water running. The toilet flushed, and the medicine cabinet opened and closed twice. Then the slippered feet shuffled softly back into the hall. They paused before his door. Price held his breath. But the next moment, the hall light snapped off and Grandmother's bedroom door shut, and did not reopen.

Quietly he rose from the bed and tiptoed across the room, grateful that Grandmother was hard of hearing. He turned the doorknob very slowly and opened his door. Peering into the hallway, he saw light still shining from under Grandmother's bedroom door. Leaning against the wall, he waited. Three more long minutes passed. Finally, the bedsprings groaned a little and the lamp went out.

Outside, the sultry air had already begun to freshen. Price drew in a deep breath. With long strides, he set out across the lawn. There was just enough light to see the wagon waiting beside the tree, where he had set it earlier that evening. He wondered where the cat was. Over the west wall, he could see a pale glow that he knew came from Mr. Murphy's kitchen window. The ten o'clock news was sounding faintly from his TV.

Good, he thought. Maybe the old man had not yet put Sinbad out for the night.

His bicycle was leaning against the garage where he'd left it, at the ready. Silently, he opened the gate. Excitement mounting, he slipped down the stone steps, carefully guiding his bike. As a last precaution, he replaced the

padlock. Then through the space he went ... into the Land
of Tolk.

King Noble, Freddy, O.P., Meepy, the two squirrels, and
the robin, were all waiting when Price emerged through the
wall. The moon was not yet up, but there was still a faint
blush along the western horizon, and Freddy had brought
a lantern. The dog sounded a sharp bark of salutation
and everyone crowded eagerly around the boy. A spirit of
adventure and growing anticipation permeated the small
group, as they laughed and hugged in greeting.

The robin fluttered onto Price's arm. "How d'you do?"
she said. "Now I get to meet you properly." Her voice was
piping and light. "My name is Toorilla."

"Nice to meet you, Toorilla." Price marveled at how the
bird, with her bone-hard beak, could speak so fluently. The
words seemed to be formed in her throat. *Like a parrot*,
he thought.

"My friends call me Trilly. You may if you like."

"Sure. Thanks for helping me today, Trilly. And you, too,"
he said, looking down at the squirrels. They were standing
upright, side by side, near his feet, nodding eagerly.

"This is my friend Sparkle," said Spark, introducing the
fluffy gray squirrel.

"It took two of us," said Sparkle, "one on each end of
the pieces of sticky stuff. But Spark and I are so in sync.
Ch-ch-ch-ch-ch..." she chattered, her round eyes suddenly
looking like buttonhole slits. Price figured this was squirrel
laughter and joined in.

"In sync?" giggled the black squirrel. "My hind paw! You
should've seen us—tails wrapped 'round the light gismo,
back paws holding down the paper, front claws peeling off
the tape. More than a few times my teeth came in handy as

pincers—and catchers. Ch-ch-ch-ch-chup." Spark doubled over, the images he recalled almost too funny to bear. "I'm ch-ch-chuckling now," he said, reining himself in, "but then it was like trying to harvest acorns in a windstorm."

Price laughed. "Wow. That would've been something to see! But getting that motion detector out of commission was *critical*. I can't thank you guys enough."

Then he lifted his arm slightly to better look at Toorilla. "You, too," he said. "When the sawdust fell down on that dwarf, I thought it was game over. Mr. Murphy would've been checking for woodpeckers, and for sure would've found the pulley. He'd have known in a second what it was for."

"Ah well," said the robin, "King Noble and I have been friends for many years. I often help him out. I can be in places he can't always go himself, you see. And robins are so commonplace. In a way, almost invisible. Enemies don't always notice me, even though I might be near enough to brush their ears with my wingtips."

"Enemies!" gasped Freddy, who had been listening to this conversation. "I never thought that word would have any meaning in Tolk."

"You said it!" O.P. joined in. "That cat is a spark looking for tinder. And there's plenty of Tolks around just waiting to catch fire."

"And more joining up every day," added Meepy.

King Noble leapt up. "Yes, the situation is grave. But now is not the time to speak of enemies. Here we are, amongst friends—with some time to pass before we must act. And Price has never been to Tolk at night. Come! Let's treat our friend to one of life's rarest adventures: a journey into the Land of Tolk after the sun has set." This announcement was greeted with cheers.

O.P. and Meepy scrambled up onto the dog's back and clung to the thick fur at the scruff of his neck. The two squirrels hurried off, one behind the other, springing lightly through the tall grass. Price mounted his bicycle and sped after them, as King Noble bounded away across the meadow. Freddy and Toorilla skimmed through the air above them.

Ahead, a full moon was rising over the eastern horizon, turning the meadow to gleaming silver. No one spoke as they rushed along. The grasses bowed before them, and swished and swayed alongside them in time with the rhythmic pounding of the dog's heavy paws and the whirring of Price's bicycle chain. Lulled by the undulating pulse of motion and sound, and by his own deep, steady breathing, Price became enveloped in a kind of calm.

Gradually though, he became aware of a sound—barely audible at first, blending with the sound of bicycle and grass and padding feet. It was a dry sound, part whisper and part whine, that rose and fell upon the night air like a peculiar, non-human sighing. What was it? Price straightened and listened.

"What's that sound?" he called.

King Noble slowed his pace. A ridiculous image sprang into Price's mind of a chorus of children gathered under the moon, dancing and playing paper on combs.

"What is it?" he asked again, baffled.

They all stopped and listened.

It sounded almost like fiddles playing at an old-fashioned ho-down, only oddly high-pitched and mechanical. King Noble lifted his nose and shut his eyes. Falling in with the rhythm, he began to recite in a deep, sonorous monotone:

The grasshoppers fiddled on the wheat berry's shaft
Singing, "Hey-ho, middle fiddle plucks just so."
The crickets sashayed while the June bugs laughed
Crying, "Why go wending, bending half that slow?

"Do you see the beetles with their feet so fleeting?
They can hurry scurry, hither thither right on tap.
And the ladybirds can, with their bright wings beating,
Bound soundly 'round the buggies in the lapse of a snap."

With the fireflies gleaming and the spider preening,
While her net is snatching, catching dewdrop punch,
Locusts joke as they hokey pokey, bees are screaming
And we'll all have funny honey later for lunch.

There's the mantis tripping, and the long legs skipping,
While the blue backs huckle buckle round by the rill.
Go onward, fiddle now, no slackward, backward slipping,
Dance while the moon looms over the hill.

Price's eyes suddenly opened wide. "It's crickets!" he exclaimed. "They're playing music."

King Noble nodded.

The music rose up all around them. The whole place was a-humming, buzzing, soaring, and snoring with the strange breezy blend of harmonies.

Then Price noticed that there were tiny lights darting in and out amongst the grasses. Fireflies! Ladybugs and beetles of all sizes and shapes moved up and down the shafts of grain in time with the infectious beat. As they danced and turned and jigged, their smooth, shiny backs flashed and gleamed in the moonlight. The grasses appeared to twinkle, as though millions of tiny, pale stars were caught in their blades. Swarms of flying insects flitted in and out, back and forth, crisscrossing paths in intricate geometric maneuvers. Sometimes they would hover just above the nodding silver-headed stalks before dipping and looping and gliding through the air, always in time with the lively, pulsating rhythm. Moonlight glimmered off their slender shining bodies and filigree wings.

Everyone listened and watched, transfixed, for several more minutes. Then, without a word, no cue nor signal given—nothing that might disturb the magic of the experience—one by one, the boy, the fairy, the squirrels, the robin, and the dog with his two unusual passengers all set off again.

They made good time. In part, they were buoyed along by that strange and wonderful music. It seemed to urge them forward. Price's every sense seemed quickened, so that he did almost fly.

Ahead of them he could now make out the ragged silhouette of the woods. Then along its bottom edge, appearing faintly at first, he could see tiny pricks of light. Before long these lights became brighter and were joined by others, more distant. Soon Price was aware of small figures milling about near the lights. The closer they came, the larger the lights grew. Now they were green, pink, blue, yellow, orange, purple, and red. A faint babble arose, like the faraway sound of a poolside on a hot summer's day. Soon they were near enough that he could see hundreds of lanterns hanging in the lower branches of the trees, with many Tolks gathered under them.

Bordering the woods, dozens of tables and stalls, draped in colorful fabrics and laden with goods of all descriptions, were laid out under the stars. The colored lanterns, strung in chains across the tree branches, were small tunnels of silken fabric, each with a single candle glowing inside—the handiwork of the fairies, Freddy explained. Dwarfs and animals, even a few fairies, were bartering and exchanging goods. It was a market!

Price dismounted. Just then Freddy alighted beside him, with Trilly perched alertly on her shoulder. The small party advanced on foot.

"There is something festive about a market at night, don't you think?" said Trilly.

"Definitely," Price agreed. "This is *way* better than any mall."

They had just reached the periphery when a she-bear, a gopher, and two dwarfs that Price did not know, hailed them and scuttled in their direction. They did not seem at all surprised to see Price—except that one of the dwarfs eyed him roundly with curiosity. But what they were really interested in was his bicycle.

"There it is!" exclaimed the gopher. "It's the same contraption I saw the other day. Chained right to a tree, it was. I can't imagine why. Told you so, didn't I? Did you see him ride up on it? Quick as a fox! By my whiskers, what is it? Oh, begging your pardon, Sire." The creature paused and removed his cap. "I didn't notice you there." He bowed respectfully to the king. The bear and the two dwarfs quickly did the same.

"So, this is the lad I've been hearing about." Speaking to King Noble, the gopher replaced his cap.

"Yes, Taber, this is Price. Price, these are my friends— Taber (the gopher), Hobbles (the bear), and Willard and Dillard." Taber affably extended a paw; Hobbles merely grunted and nodded. The two dwarfs echoed each other in quick succession.

"How d'ya do?" and "How d'ya do?"

Price smiled shyly as he and Taber shook hand-in-paw. He noted with interest that the dwarfs were identical twins.

"Take a look at this!" Formalities dispensed with, Taber immediately returned to the matter of the bicycle. They all crowded around, poking and prodding it. Price was obliged to show them how the gears worked and took a couple of turns around on the grass.

But, eager to explore the market, he at last got out his lock and chain and secured it to a tree, along with his back-pack. The gopher, the bear, and the two dwarfs said nothing as they looked on, but they seemed disappointed—even a little hurt.

"I'm going to need it later," Price explained.

"Aye," Taber responded doubtfully.

Toorilla flew up into the branches of a nearby tree. "I'll stay close by," she called down to Price. "I'll warn you when it's time to go. Now, you must hurry along."

"Come on," Price whispered to Freddy. King Noble was busy mingling with his subjects, and the squirrels had scampered off shortly after their arrival. O.P. and Meepy, best of pals, skipped away, arm-in-arm. Quickly, the fairy hung her lantern on a tree branch and the two set off together.

The first thing they saw was a long colorful table, about six inches high, surrounded by a bevy of mice. It was piled with bolts of cloth and doll-sized sewing 'notions,' as Grandmother called them, threads and buttons and things, in great variety. The chattering mice were busily examining the fabrics and trimmings. Price instantly thought of an old-fashioned audiotape playing in reverse, and couldn't help but laugh.

A rotund little field mouse sat at a table next to them with his feet up on a stool. He had a small display of what appeared to be wooden blocks. Price bent down to get a better look. They were actually tiny hand-carved wooden boxes of the most intricate and detailed workmanship.

"Can I take a look?" asked the boy.

"Certainly." The mouse had long whiskers, neatly combed and curled up at the ends, and he wore a starched white shirt under a fancy embroidered red vest.

Price selected a box and held it close to his face. It was about an inch square with the image of a rabbit's head carved on top. The tiny lid fit with machine-like precision.

"Wow." The miniature carving with its thread-like lines and curves was amazing. Carefully he replaced the box and picked up another. This one was larger, with a tiny grove of aspens carved on it. He wished that he had his magnifying glass, so that he could look more closely at the infinitesimal detail.

"Wow! I'd really like to have this."

"Hm. That particular box *is* rather special to me." The chubby mouse rubbed his chin. "Do you have anything you could trade?"

"Trade? I..." Price dug into his pockets, but since he had put on clean jeans, he came up empty. He tried the back pockets just in case. There he found a single Canadian nickel. He pulled it out.

"I've got this," he said. "It isn't much."

"Let me see." The rodent extended a bony paw, and Price handed him the coin. "Hm. A beaver. I like that." He turned it over. "And who is this? A fairy queen?"

"It-it's a queen ... yup."

"But what in Tolk is it made from? I've never seen anything like it." He bit the edge with his two prominent mouse incisors. "This is hard! And so shiny and silv'ry. What do you call it anyway?"

"It's nickel," said Price. "It's a metal. There's lots of it where I come from."

"You don't say."

The mouse held the coin at arm's length and scrutinized it. "This would look nice hanging on the wall over my bureau." He scratched his forehead. "And I could turn it over from time to time and change the picture. All right. It's a deal!"

"Great!"

The exchange was made, and as Price ambled away, he and the mouse both examined their new possessions, each extremely pleased.

"May I see the box?" asked Freddy.

"Sure." Price handed it to her.

"It's very tiny," she said. "What good is it to you?"

"I like it because it *is* so tiny. Where I come from, nobody could carve anything this small with so much detail. Not by hand, anyway. It's a treasure."

"I like it, too," Freddy said. "I like poplars. To me, it's as if every leaf in a poplar tree has its own downy little voice. They chatter away, and I can imagine that they're gossiping about all the 'dramas' happening around them in the forest, and laughing." She stopped suddenly and hung her head, blushing. "That's very foolish, isn't it?"

"No! That's not foolish at all. We've got a huge poplar in our yard." Price retrieved the box and stuffed it into his pocket, being careful that it went right to the bottom. "My dad and I are going to build a tree house in it someday. Come on. Let's explore."

He took Freddy's hand and together they wound in and out amongst the stalls.

The boy was not in the least aware of how his kind words and the touch of his hand had affected the small fairy. He didn't know that no one had ever held Freddy's hand before. At first, she was startled, and seemed almost afraid to breathe. But then a small smile crept over her face, as though, perhaps, she liked the sensation. Freddy, of course, knew no name for this exciting, but unfamiliar feeling. But there is a name for it: That name is Joy.

The colored lights and the sounds of the market reminded Price of a carnival. And he was still very much in awe at finding himself in the midst of intelligent, walking/talking animals, not to mention the dwarfs and giants and fairies. It all seemed like a wonderful waking dream.

"Freddy...?" he asked, looking around curiously, "Why are there hardly any fairies here? And I don't see many giants ... or any elves at all. In fact, I've never even met an elf face-to-face."

"As I said before, we fairies are shy and as a rule, keep to ourselves. But the elves," Freddy explained, "are positively reclusive. They shun any company but their own, and always stay hidden, deep in the greenwood. Elves are creatures of the woods, you see ... just as the fairies and birds inhabit the skies and treetops.

"Besides that," she went on, "elves aren't very useful. They don't spin or weave like the fairies do, or make tools and things like the animals and dwarfs, who are creatures of the earth. Even the giants are more industrious. It can take years to develop a friendship with an elf. Most people don't take the time. And the elves themselves just don't care."

"Then I guess I could never meet one," sighed Price.

"King Noble could introduce you," Freddy suggested. "He knows all the elves."

"Good idea." Price made a mental note.

"The giants," she went on, "are too large for our markets. They have their own. Everything there is ... well, gigantic. But also rather..." Freddy searched for the right word, "mm ... crude." Her eyes met Price's and they both laughed, no doubt recalling the day they'd spied down on the giants in Drumbleton.

"Mostly they exchange pumpkins and big loads of corn. And shirts, trousers, and things made from sackcloth." She giggled, as if picturing all of this in her mind.

Next they saw a long table, spread with spools of yarn and woolen goods. Five fleecy ewes were sitting in a row along one side, busily knitting. Occasionally one would glance up over the top of her flying needles. But they never paused, even for an instant. Price was amazed at how the sheep were able to so expertly grasp and manipulate the knitting needles with their hooves.

Price and Freddy continued along. There were displays of tools and household furnishings, dishes and pans. Each of the items was functional, even primitive, in its design, but the craftsmanship was always very fine. There were shoes (some of them very oddly shaped!) and belts, bags, and bindings made from tightly woven, tough-looking fibers. Price was surprised, when he handled them, to find that they were actually soft and supple. There were coils of rope, millstones, copper scythes, and sacks of grain and meal. There were tables laden with fresh fruits and vegetables.

But his eyes were instantly drawn to the tables of delicacies and baked goods, freshly made. The aroma and sights were tantalizing, and Price was beginning to feel hungry. He had no more coins with him, but he was pretty sure that no money was being exchanged. He watched as creatures sipped cold punch and carefully selected the choicest fruitcakes, pies, and biscuits. How he wished he'd brought along a few other items he might have bartered. He sighed. All so near, but without something to trade, so out of reach.

Then he noticed that, although there was actual bartering taking place, often the vendors would simply give something away for a compliment, as though that in itself was reward enough. Price had just begun to consider the possibilities of this discovery when a tall, lanky rabbit-girl, seated on her haunches at a table laden with salads, beckoned to him. He approached, and she stared, her velvet nose moving up and down, as if sizing him up.

"You're that boy I've heard about," she said, her ears tilting forward. For a moment, Price expected her to thump her back feet, warning those around her, but she suddenly relaxed.

"You seem safe enough to me," she said. "Are you hungry?" Price nodded.

"If you want salad, you may help yourself, although if you're like the dwarfs, you won't. To a dwarf, it's an insult to even look at a salad."

"I like anything," said Price, and selected a rolled-up lettuce leaf. He took a bite. Inside were spiced tomatoes, onions, and peppers. It was delicious. "Mmm. Thanks," he said. "This is good! It tastes kind of like salsa."

The rabbit, whose name was Drusilla, had never heard of salsa, but her pleasure was evident. She looked on with approval as Price sampled celery stuffed with something radish-y and then tried salt-and-vinegar sliced cucumbers. Everything was delicious.

Before long, he had consumed honey-clustered sunflower seeds and honey-oat muffins from a stall managed by two black bears, Martha and Mandrake. He'd had a tall cup of berryade and eaten a generous portion of wild plum cake—baked and served by none other than Dot Arbuckle. It was pleasant to see a friendly, familiar face. A striped cat and a small gray fox fed him baked potato with butter and salt, along with a hot, sweet, milky drink, reminiscent of vanilla. Price thought it was odd, but nice, to see cats and vixens serving up potatoes. He couldn't help but smile—inwardly, of course.

Freddy gaped. "How can you eat so much?"

"But it's all so good," Price said, patting his stomach. "I guess that's something you have to learn about boys: We love food."

Freddy shook her head in amazement.

But after eating three or four wedges of savory cheeses, offered by a cow named Clarisse and a goat named Constance, even Price was feeling stuffed.

"I don't think I can eat another bite," he groaned, clutching his belly. "O-o-h, I wish you'd stopped me, Freddy, before I ate so much."

"Me? What have *I* got to do with it?" She studied him out of the corner of her eye.

Price thought a moment. "Point taken. You're right—I am the boss of my stomach."

They grinned at each other.

A crowd was gathering just ahead of them, consisting mainly of dwarfs, animals, and a few giants. They were grouping in twos and threes, sitting on the grass before a smooth, raised plateau. It was surrounded on three sides by trees and lit by eight large, flaming torches set at equal distances against the backdrop of the forest. Price guessed that this was a natural amphitheater. He quickly forgot his stomach, realizing that something new was about to begin.

He could hear O.P.'s unmistakable voice rising above the general rumble, then caught sight of him and Meepy sitting at center front—although, due to their small size, barely visible in the crowd. Clearly, the pinecone man was in his element.

"Let's sit over there," Price said, pointing to their friends.

O.P. grinned and wriggled over as Price and Freddy plopped down on the grass beside them. "Take it easy!" He cocked an indignant eye at the boy. "Gee. Thanks for not sitting on me." He tilted his head back so that he could look 'down' at them over his painted nose.

Then he began rambling excitedly, "The famous *Four Flying Fers* are performing tonight! The last time I saw them, Ferly and Fermont had Ferton by the paws, stretched out between them, like a safety net," he gestured with his two arms. "They flipped Ferby off Ferton's back and he did a triple loop, spin, and low glide, right over the crowd. Pheww-w-w." One white felt hand became a glider. "You should've seen it!"

"What're you talking about?"

"Flying squirrels." O.P. looked askance at Price. "Acrobats, acrobats. You know."

"Oh. Right."

Just then the two beavers, Buckley and Frip, came rushing out onto the platform juggling what appeared to be six round, hairy balls.

Price craned his head forward. "What the heck are they juggling?" he asked.

"Probably muskrats," said Freddy. "It's hard to tell. They're curled up."

The furry balls were being tossed about, the beavers catching them neatly in their forepaws or hind-paws, occasionally cradling one in a tail and then flipping it deftly into the air. The fur ball would land squarely on the tail of the other beaver, who might at that moment have just turned his back or be standing on his head. The crowd laughed and applauded, as did Freddy and Price.

"Woo-hoo!" O.P. whooped. "That's what I call 'telling tails!'" Meepy clapped a paw over his mouth to stifle a squeaky laugh.

By that time, the two beavers were bowing energetically. And Freddy was right—six muskrats uncoiled and hand-in-hand skipped to center stage, waving and bowing.

Next came the acrobatic squirrels, who repeated the amazing stunt O.P. had described. It was Price who whooped this time. "Ee-haw!" he shouted.

Then a giant man came on stage and began a stand-up routine that was unbelievably bad, though the crowd laughed politely, even jovially, at the terrible jokes. The giant's big face was aglow with the pleasure of being the center of attention. Price glanced at Freddy, who rolled her eyes and giggled.

"Now I'm going to tell you a really true story," boomed out the kettle-drum voice. "This very night, I met Dimble the Dwarf at the market. He tol' me that he'd just turned down an invite to dinner from Bill Bear. 'Impossible!' says I. 'A dwarfie *never* says 'no' to dinner.' 'But I *did!*' he said, 'after I heard there wasn't much room at Bill Bear's. And you know how dwarfies loves mushrooms. Hee, hee, haw!" He slapped his barrel of a thigh. "*Much* room? *Mushrooms?* Get it?"

Price cupped a hand to the side of his mouth and whispered to Freddy, "I can't take much more of this."

"Then I have an idea," she said, breathless with excitement. "Let's go to the Bluebell Bower. You can meet my kinfolk." She gripped his hand tightly.

"Sure." He glanced at his watch. "We only have about an hour left. Is it far?"

"Not at all. Most of the fairies will be there already. And if you've never seen it, you can't even imagine the wonder of fairydom at night."

"Then let's go."

With quick goodbyes, they left O.P. and Meepy rolling on the grass, faking nausea and giggling.

All this time, Price had been so caught up in the novelty of the evening's adventures that he hadn't noticed the suspicious looks cast in their direction, or the occasional exchange of a wary, mistrustful glance, or the passing of some whispered remark. And Freddy, so enrapt in her newfound joy, never saw the eyebrows raised or the brief frown swapped from one to another; she never heard the animated conversations that suddenly went into a stall. And they certainly never noticed one or two dark shapes silently slip away into the shadows, bent on some private and secret errand. No, they saw none of these things. But Toorilla, from her perch, well-hidden under the canopy of the evergreen boughs, did see all of this, and more.

Chapter Nineteen:
Bluebell Bower

With Freddy in the lead, they hurried down a moonlit path that meandered through the evergreens. Soon they came to a grassy meadow surrounded by the woods. By day, it would have been a shimmering emerald green. But on this night, millions of tiny silver bells—bluebells they would have been in daylight—dotted its expansive train, glinting under the moonlight. In the center, stood a magnificent arbor—a great arch of slender, interwoven branches, covered in a mass of clematis vines, thick with blossoms. Moonshine had turned the large purple flowers into clusters of platinum stars.

At first Price didn't see the fairies, seated randomly by ones and twos, half-buried amongst the wildflowers and lush meadow grasses. But they hadn't noticed him either. As still and as intense as statues, each beautiful oval face— smooth and white as eggshell, framed in a halo of shining hair—was directed upwards toward the sky. Overhead, in a swirling, shifting mass, was the most magnificent display of Northern Lights that Price had ever seen. And he could hear a soft, rushing sound, like the sound of the wind scattering snow crystals against a window.

Price was familiar with the Northern Lights, including their strange, ethereal music, but this was more amazing than anything he'd ever imagined. The heavens were a churning, seething blaze of light that was steadily increasing. Like wildfire, the roiling pastel flames were licking up the stars, consuming even the black of night.

The sound, too, was extraordinary. At first it had been like the many voices of the wind, whispering together. Then it began to sigh—long, elastic sighs. Finally, it surged forth, like the swell of an organ, filling the night sky with its majesty.

Price was on the verge of speaking when he suddenly noticed that the swirling mass of light was shattering into very small but distinct shapes. At first they resembled small, spinning firebrands, each balanced on a point with streamers of light spiraling out around it. As they came nearer, the revolving shapes lengthened into glowing spindles. Gradually, the spindles evolved arms and legs. He could see that some of the figures were leaping about and cavorting in mid-air.

Price's lips rounded as if framing a question, but nothing came from his mouth. He wanted to catch Freddy's eye, but found that he could not pull his gaze away from the spectacle above them.

"Oh, Price! How lucky that you're here tonight. Look! The Peri dancers are coming!"

Yes, it was true. He could now plainly see that the small, lithe figures were dancing.

"Are they fairies?" he asked.

"Of course. They're the fairies of the night sky—of the Aurora Borealis. I believe, when they're very high up, they're visible even in your world. Have you ever seen them?"

Still deeply enthralled, Price did not reply.

The dancers were descending on what looked like a carpet of stardust that had scrolled down to the foot of the arbor. Now he could see that they were not flaming at all, but that a radiant halo of light surrounded the graceful form of each dancer. One by one, the fairies pirouetted daintily to the ground. They continued to dance, their small, quick feet just grazing the tops of the meadow grasses. These fairies did not have wings; they didn't seem to need them. Soon all the dancers had gathered in a circle around the arbor.

In perfect symmetry, they rose up on their toes, leapt into the air, crouched down low, turned, or gracefully extended a limb. Their music, which seemed to emanate from the stars themselves, had no real melody but was a revolving progression of harmonies that rolled on and on, with no beginning and no end, much like the fairy ring itself. And like the music, the fairies' movements were circular. The dance wound around and around, repeating the same series of elegant gestures.

The other fairies gathered nearby to watch—some flying, some on foot. Freddy and Price joined them. The hypnotic charm of the music and the seamless, fluid movements of the dancers eased the anxiety Price had felt earlier.

Freddy was watching him closely. His brown eyes were wide and staring, his lips caught in a half-smile. He was obviously entranced by the scene before them. "I've never seen anything so beautiful," he said. "The Peri dancers are like angels!"

"Oh no. They're not angels," Freddy corrected. "They're fairies." But Price didn't seem to hear.

In fact, Freddy appeared to be the only one there who was not entirely caught up in the spell, either as performer or spectator. And seeing her friend so completely captivated by the ritual dance of the fairies made her uneasy. She caught his arm and shook it. "Price!"

Without even glancing in her direction, the boy gently disengaged her fingers. "Not now, Freddy. Wait 'til the dance is over." He moved a few steps closer to the fairy ring.

The dance never really ended. Each fairy, in turn, tripped airily to the foot of the arbor where he or she reached up two slender arms and spiraled upwards into the cloud of cool milky light. One by one, the dancers ascended the trail of stardust in the same manner that they'd come. Gradually the graceful forms of the Peris blended with each other, blurring into a mass of swirling, luminous colors.

The music, as well, was dying away to a gentle shushing, like the faded texture of voices speaking nearby when you are drifting off to sleep. Soon, only a few faint wisps of light were still visible.

Price found himself staring transfixed at a darkened sky that was now speckled solely with the millions of stars. They seemed somehow inadequate after what he had just witnessed. He blinked several times and shook himself. Had it been a dream, he wondered. It felt like a dream.

"Price." Freddy tugged his arm again and pinched him.

"Ow! What was that for?"

"Come back," she said. "You're somewhere out in space."

"You're right about that! Where did they go, Freddy? More to the point, where did they come from?"

Freddy's large eyes thoughtfully scanned the empty sky. "I'm not certain," she said. "Legend tells that the Peris once lived on land, but all they ever wanted to do was dance. They would dance all night, every night. Then one of them discovered a ribbon of starlight leading up into the sky. He ascended it dancing, and all the others followed. There they have remained ever since, caught in an eternal round of dance." Freddy paused. "That is what the legend says." She frowned. "But I don't believe it myself."

"Who do you think they are?" asked Price.

"I think they're spirits."

"Spirits? Really?"

"Yes, I believe they're the spirits of fairies yet unborn."

"Doesn't anyone ever go up to them and speak to them?"

"They never stay long enough, and they never pause in their dancing for even an instant. But tomorrow—just wait and see—tomorrow a flower will open and a new fairy will have arrived."

Price studied her face for a moment. "You seem so serious. Isn't it a happy event when a fairy is born?"

"Oh yes!" said Freddy. "There is always great rejoicing when a new fairy comes. But..." She bit her lip. "I can't explain it. It feels like I'm missing something. As if I know what it is, but I just can't remember."

She then turned abruptly to face Price. "But right now that doesn't matter. Right now, you're here with me, and I'm going to take you to meet my kin." She smiled.

"Then let's go," said Price.

Hundreds of fairies were visible now as lighted torches were being set on posts in a wide circle around the glade. Price also noticed three tall flagpoles, each with a long, silken banner at the top, wafting in the faint breeze.

"What are the banners, Freddy?"

"Each one displays the emblem of a fairy clan," she explained. "My clan are the Fairchilds. Our emblem is the lily. The Fairborns' is a purple iris. The Fairbes' is the wild rose."

The fairies were flying low or hovering just over the ground, but Price could see that they were all heading towards the arbor. Like dozens of free-floating dandelion tufts, they were coming to rest in the grass, settling within the circle of light.

Two fairies sat at the very top of the arbor's leafy arch. Several more were clinging to its sides, their filigree wings displayed for all to see, glistening in the torchlight as they fluttered, ever so slightly. Price and Freddy were the only ones approaching on foot. A number of fairies glanced at them curiously in passing. A few smiled vaguely, but no one spoke to them. They seemed to be waiting for him or Freddy to make the first move.

Freddy found a spot not far from the arbor, large enough for the two of them to sit down together. Laughing now, she immersed herself in the soft, aromatic meadow plants. Price flopped down beside her and looked around, a bit self-consciously. Many of the fairies sitting nearby were also watching him. Without exception their features were perfectly formed, but he could read nothing in their expressions. He wondered what they were thinking.

"Look." Freddy nudged him and pointed towards the arbor. One of the fairies seated atop the arch was holding a harp; the other held a wooden flute, already poised, her lips drawn together at the mouthpiece.

The flutist began to play, and a soft, breathy melody floated out. The notes ran up and down freely in ripples, like a breeze rifling through a tall stand of rushes. Then the harp introduced a gentle, rocking rhythm, and the free-running tones of the flute immediately fell into line. It was like listening to a duet performed by the hollow chuffing of the wind against a background of softly sifting raindrops.

Part II: The Rescue

Now, the harpist began to sing. His voice was high and pure, not the mature voice of a man but that of a youth.

> *The fairies' Art doth reign supreme,*
> *And none can match their feats.*
> *They sing and dance with grace not seen*
> *Among the lesser beasts.*
>
> *Who else can rise on pointed toe?*
> *Who else can strike the lyre?*
> *Where fairies, there doth Beauty go,*
> *And Beauty doth inspire.*
>
> *It's true that birds can catch the air,*
> *And soar with certain skill.*
> *Yet who but fairies hover there*
> *And halt or roam at will.*
>
> *And though they say the skylark sings*
> *With rare and beauteous tone,*
> *It's only fairy music brings*
> *A meld of harp and song.*
>
> *And where the beasts live underground,*
> *And cleave to moss and root,*
> *In fairies' den the flowers abound,*
> *With blossoms underfoot.*
>
> *The net that's spun on fairy loom*
> *Is silk so fine and rare*
> *That petals on the rose in bloom*
> *Seem coarse when you compare.*

The fairies' tongue is kissed with gold,
And poetry is blessed,
As rich the epic tales unfold
Far finer than the rest.

Ah, fairies' Art is sweet and pure,
And eases every care.
It is the gift of Beauty sure
To please us everywhere.

As the song ended, the fairies applauded and smiled, displaying rows of small, perfect white teeth. Price clapped, too. But compared to the Peri dancers, the performance seemed somehow pale and insignificant. Freddy didn't applaud; she seemed distracted. All at once she stood up.

"Come on." She took him by the hand. Many pairs of large, slanted, sober eyes followed them as they made their way through the fairies and the wildflowers. "I am taking you to meet Laefay. She is the chief fairy of my clan." They moved away from the arbor, where the harpist and flutist had just struck up another tune—a merry tune this time— and headed towards the edge of the clearing.

It would be hard to believe that any one fairy could stand out from the rest—they were all so beautiful—but Price suddenly caught sight of a young woman seated on a rise who was exquisite.

All of the fairies, even the boys, were naturally very small and slight: immature, Price thought, not quite grown up. But this fairy was somewhat taller, with long silver-blond hair. She wore a silken tunic of wintry white that draped elegantly over her arms and bodice and reached down to her ankles. Her skin, too, was as white as marble. Her eyes were sky-blue; her lips and cheeks the pale pink of advancing dawn.

As a rule, a beautiful face didn't mean that much to Price—he preferred the easy companionship and warm heart of a friend—but as soon as he caught sight of this white fairy, he could hardly take his eyes off her.

There were several other fairies sitting on either hand—members of her party, Price thought. They were very attentive to her. She was like a diamond set amongst pearls, and Price noticed that he and Freddy were moving pointedly in her direction.

At that moment the fairy's large, blue eyes were coolly perusing the collective assembly, and as a matter of course, her gaze fell upon Freddy and Price. A sort of detached interest flickered behind the blue eyes as she watched the two approaching. As soon as they were close enough, she smiled and graciously extended a hand in welcome. It was the warmest reception they'd received from anyone in fairydom up to that moment.

"Winifred." The fairy's smile broadened as she greeted the little fairy, almost with affection. "So, you've brought the boy to our assembly, as you said. You have always been one to surprise us with your unique ways. Yes, you have always been the daffodil amongst the lilies, isn't that so? Thank you for bringing him." She turned to Price and extended her hand. It was soft and cool to the touch.

"Thank you for coming. We have all heard of you, Price. King Noble speaks highly of you. You are welcome here." She released his hand and motioned to the party on her left to make room.

"Please sit here. My name is Laefay. Winifred is my ward, you might say. I watch over her, as I do all of the Fairchilds."

The other fairies stole furtive glances at Price as he and Freddy sat down. He smiled politely to all around, hoping to encourage them. Several of the fairies smiled back, guardedly.

"And how are you enjoying your journey into the Land of Tolk?" asked Laefay, partly to make polite conversation and yet certainly out of curiosity as well. Strangers were as rare here as beardless dwarfs.

"I like it. It's really beautiful here. I like the fairies and the talking animals, and I've made some friends." He glanced at Freddy, and she blushed.

"I would think that you'd never want to leave," said a boy with curly red hair sitting to the right of Laefay.

Price shrugged. "I don't really have much choice about it."

The redheaded boy looked surprised. "And why is that?"

Price scratched his ear. These fairies were like Freddy, asking too many questions.

"There's nothing to stop you from staying if you want to," the fairy went on. "Now that you've been to Tolk, you have every right to remain."

"I'm sure the friends you mentioned would be very happy if you chose to stay." Laefay's smile was constant, and she spoke as though remaining in Tolk was a foregone conclusion. "How did you like the music?" she asked, shifting the conversation in another direction.

"I always like music." Price was glad to change the subject. "My mom plays the piano, so I've grown up around music."

The fairy's smile collapsed and the blue eyes stared. "Puh-yano? I've never heard of such a thing."

"It's a musical instrument," he explained. "It has keys that you strike with your fingers. I tried learning when I was younger, but I was hopeless."

"Ah, a musical instrument." At the mention of something she understood so well, the smile reappeared in full force.

A few more fairies had gathered around them now and were listening so closely and with such expectation that Price felt compelled to go on.

"My dad and I are about as musical as stumps." He smiled wryly. "We sing like crows and keep a beat like a couple of loose shutters flapping in the wind. But we really know how to annoy my mom ... when we're traveling in the car." Price stopped. "Oh." He suddenly realized that the fairies would have no idea what a car was.

But Laefay threw back her lovely head and laughed. She, at least, had caught the gist of the story without understanding all of the details.

"So, you belong to a family then, in the world that you inhabit? We have heard of mothers and fathers and families, but no such things exist here in Tolk. They are not needed, you see."

"How do you grow up, then?"

"We all learn together, and of course, none of us ever dies. We are all happy. There is no real sorrow here. There is not even much toil or hardship, at least not in the way that you know. Naturally, we must work and do our part, but in Tolk there is not the opposition that exists in your world. Our crops don't fail, our orchards are always filled, our streams never run dry. The days may be warm, but they are never too hot. We may be cool, as in winter, but we've never known the bitter cold. Mortal pain, suffering, want—those are concepts that we understand only in the abstract. We've heard something about them, from King Noble, but we've never experienced them—at least not to any large degree."

"Oh, that's not true," interjected a fairy. "*I've* known hardship. Just last week three warps broke on my loom. I was up to my knees in rushes half the morning looking for some good reeds to replace them. What's worse, my wingtips got wet and I was grounded for the rest of the afternoon!"

Laefay looked at Price and smiled knowingly, as if to say, 'You see what I mean.'

"Me, too," complained another fairy. "I've tried everything, but I can't think of a single word to rhyme with 'gossamer.' How can I finish my poem in time for the jamboree?" The fairy looked around. "Does anybody know a word that rhymes with 'gossamer?'"

Price glanced down, hiding a smile.

Then the redheaded fairy quipped, "*There is no rhyme for gossamer, so I suggest you toss the word!*"

Everyone laughed, including Price.

But then he recalled how he and his mom had washed and vacuumed out the car in the heat the other day, before they'd gone to pick up his grandmother. How uncomfortable it had felt with the sun beating down.

"No hard chores," he mused out loud. "No homework, no school. I wouldn't have to worry about getting a job when I grow up. I could just hang out with my friends all day and explore. It'd be fun."

"Oh yes. We have lots of fun." The redheaded fairy was speaking again. "We sing and dance; we play together and make up stories and poems."

"Stories?" Price was interested. "What kind of stories?"

"Stories about soaring over the treetops and over the sea." The fairy's face was alight. "Stories about the woods and the valleys and the mountains, and all the living creatures of Tolk."

"But we have all of those things where I come from, too." Price was speaking to himself as much as to the others. "And I can do anything there that you can do here—and more."

"No you can't," objected the redheaded fairy. "You can't fly. You don't have any wings."

"Sure I can. I can fly in an airplane, or in a helicopter, or on a hang glider—or even by hot air balloon. But come to think of it, it's here in Tolk that I really can't fly." Price had a sudden thought. "Do you draw here?"

"Draw? You mean water?" asked the redheaded fairy.

Price laughed. "No. I mean, do you draw pictures?"

"Oh yes, of course. We fairies are weavers and we weave patterns and pictures into cloth. The dwarfs and some of the animals use tools to carve shapes out of wood. Some even use ash and cinders on parchment to make portraits. But..." He made a dour face. "Such methods are far too coarse and dirty to be of any use to fairies."

"Oh." Price was a little disappointed.

"Do you know...?" Laefay's beautiful blue eyes, already very large, had suddenly grown enormous, as though she had just recalled something incredible. "There *was* a fairy once who left Tolk, of her own free will. She was not a Fairchild, and I didn't know her well, but I knew *of* her, and it is a fact. We try not to think about her or speak of her often, but your being here tonight has brought the matter to my mind. Can you imagine anyone doing such a thing?"

"But *why* did she leave?" asked Freddy, speaking for the first time.

"I believe it had something to do with a book."

"A book?"

"Yes. Some sort of book found its way here from the world of humankind. How this could have happened, I cannot imagine. She stumbled across it and read it. It unsettled her and she couldn't rest until she'd gone into your world. She wanted to learn for herself whether the things she'd read in the book were true. She has never returned, and now, I would imagine she must be very old or perhaps even..." the pretty face grimaced. But then she continued airily, "No one knows what became of the book. And ever since, we fairies no longer read human writing. Of course, the older fairies still remember how, but the younger ones have never learned." She turned her wide blue eyes on Price, "I rarely read anymore," she said, "but I can recite hundreds of lines of poetry that I have memorized." She studied the boy's face for a minute.

"Surely you won't leave Tolk now. Surely you will not return to a place where there is hardship and death and ... and something far worse, I've heard." She leaned closer to Price and lowered her voice to an intense whisper. "*Evil.* I am not exactly sure what that is, but the very thought of it makes me tremble. King Noble has said that it exists, even thrives, in your world."

Price didn't know what to say, but he noticed that all of the fairies were watching him now with the most absorbed curiosity. "It's true," he admitted.

Evil? He'd never really considered it before coming to Tolk. Now the subject had come up again. These fairies didn't seem to know what it was, and Laefay was evidently very much afraid of it, but they were certainly uncommonly curious about it. He thought of Javelin Man and the scores of superheroes and villains he'd read about in comic books. But that was all in fun. Was evil fun, then? Price looked at Laefay.

"You're right to be afraid. Evil can be very dangerous. But ... I think that it can also be kind of attractive. And exciting."

Laefay looked shocked. "Attractive!" she exclaimed. "I have heard that it can destroy you!"

Price squirmed. This was out of his league. "Only if you let it. No one has to be bad. But, it's there all right, if you're looking for it ... and even if you're not."

Laefay sat up straight and ran her eyes, unseeing, over the assembly.

"I'd rather be here, I think, where I'm safe." Several of the other fairies quickly agreed. "I would never go where I might be destroyed and where in time I must surely die." She scrutinized Price. "That's why I think that you won't leave, either. Surely you *must* remain in Tolk now. It would be foolish to do otherwise."

Price was silent. He thought about his mother and father and his grandmother and grandfather. At that moment he felt a loyalty to them that he hadn't known existed, since it had never before been tested. When he responded to Laefay, he was surprised at the deep well of resolve that flowed from his heart.

"I have to go back. I know it's hard for you to understand, but staying here in Tolk is completely out of the question."

"No!" Freddy jumped to her feet. "No!"

Everyone stared at her in surprise, especially the fairies, who weren't used to any kind of open display of emotion. Freddy was breathing hard and tears had even welled up in her eyes. "No, Price. If you go back, then *you* must die!"

Price sensed the hurt and fear that had sparked this outburst and wanted Freddy, of all those present, to understand what he was driving at. But he was at a loss as to how to explain.

"But ... but Freddy, don't you see? It's just that ... there are some things worth dying for."

The fairies had all fallen silent, except for Freddy. Through clenched fists pressed against her cheeks she began to sob. Price looked around at the others, searching for some assistance, for even a glimmer of understanding, but every pair of beautiful slanted eyes staring back at him was uncomprehending.

Then suddenly, "Chirrup! Chirrup!"

Price looked up. It was Toorilla perched nearby on top of the flagpole.

"Chirrup!" she repeated. "It's time!"

Chapter Twenty:
The Rescue

The moon was merely dime-sized now and well advanced in the western sky, yet it cast a silvery sheen over the garden. The cat, his orange coat dulled to tarnished copper, was plainly visible on the back steps, apparently asleep. He did not notice the gate that led into the space slowly open about ten inches. Nor did he appear to be aware of any slight shiftings in the shadows here and there amid the murky shades of night. Then, suddenly, the tip of his tail twitched and his eyes snapped open. For a moment all else was perfectly still—only the glowing yellow orbs darted warily from side to side. He could see many small, bright eyes watching him from deep within the shadows of the lush garden.

Well, well, he thought. I *didn't expect so many to come. Still, no matter. None of them are any match for me.* He snorted. *What fools they are to risk their lives!*

Suddenly the cat's head jerked up and his tail began to lash. He had noticed movement in the poplar tree. With his excellent night vision Sinbad could easily make out the figure of a boy creeping along the large bough overhanging the dwarfs, face-paint and dark clothing notwithstanding. The sinister yellow orbs narrowed. Slowly he rose and strolled over by the dwarfs, where he began to pace, back and forth, staring up into the tree.

Then his ears pricked. He could hear some vociferous chewing coming from somewhere on his left, near the lilac bushes. In the gloom, he could just make out the shape of a beaver gnawing noisily on the bark.

Sinbad, of course, was well aware that the garden was Mr. Murphy's shrine—his monument to the world. Should any harm come to it, he knew that the man's rage would be a thing to be reckoned with. Annoyed, he bounded over, but by the time he'd reached the bushes, the beaver had sauntered away and slipped noiselessly into the pond. The cat bared his fangs and hissed an angry warning after the disappearing flat-tail.

But his attention was quickly diverted. Five chattering squirrels were running helter-skelter through the border plants, heedless of the damage they were causing.

Just what do they think they're doing? thought Sinbad, steeling himself. Squirrels he could deal with, even squirrels from Tolk. They would not live to see another day. And in the morning, wouldn't Mr. Murphy be pleased to find their corpses piled in a neat stack on the patio. The cat sniggered as he slunk down and darted nimbly across the lawn.

A blackbird suddenly dove out of the inky sky and nicked his ear. Three others swooped down and began pecking at his tail. He wheeled round, but before he could pounce, the birds had flown off. And when he turned back to the squirrels, they were gone too.

Great leaping giants! What was that he heard now? More gnawing! This time it came from the vegetable patch. Mice. He had just begun to slink in that direction when he noticed something out of the corner of his eye, something swaying gently, suspended by a rope, rising slowly from the ground. It was one of the dwarfs!

Sinbad sat back on his haunches and let out such a yowling and a caterwauling that it made Price cringe. It was like turning up the volume on a creaking door hinge. It was worse than the tuning of the junior high school band, worse than the sound of tires screeching to a halt on the freeway, worse even than a squalling baby. Price promptly lowered the dwarf back into place.

The racket continued until at last an upstairs bedroom window-screen banged open and out shot Mr. Murphy's head, blinking sleep from his eyes. "What in tarnation is going on?"

Price held his breath and didn't move a muscle. The cat began yowling again as he slowly circled the dwarfs. Squinting, Mr. Murphy quickly scanned the premises. Not satisfied, he ducked inside, and a few seconds later, reappeared at the window with a flashlight.

Price, meanwhile, had taken advantage of his brief absence to crouch behind a leafy fan. Sinbad went on howling and pacing. Then the cat sat down and stared hard up into the tree, still screeching. Mr. Murphy shone his light into the dark, dense foliage. The beam ran up and down and from side to side, pausing here and there as it tried to penetrate the leafy depths of the tree. A couple of times it skimmed the back of Price's shirt and a piece of his hair, but the old man never saw him.

Sinbad hunched his shoulders and made for the tree.

He's not going to get away with this! he thought, *I'll force him down.*

Suddenly there was a squeak and a rustling noise. A mouse scurried out from the shadows and ran pell-mell across the lawn. The light caught him just as he disappeared behind a caragana shrub. It was Meepy.

"A mouse! And a big fella. So *that's* it. You get that mouse, Sinbad, you hear? I don't want no mouse pinching my peas or wrecking my bulbs. You do your job now and get me that mouse!"

Sinbad gaped. This was *not* what he'd had in mind! Yet now he had no choice but to dash off in pursuit behind the shrubbery where Meepy had disappeared just seconds before. Of course, by that time the mouse was out of sight and well hidden.

Grumbling to himself, Mr. Murphy pulled in his head and savagely yanked the curtains across the open window. Shortly after, a disgruntled Sinbad re-emerged from the bushes, casting his eyes around warily.

For about a minute the garden was silent. Then it suddenly transformed into a hive of activity. Two gophers began chewing the stems of the tiger lilies. Rabbits nibbled the lettuces; a muskrat took a couple of generous bites out of a lily pad; squirrels and skunks were playing tag, charging through the marigolds and pansies and petunias. The dwarf, dark-green twine looped around his middle, was once more being lifted gently into the air. The caterwauling began again—only this time even louder and more desperate. Price lowered the dwarf.

For the second time the bedroom curtains were flung aside, and Mr. Murphy's angry face appeared at the window. Instantly the garden became perfectly silent and unmoving.

"Shut up, you confounded feline! You want the neighbors to call the cops? What's the matter with you? Can't you catch one paltry little mouse? Any more of this, and I'll be putting you down the basement for the rest of the night!"

The yowling stopped dead. The basement? The basement! So! That was their game. Get the cat out of the way. Toss the cat down the basement. *Now I see,* Sinbad thought grimly. He sat down to think.

Satisfied that the cat had finally shut up, Mr. Murphy closed the screen and lowered the window, leaving it open about six inches. Again he yanked the curtains across. Immediately the gnawing and scuttling and burrowing began again in earnest.

But by now Sinbad knew exactly what to do. He grinned crookedly. *Oh, they think they're so smart ... but no one's as clever as me. Fools!* He sneered. *After all, there are two dwarfs. I can easily get Murphy's attention if one of them goes missing. And mark my words, I am not going down the basement.* In the meantime, he had determined to silently stalk and kill as many of those ignorant Tolks as he could—regardless of the damage they did to the garden. He was sure that Mr. Murphy would reward him when he discovered the spoils the next morning. Besides, the old man could not deny that he had tried to warn him.

There was just one snag. Sinbad scowled. If only he could be sure that wretched boy got caught. But how to get him out of the tree? *Hmm,* he thought. *I wonder just how brave—and stupid—he really is.*

He turned his attention first to the skunks. *Skunks are slow,* he calculated. *An easy mark.* It occurred to him that the skunk's spray, instead of smelling like fresh spring air as it did in Tolk, would be repulsive. *Well the skunks don't know that,* he reasoned, *and if they do spray me, it will only make it easier to alert Mr. Murphy.*

With head down and on silent feet, the cat started towards them. There were two, burrowing randomly under a carpet of blossomy ground cover. Carelessly they tossed up pieces of torn root and small clots of dirt.

As soon as the cat's intentions were clear, two large jays swooped down, aimed directly at his face. Sinbad flinched, taking a nasty peck on the forehead and on the neck. The birds retreated skyward to renew their assault. But this interruption had only deterred Sinbad for a few seconds.

Again the cord tightened around the dwarf's belly and slowly he rose up from the ground. But Sinbad paid no attention. Squirrels began chattering in the rhubarb patch, jumping up and down, shredding the broad leaves with their sharp toenails. Sinbad ignored them. With single-minded purpose he continued on a direct path toward the skunks. The two animals scurried away as fast as they could, each going in a different direction. Without missing a beat, the cat singled out the stouter, stodgier of the two.

Watching from the poplar tree, Price stiffened in alarm as it became apparent what the cat was up to. The distance between predator and prey was shrinking rapidly. Quickly, he lowered the dwarf.

He was just about to swing down to the rescue when Meepy darted out from under a juniper bush, not more than five yards from the cat's nose. There stood the mouse, glaring into the creature's yellow eyes, taunting him. Mr. Murphy's last words, "Get me that mouse!" echoed in Sinbad's mind. *Ye-e-s, the mouse*, he thought. *And I happen to hate this lying, spying mouse.* He was off in a flash.

Meepy was lithe and quick, but being unfamiliar with the garden, wasn't sure of the way. And with Sinbad fast closing the gap between them, there was no time to get his bearings or make a plan. The next thing he knew, he was barreling blindly across the yard, literally running for his life.

Suddenly he found himself skirting the edge of a flower-bed that loomed unexpectedly in his path. The bed arched around in a long curve, and before he realized it, Meepy had turned and was heading back in the wrong direction! Sinbad angled and cut sharply across the rapidly shrinking distance between them. Then the cat dropped to his stomach, viper-like, preparing for the attack. Straight as an arrow, he seemed to glide across the grass.

Meepy was now facing the stone wall between Mr. Murphy's yard and Price's, near the corner where it met the short wall connecting to the house. There was a gate in the short wall, the same gate through which Price and his mother had first entered the garden a few days ago. Meepy's only hope lay in reaching the gate. He could easily escape underneath, giving him a few precious seconds to find cover before the cat made it over the top.

But then, with a mighty bound, Sinbad hurtled his body through the air and landed with a light thump, squarely between mouse and gate.

Meepy quickly scuttled behind a bush that grew in the corner where the two walls merged. But now he was trapped—trapped behind the bush with no way out except into the clutches of the waiting cat.

Meepy let out a plaintive squeak for help.

That's it! thought Price, straining to see in the darkness. *Mr. Murphy or not, I'm going down.*

For the second time, he was just about to swing to the ground, when suddenly they heard a deep-throated growl as a huge, dark figure lunged over the wall and landed with a heavy thud. Price recognized at once the thick, luxurious coat that gleamed duskily in the moonlight.

Snarling, black lips curled back, King Noble made toward Sinbad. The cat shrank back. Bristling with indignation the dog hunkered down, the long hair on his spine rising in anger as he faced the stunned animal at eye level. Then he advanced, snapping and growling, bearing down like a demolition machine.

Sinbad began to back away, but each step only took him nearer to the house, leaving no possibility for a hasty retreat. Soon he was up on the patio. In desperation the cat lurched to one side, but King Noble was too quick. He lunged and the trap-like jaws caught the creature by the scruff of the neck. He shook him violently. Then he swung the cat from side-to-side—once, twice, three times—and flung him hard against the wall of the house. There was a sickening thump. With a bound the dog stood over the fallen cat, straddling him, his great forepaws planted firmly on either side. Now it was Sinbad who was trapped.

Then King Noble lifted his magnificent head and released a long and terrible howl.

The sound carried for blocks. There was more than one human in the neighborhood who scrambled out of bed and searched anxiously out of the window. There was more than one child who woke with a start, and huddled nervously under the covers. There was more than one earthly creature that sought refuge under the sofa, or doorstep, or beneath the pile of rubbish behind the tool shed.

Mr. Murphy, however, literally jolted out of his bed. Again, he flung aside the curtains and pushed up the window-screen. He could only gape at the sight that met his eyes.

"What th-! What is it? A wolf? No, by crackers, it's a dog!" The old man fumbled for his robe and slippers, grabbed his flashlight, and hastily made his way through the darkened house. By the time he stood at the back door, King Noble was leaving by the rear gate that led into the alley. The animal calmly turned and looked back, as though he actually wanted to be seen. Then he was gone.

Mr. Murphy's jaw dropped. "By the devil, how d'you suppose that gate came to be open?" Shaking his head and muttering to himself, he hurried out across the yard. The beam from his flashlight jagged from side-to-side, but not one small animal was caught in its light. He made a cautious scan of the alley. Then, still dumbfounded, still grumbling, he shut and bolted the gate.

"He won't get back in here. Not tonight. I must be losing my mind. I could've sworn I'd closed that gate." Shaking his head, he started toward the house. "Never saw such a monstrous Alsatian in my life. Must have scared the innards out of that cat. Thought it was the sound of the last trump when I heard that howl. Darn near curdled my blood!"

By this time he'd reached the patio. Even if he hadn't been so distracted, it was too dark to have noticed any of the damage done to his garden.

Dark? The thought must have occurred to Mr. Murphy. He stopped short and squinted upwards.

"What the...?" He aimed his flashlight at the light fixture. "Why, of all the...!"

Then, reluctantly giving in, he focused the light on Sinbad, still cowering against the house. "Come on, you big bag of orange chicken feathers. No point leaving you here scared half out of your wits." He gave the cat a nudge with his foot.

"Just look at you," he said, as he opened the back door. The animal grudgingly crept over the threshold. "I'd say you're lucky that beast didn't eat you alive. Ah well..." With a long, weary sigh, he followed the cat inside. "We'll take a closer look at those battle scars. Then you're heading downsta—" The door shut with a bang. They were gone.

A few seconds later the kitchen light switched on, and after about five minutes, switched off again. The next thing, they saw the bedroom light come on upstairs and Mr. Murphy's silhouette appeared at the window. This time he closed it all the way before drawing the curtains. The light snapped off.

Instantly the still, silent garden sprang to life. One dwarf began rising steadily from the ground. Soon he disappeared into the tree. A few minutes later the second one had vanished. One by one the animals slipped through the gate, into the space, and back into Tolk.

Spark stayed behind and held the flashlight while Price unscrewed the pulley and removed it. Then, while the boy was putting everything into his zipper bag, the squirrel scurried up the brick wall of the house and removed the black tape from the light fixture. That, of course, meant that the light came on, and stayed on for a couple of minutes. But there was no Mr. Murphy and no cat around to see. With his hind feet and front paws, Spark managed to squish the tape into a sticky ball. Once back in the tree, this also went into Price's bag. Last of all, they coiled up the green rope.

Soon everything had been lowered safely into Price's yard. The dwarfs and the gear were piled hodgepodge into the wagon, and as quietly as possible, the boy, the squirrel, and a few remaining animals hauled the lot down the stone steps. Then ... home at last.

Part III:
Sinbad Exposed

Chapter Twenty-One:
A Happy Reunion

All this time, a small party of friends and kin had been waiting anxiously on the other side of the wall. There had been a lot of fretting and fidgeting and pacing back and forth. Minutes had seemed to stretch into hours, and the passing of an hour had become almost unbearable. Then finally, with wagon in tow, Price emerged triumphant into Tolk. All eyes focused eagerly on the wagon and its disheveled occupants. They heard a moan, followed by a grunt, and then with a flip-flop, two uncomfortable but very much alive dwarfs tumbled onto the ground. Immediately a cheer went up.

Dori blinked, staring in wonder at the crowd gathered there to greet them. "By my whiskers, it's the middle of the night. And there's Dileen! Dileen, what're you doing here?" He glanced around furtively. "And where's that flaming cat got to? What th-? Smoot! What're you doing?" Dori's stout leg was draped across his friend's shoulders, his big square boot resting heavily on the back of Smoot's neck. Smoot, flat-out, face-down, couldn't lift his head.

"Mmph."

"What? Speak up! Oh—beggin' yer pardon." Dori removed his foot and a startled Smoot scrambled to his knees. Sputtering and blowing, he dislodged the dust and grass from his mouth and snorted through his broad nostrils. "Confound it, Dori! Watch what yer—" He stopped and gaped in bewilderment at the beaming crowd. Another cheer rang out, but the two dwarfs just sat there, dazed and gawking.

Price spotted Freddy, and then O.P., who was lounging on the fairy's shoulder, taking it all in with a calculated disinterest. But Freddy clapped her hands and laughed joyfully at the dwarfs' antics. Price hurried to her side.

"This is a happy reunion," he said. "Wait 'til I tell you what happened!"

The fairy wrinkled her nose distastefully. "Not until I wash off that make-up. Your face looks like it's carved out of an old brown tree trunk. I don't like it a bit."

"What do you mean?" objected O.P. "If you ask me, it's a distinct improvement. I think wooden heads are attractive. I'm glad to see they're coming into vogue. Of course, yours is only a façade. Nothing to compare with the real thing. Hee, hee."

Freddy giggled. "Come with me." She led them to a place where she had already hung a lantern on a bush and prepared a copper basin of water. Price sat cross-legged on the grass while Freddy, using a silken cloth and a small jar of ointment, carefully and tenderly washed his face. Kneeling down, the fairy worked right-handed while O.P. slouched on her left shoulder and watched, giving directions. Freddy didn't need any instructions, but she smiled and followed them anyway. At that moment she was too happy to complain.

"That smells nice," commented Price. "Sort of like ... newly mowed grass. What is it?"

"The fairies call it Wheedleberry Balm. It's oil pressed from the seeds of the wheedle plant," explained Freddy. "We fairies use it on our wings to make them shine. Some fairies use it in their hair to give it luster. But..." Freddy rolled her eyes, "not me. It attracts bees. They think I'm an enormous yellow blossom. It's such a nuisance!"

Price laughed. "The wheedle plant?" He scratched his ear. "You'll have to show me sometime."

"Show you?" Freddy dropped her working hand. "Then ... you're not going away after all?"

"Well, I was hoping King Noble would still let me come and visit. Why wouldn't he?"

"Yes, I suppose he would." Freddy was thoughtful. "But eventually you will grow older and forget us."

"I'll never forget any of you. You're my friends. Next to my family, you're the best friends I've ever had."

Sadly, Freddy understood the truth better than Price. He would forget them, she knew. But she said nothing. With a sigh, she resumed the delicate operation she had begun on his face.

O.P. did not like this somber shift in mood. He squirmed. "Of course he'll come here all the time. I expect he'll be pestering us nearly every day. What could he possibly find to do *there* that could compare in any way to the fun he can have *here*? All this talk of growing older is nonsense!"

Freddy glanced sidelong at the pinecone man. She had, no doubt, sensed that he was trembling. But again she said nothing.

"Right," said Price. "Now, listen. You've got to hear what Meepy did. He was amazing!"

At the mention of his friend's name, O.P. sat up straight. His black painted eyes grew larger. "Did Meepy *do* something?"

"Oh yes. He was awesome. He risked his life. And King Noble—he was magnificent! I'll tell you all about it."

The pinecone man was trembling all over now. Without a word, Freddy gently lifted him from her shoulder and set him on Price's arm. Then, turning, she rose, emptied the basin behind a bush and carefully dried it with the cloth.

"At first we had Sinbad completely duped," Price went on. "He was running back and forth like he was torn between a goldfish and a canary. But then he caught on. And he was going after this skunk. But wait. I have to back up. Mr. Murphy—"

Then suddenly they heard the sound of a large animal bounding through the tall grass, coming their way, and all three heads swung round in that direction. Seconds later King Noble galloped out of the shadows with an elated Meepy clinging to his neck. Like the conquering hero of old, he halted triumphantly before them. The telling of the tale, it seemed, would have to wait.

As soon as Meepy saw his friends, he jumped down. At the same time, O.P. slipped off Price's arm, and laughing, he and the mouse did a little jig around each other several times.

Price faced King Noble. The first faint blush of dawn had just begun to stretch thinly across the meadow and caught the rim of the dog's coat in a soft halo of light. Lovingly, he licked the boy's face, while Price threw his arms around the animal's strong neck and hugged him. Then, and for perhaps the first time in his life, the boy cried real tears of gratitude. No words were spoken, but only a stone or a clot of dirt would not have sensed their joy.

The sun had risen completely when Price crept in through the back door. Upstairs, Grandmother was still asleep. Cautiously, he made his way across the creaking floorboards to his room, where his digital clock dutifully informed him it was 5:46. Price groaned. He wanted to flop down on the bed right then and there, but knew it would look suspicious. What if Grandmother looked in on him and found him dressed in his black clothes? Quietly he slipped them off and stuffed them into a drawer. Then he pulled on his pajama bottoms and scuttled his zipper bag and tools out of sight behind the closet door. By now, he was giddy with fatigue and crashed onto the bed.

Still bleary-eyed, he did not present himself downstairs until nearly one o'clock in the afternoon. Grandmother was in the kitchen drinking iced pop. She glanced up at him sharply. Even she realized that this was unusual.

"Price. I was getting worried. Are you okay?"

"I'm fine."

Grandmother's eyes quickly ran him up and down, and she didn't seem convinced. "There's some fruit salad in the fridge. Why don't you make yourself a peanut butter sandwich?"

Price yawned and sat down at the table. He thought about stuffed mushrooms and honeyed muffins and Dot Arbuckle's wild plum cake. "I'm not that hungry," he said. "I guess I'll go to the park. D'you mind?"

Grandmother did not reply. She couldn't help but notice his uncombed hair and the dark circles under his eyes.

"Not hungry?" She put a hand on his forehead. "No, I don't think you should go outside today," she said. "My guess is you're coming down with something."

"I'm fine."

"Still, I think you'd better stay in until I'm sure of it."

And thus a deflated Price was confined to the house for the rest of the day.

Later, Grandmother was relaxing in the living room, reading, feet up on the ottoman, while Price distractedly thumbed through a comic book. Finally, giving it up, he pushed it aside. Grandmother looked up at him over the top of her glasses.

"You missed all the excitement this morning."

"Excitement?"

"The police! Next door. Seems there were vandals there last night. It does make one a little nervous, I must say. They stole some lawn furniture, of all things. And I understand they did some damage to that beautiful garden. Such a shame!" She sighed and shook her head. "I just can't understand that kind of behavior."

Price didn't say a word, but felt his face redden.

"The police came here and spoke to me, but I hadn't seen or heard a thing all night. Except for the most frightful howling from somewhere. I thought it must be a dog, but it sounded like a wild beast." Again she shook her head, thinking it over. "If that animal could talk, I'm sure it could have told them a thing or two. And if I heard it, surely you must have heard it, too?"

Not trusting his voice, Price nodded the affirmative. He cleared his throat. "Uh, Grandma, do you mind if I go outside now? Just in the yard. I want to take a look."

Grandmother chuckled. "Well, it seems your curiosity is in good health. Go ahead." But then she frowned. "You still haven't eaten a bite."

"I'll grab an apple on the way out."

He was gone.

Munching on the apple, Price found a spot in the poplar tree where he could see Mr. Murphy working in his garden, trying to repair some of the damage. He was kneeling down, clipping away at broken pieces of plants, tossing them into a trash bag. His expression, severe at the best of times, was now dark and brooding, and that strange light in his eyes was smoldering. Price noted that Sinbad was nowhere in sight. Would he dare to venture into Tolk so soon after last night? At one point, the old man happened to glance up and saw the boy watching him from the tree, but he was too preoccupied to really notice or care. The thin, dry lips moved constantly as he muttered to himself. Occasionally he would stop and scratch his bald head or rub his eyes.

It was obvious that Mr. Murphy was flummoxed. Stiffly, he rose to his feet.

"Footprints!" Price heard him mutter. "Animal footprints." Then something new caught his eye. He strode over to the lilac bush. "I'll be darned if this isn't beavers' work!" he exclaimed. Turning to the pond, he frowned, staring at his lily pads. Then he bent over his tiger lilies, to get a closer look, and shook his head. Finally giving it up, he breathed out a long sigh. "What ... *what* in tarnation happened here?"

Chapter Twenty-Two: Who Price Met and What He Found

The next morning, before Grandmother had even set a foot out of bed, she was wondering about Price. "Something's up," she said out loud. "He was so restless yesterday—like a caged bird."

She stepped into her slippers, fastened her bathrobe, and tiptoed into the bathroom. Imagine the look of surprise on her face when, through the open window, she saw Price standing in the poplar tree. He was staring across the wall into Mr. Murphy's yard.

She chuckled to herself. "My goodness! Wouldn't life be dull if our neighbors never had any problems?" But apparently he was feeling better. And that was good, because the lawn needed mowing.

For his part, Price had noted only two things of interest in his examination of Mr. Murphy's garden. Namely, that the cat wasn't there, and at about eight o'clock, Mr. Murphy had driven off in his car.

It was nearly lunchtime before Price had finished his chores. Luckily Mr. Murphy still hadn't returned. Price came inside and washed his hands at the kitchen sink. Grandmother sat at the table grating carrots for a salad.

"Mind if I take my lunch to the park this afternoon, Grandma?" he asked.

"Are you feeling better then?"

"Never better."

"Then of course you may."

"Great. I'll pack enough for two."

Grandmother looked up at him over the top of her glasses. "You know, you're welcome to bring your friend home any time you want."

Price had no idea how to respond to this, so he said nothing. Fifteen minutes later, with two lunches in his pack—plus a little extra for O.P.—he and the bicycle were gone.

Price immediately set out across the meadow, his legs vigorously pumping the pedals of his bike as he pursued his own thread of a trail, which was still faintly visible. His first thought was to head to the Muskins'.

But when he arrived, no one was home. A few minutes later he was knocking at the Arbuckles' door, but no one was there either. Of course, nobody was expecting him just at that moment, but all the same he felt let down. He decided that he might as well go exploring down by the river. That was, after all, where he'd first met Freddy.

He soon found a rocky, twisting, downward path, where the river was flanked on either side by giant firs. Before long he caught glimpses of sparkling water between the dark shelves of evergreen boughs.

He hadn't gone far when he heard a rapid footfall thumping along behind him. But when he stopped and looked around, no one was there. *It must be a dwarf*, he thought.

Who else has such a heavy tread? I can hear it before I can even see anybody.

On an impulse, Price ducked behind a large tree and crouched down. Tall ferns grew thickly around its base, giving him additional cover and a bit of visual leverage. The footsteps paused. Peering through fronds of fern, he still could not see anyone. The footsteps began again. A few seconds later, sure enough, a dwarf came padding into view around a bend in the path. It was no one he recognized.

Red-faced and hairy, the dwarf hurried along on thick, stumpy legs. Then he stopped at the very place where Price was hiding. The boy crouched down a bit more. A few seconds later the dwarf was on his way again, but now Price was watching the back of the stocky, burly little man. He decided to follow him.

Every twenty paces or so, the dwarf paused and looked suspiciously all around. Whenever this happened, Price had to dive for cover. But he kept his distance and used the bushes and trees for camouflage. It was lucky that the dwarf was heavy-footed, and that high above them a soulful breeze soughed through the tall pines, conveniently covering any sound that Price made.

Once again the dwarf stopped dead in his tracks. Price ducked out of sight, but had a good view of him through a gap in the foliage. The dwarf turned, checking behind and on all sides. Then suddenly, he disappeared.

Price continued to watch for a several seconds, thinking that the dwarf would pop up again or that he would hear some telling sound. But nothing happened, and he heard only the vapid sighing of the wind and the restless creaking of the ancient firs, like the bones of old men stirring in their sleep.

Bewildered, he stepped out from his hiding place and went to the exact spot where he had last seen the dwarf. The trail veered sharply to the right here, but was plainly visible from where he'd been watching. He couldn't possibly have missed seeing the dwarf, if he had continued along the trail. Just to be certain though, he quickly ran in that direction. The path followed a consistent, oblique course down to the river. His eyes scoured the empty trail in vain. There was no sign of the dwarf. *He couldn't have gone this way*, Price reasoned and retraced his steps.

He tried to puzzle it out. Had the dwarf dived into the bush? Was he at that moment watching Price from some hidden enclave? The boy listened up sharply. Now he wished that the creaking boughs and mournful sighing of the wind would stop, as he strained his brain and every sense for some hint of what might have happened.

Then he actually did hear a faint, dry rustle coming from somewhere behind him. Wheeling around, he caught sight of some slight movement. But it wasn't the dwarf. What he saw was a flash of orange fur.

Price shut his eyes and inwardly groaned. He had no desire to confront Sinbad just then—or ever. But then he heard a scuffling, leafy sound and an elongated snake of orange fur slithered out from the underbrush. The cat squinted up at him.

"What are *you* doing skulking around here?" he sniveled. "I thought you'd finished what you came for. Why don't you go home now and stay there?"

Price was amazed at the transformation. Just two days ago Sinbad had been puffed up and pompous, but now he slunk low to the ground, his whole being somehow diminished. But the greatest change was the look in his eyes. Before, they had gleamed with conceit and selfish pride; now they glowered with a stark hatred. Price had never before seen such a look, and it was truly frightening. Instinctively, he drew back.

This reaction restored some of the cat's battered ego. He sneered. "I suppose you thought you'd seen the last of me. Believe me, the fight's not over yet. I have my allies, you know."

Price looked around. "Really? I don't see anyone."

The cat stiffened in anger. "You *shall* see!"

"Right," Price scoffed. "I'd like to see you even *try* to stand up against King Noble."

Sinbad recoiled at the mention of the dog's name.

"Just you wait!" he sneered. "I have a plan of my own. And if I must be miserable, then mark my words, all of Tolk will be miserable with me." With that the cat turned on his heels.

Price watched the long, tawny shape worm its way back up the trail. Never before had he witnessed such an overwhelming hatred, and it had unnerved him. Several minutes passed before he could breathe normally again.

But then he gritted his teeth and applied himself once more to resolving the mystery of the disappearing dwarf. He returned to the place where he'd last seen him. Crouching down, he carefully examined the mossy ground. It did seem a little compressed here, as though a heavy foot might have recently trod upon it.

And this is definitely a freshly broken twig, he thought, noting a flimsy branch of honeysuckle dangling loosely before his face. He pushed it aside. Just beyond, some of the slender, woody stems had been deliberately cut and a kind of slit had been forged through the bush. He wriggled behind the loose branch and sidled in through the gash.

He found himself in a passage flanked on either side by dense, scruffy brush. An avenue, about four feet across, had been roughly hewn through the vastly overgrown honeysuckle. But where the trail should have gone up, instead it led directly down into what looked like the mouth of a cave.

Price did not think twice about stepping into the open cavity. It led into a channel that appeared to be a natural fissure running through solid rock. Staying within the shadows along one side of an irregular stone wall, he started down an uneven, stony path. It was dark in the passage, but just ahead, he saw a faint glow emanating from an unknown source. A minute later he passed a lighted torch, invisible from even a short distance away, because it was set inside a small crevasse.

Then someone must live here, he realized and was suddenly keenly aware that he was trespassing. Yet the idea of turning back never entered his mind.

He had covered only a few more paces when his ear caught the muffled sound of voices. One, two, three different voices were speaking in turns. But if they were familiar, they were too distant to recognize. Then a fourth voice, a deeper voice, was added. Price suddenly remembered Sinbad's words. "I have my allies," the cat had said.

Who were these allies? What if he'd stumbled upon the lair of some of King Noble's enemies?

Chapter Twenty-Three: Inside the Cave

Enemies! The thought provoked a small stab of fear. Price edged closer to the cavern wall, as if he could meld into its vague, shadowy convolutions. The palms of his hands felt sweaty as they skimmed the rocky surface, but the contact provided a kind of cold, sheltering presence.

I want to find out who lives here, he thought. *Maybe I can learn something.*

He had gone about another ten yards when the tips of his fingers nudged something wooden just above his head, making a soft scraping noise. Startled, he glanced up and found that he had disturbed a large, rough picture frame hanging on the wall. There was a lantern, like the ones he'd seen at the market, mounted over the picture to highlight it, but the lantern was not lit. In the gloom, he could just make out a sketch of five gregarious-looking bears linked arm in arm in jovial camaraderie.

"Bears!" he whispered out loud. "Then this must be the den of some bears." The revelation was not reassuring. *Five of them,* he counted. *At least five.*

A faint glow some distance ahead indicated a bend in the tunnel. As he sidled in a few more paces, he noticed the voices were becoming louder. He still didn't recognize them, but he could now pick out the odd word or phrase. His ears caught '*Sinbad*,' '*great thunder bolts!*' and '*I say it's treachery!*' None of it was the least bit enlightening.

"Who goes there?" An enormous bear suddenly lumbered out from around the bend. He rose up on his haunches, his massive body filling nearly the entire height and breadth of the cavity.

"I could smell you coming!" The bear sniffed loudly and his eyes pierced the shadows. "Who are you? You're not a dwarf."

Price stood stock-still, afraid to open his mouth. But he quickly realized it was inevitable. "It-It's Price Evans," he said, stepping ahead to where there was more light. "Look, I'm sorry. I know I'm trespassing, but I'm just trying to find my friends."

"Price Evans? Are you that *boy*, then?"

Price nodded.

"Well, come on in. The meeting's nearly done, but we were hoping you'd still make it."

Just then Price heard a deep, mellow-toned voice that he knew well. He blew out a breath of air and relaxed. It was King Noble.

"Name's Paxton ... guard duty, you know. Hope I didn't give you too much of a fright."

"Yeah, a bit," Price confessed, stepping forward. "But you're doing a great job."

He found himself standing at the mouth of a cavern, shaped roughly like an enormous mushroom cap. The interior walls were ragged and uneven, and it was lit by torches like the one he'd seen coming in. It was just large enough to hold the assembly of about fifty bodies, great and small, that were gathered there—including, Price noted, about half a dozen large bears. King Noble was seated prominently within a small cleared area, in plain sight of everyone.

Price saw others he knew, including Freddy. She was with Laefay and the redheaded fairy he'd met on the night of the rescue. And O.P. was with the Muskins, sitting cross-legged on the hard stone floor, elbows (of a sort) on his knees and non-existent chin resting in one white, felt hand. He was close enough for Price to see that his painted eyebrows were knit together and his round eyes were half shut, as though deep in thought. In fact, the entire assembly was caught up in the proceedings and no one noticed him.

Price's attention was quickly drawn to a dwarf, whom he recognized as Dori. He was earnestly addressing King Noble. With his short arms he made broad, sweeping gestures, indicating that the rest of the company was included in what he had to say. Not wanting to interrupt, Price stayed out of sight, within the shadow of the cavern's entrance.

"I can't understand it!" Dori's voice rebounded off the stone walls of the chamber. "Smoot and I have been life-long chums!" He wrung his hands in exasperation. "Our greenwood dwellings are side by side. We've planted and gathered mushrooms and squash on the same plot of ground since we were hardly bigger'n button mushrooms ourselves. I couldn't even count the hours we've spent playing at Trick Sticks and Knuckle Balls." He winced, as though in pain.

"I just can't understand how he can go on defending that lying cat, after what he done to the both of us. Ah, yer Majesty..." He spread his palms like a beggar begging alms and his big, droopy dwarf eyes searched imploringly. "Sometimes I think it's more than I can bear!" Dropping his arms, he hung his head and heaved a deep, trembling sigh.

King Noble exhaled slowly. "Have you tried to reason with him?" he asked.

"Aye. Over and over. He won't listen to me! He keeps insisting there's a life of ease, brimful with unheard of riches within our easy grasp. 'If we can't go to men for it,' he says, 'then men can bring it to us.' But I says, 'Maybe it's a lie. If that cat lied to us once, how can we ever trust him again?' I says, 'We've got a good life already. Why fix what ain't amuck?' Then he says, 'I'm all for leisure, treasure, and pleasure,' and he laughs. 'Get off your corn shuck,' says I, 'You may think you're clever, but I say you're *never!*' Then he says my head is stuffed with toadstools!"

Dori's broad, open features were stricken with a look of profound sadness. "Ah, to think it should come to this: bosom friends given to such common name-calling."

The corners of the dog's lips lifted in a sad smile and he shook his head. "You've been a good friend, Dori—you've done what you could. And you are absolutely right. The ways of men were never meant for us. It would be a grave error indeed to invite humans or the human way of life into Tolk." The dog shut his eyes then, deep in thought.

After a moment, he stood and addressed the entire company.

"Hear me now ... and hear me well," he said. "Sinbad is both deceived and deceiving. Believe me, there are things in the outside world that would be better for us not to know."

The dog's voice was not loud, but the weight of his message penetrated to the core of each listening mind. "You do not understand the ways of men as I do. Should humans come here, Tolk would in a very short time become as the Earth, mortal and corruptible. And, in the same stroke, we would become as the poor, dumb creatures of the world. There is no life of absolute ease and plenty. That is contrary to natural law. And humans, in spite of all their conveniences, bear heavier burdens than you or I can even begin to comprehend." He paused, giving everyone time to ponder his words. All were silent for several minutes.

Then the small voice of a marmot piped up. "But, Sire ... what if Sinbad is right? What if some of those vicious beasts, those predators he spoke about, *do* find a way into Tolk? Begging your pardon, Sire, but even we don't know where these gateways are. Only you know, and they aren't fortified, or even watched. What would happen to us then?"

"Those animals Sinbad speaks of are creatures of another sphere. They exist only in the mortal world. Besides, no one who is not of Tolk can come here unbidden. No one! It is a law that has been in place since the beginning of time. Of course, you're not prisoners. You can leave if you choose. You must remember, though, that coming back is not a sure thing. My friends, you *must* believe me when I tell you that there is no danger from outside that can find its way here to harm us. But..." his voice dropped darkly, "I perceive a danger from within."

"Sinbad!"

"Sinbad."

"Sinbad."

The name reverberated softly from one to another.

"That cat's going to keep right on stirring up trouble," someone said.

"And trying to trick us."

"Yes ... and the tragedy is that so many of our friends believe him."

"That's so! Why, only yesterday he told Mertyl Bear and me that you don't care about us, King Noble, because if you did, you'd want us all to live in big houses with *servants* to wait on us. But I told him right out, there's no such things!"

"He keeps on saying that King Noble is useless and broken down, like an old bucket, full of holes: Can't keep the water in, can't keep the crickets out. It's all such wretched, wretched lies!"

"Aye. He told Frip, who told me, that King Noble is just trying to keep us from betterin' ourselves, from gainin' treasures of knowledge and wealth that we can't even imagine. Well, says I, 'I got all the knowledge and wealth I'm ever going to need ... or want.' I like things the way they are."

"Those we used to call our kin and friends are fast becoming our enemies."

"He *has* to be stopped."

"But what can we do? He won't listen to anyone. We can't force him to stop talking. It would be like trying to stop the wind from blowing."

"Yes, but this wind is blowing bad seeds onto the soil of our own dear Tolk!" Dot Arbuckle suddenly stood up and pressed two tight fists against her breast. "They're the seeds of lying, and wickedness, and ... and death!"

"We must be rid of him!" someone shouted.

Fender jumped to his feet. "Aye! And if we don't, then we're all—*all* of us—doomed!" The dwarf's wide features had reddened in anger and fear, the whites of his eyes showing all the way around. "Doomed, I say! Things will only keep gettin' worse, 'til fine'ly ... he'll bring humans here, sure as sure. And when that day comes..." Fender could not find words to describe the terrible fate that he knew was inevitable. He swallowed hard. "Doomed, I say!"

"Yes. We *must* get rid of him! We must drive him out! Away! Far, far away!"

King Noble was staring bleakly over their heads. The others did not know it, but he was looking back in time. He was remembering a friend he'd once loved and admired—one who had borne the proud and honored name of 'Flame.' The dog shook himself, as if he could shake off both the memories and the reality.

"Yes." His large brown eyes were heavy with grief. "It's true. We must drive him out. And we must seal up the portal that he is using, *and* abusing ... forever."

A deep silence hung over the assembly, as the simple Tolks grappled with this terrible, new idea: the permanent and irreversible expulsion of a fellow creature. Why, even a few weeks before, the very thought would have been incomprehensible.

"But how?" Millie Muskin asked timidly.

King Noble shut his eyes. "How indeed."

When the eyes reopened, it was plain that they saw clearly the path that lay ahead. He leapt up and declared in a loud voice, amplified by the walls of the cavern, "I will call a meeting! An assembly! *Everyone* must attend. Everyone—without exception! A special patrol will be organized to ensure that no one is left out. The Tolks must decide for themselves where their loyalty lies—whether to me, or to Sinbad." Then he looked around, searching the maze of faces. He singled out Freddy. "Winifred Fairchild, I now call upon you to come and stand before me."

The fairy was so stunned by this completely unexpected solicitation that she couldn't move. "Come, Winifred," King Noble said kindly. "There is nothing to be afraid of."

With knees quaking, somehow Freddy's legs carried her before the king.

"Freddy, I am putting you in charge of organizing the special patrol."

The fairy was speechless.

"I have been watching you. I've seen how you speak to the others about me, gently persuading them to come to our side. You are loyal and faithful. I know I can trust you to work hard. And you will have to. You must be certain that every living creature is accounted for. Now ... go to! There is no time to lose. You have only four full days. In four days, there must not be one egg left in the clutch, not one soul missed. On the afternoon of the fourth day, we will all gather at the place the fairies call the Moon's Platter."

The king's eyes again searched the crowd.

"I now call Meepy Muskin to stand before me!"

Shaking visibly, Freddy returned to her place next to Laefay. The beautiful white fairy greeted her with a radiant smile.

"Congratulations, my little daffodil!" she whispered. She grasped the smaller fairy's hand and held it tightly. In spite of herself, Freddy felt her cheeks flush. It was a mixture of gladness at having been called to serve her king and her fellow Tolks, and the uncertainty of inexperience in a new role.

In low tones King Noble spoke briefly to Meepy. The mouse nodded two or three times as he gleaned some vital instruction. Then he straightened, clicked his heels together and clapped his right arm across his chest, military fashion. Then turning neatly on his heel, he scuttled from the room, mouse fashion. He rushed right past Price, and in his haste, never saw the boy standing in the shadows at one side of the entrance.

King Noble again faced the assembly. "My dear children!" he addressed them. "From this day on, to me, it is as though you are my own flesh and bone, the children of my heart. My children, I must leave you, for there is a matter that requires my immediate attention. You must now listen to Freddy. I know that she has important directives for each of you."

With a bound, King Noble disappeared into the tunnel's dark mouth, leaving Freddy, quite unexpectedly, and to her great dismay, at the hub of the wheel.

Once out of sight, King Noble turned and faced Price. The boy hurried over and wrapped his arms around the dog's strong neck, affectionately ruffling his thick coat. The dog flicked a warm, damp tongue across the boy's cheek.

"And what do you have to say for yourself?" he chided gently. "We missed you yesterday."

"And I missed all of you, but you see, I was so worn out after our awesome adventure that my grandma thought I was sick."

"Ah. Then it's the 'Case of the Vigilant Grandmother' is it?"

"Yes, that's it."

"Now, out with it. Tell me what you know."

"Well, I know that you're planning a big meeting in four days and that everybody has to be there, or else. And I know that Sinbad is getting a permanent change of address. But *he* doesn't know that."

King Noble nodded. "Then you know enough."

Price was suddenly serious. "I ran into Sinbad, just before I got here."

"Yes?"

"He claims he has allies. He says he has a plan."

"A plan? Hm. He may have been posturing."

Price nodded. "Have you seen him, since … you know…?"

"No. No, I haven't. He seems to be avoiding me." The dog clucked his tongue and looked away.

"Well," Price went on, "he … he's changed."

"Changed?" King Noble frowned. "That's not surprising," he said, "considering he suffered such a bitter humiliation—scarcely two days ago. It must have disturbed him greatly. Is that what you mean?"

"Not exactly..." said Price.

"In what way then has he changed?"

Price searched his mind for the right words. "If..." he began slowly, "if hatred were an iceberg, then he's standing on top of the biggest iceberg I ever saw. But the bulk of it, the part you can't see because it's under the ocean, is ten times bigger than you can imagine."

King Noble shut his eyes, and Price heard a low rumble, like a groan of exquisite pain, from deep within the canine throat, that made goose bumps rise on his arms. When the dog looked up at him, his large, soft eyes were moist. If dogs could cry tears, Price knew at that moment, King Noble would have been weeping.

"Until now I had still clung to the hope that there might be a chance for Sinbad," he said, his voice thick with grief. With a defeated kind of sigh, he stared at the ground.

"Do you know where I must go now?" he asked, looking up.

Price shook his head.

"The time has come when I must confront the creature with his destiny. But you cannot tell the others."

"Of course not ... if you say so."

"I do. Now you must go to Freddy. She will need all the help you can give her."

"Sure."

But Price continued to watch as King Noble, head and tail down, ambled slowly toward the pale slash of sunlight at the mouth of the tunnel. It was obvious that he took no pleasure in the task that lay ahead.

Chapter Twenty-Four:
The Invitation

Once outside, King Noble's expression altered dramatically. His jaw tightened, his eyes focused intently, and if one looked closely, the hint of two pointed fangs appeared along the lip line. A fervent and grim determination had gripped his being. Nothing mattered now except the loyal and lovely flock he'd left behind. And the truth was that, in a very real sense, all of their lives depended on him.

He lifted his nostrils and quickly located the scent. With nose to the ground, he set off at a remarkable pace, dashing through woods and charging through brush with the determination of a locomotive. Yet his progress was as noiseless as thought, as though it was the mind itself that willed him through the tangled terrain.

Sinbad, Smoot, Duff, Buckley, Frip, and many others were hunkered down in a small covey. Duff sat hunched over with his knees drawn up to his chin, so as not to crowd anyone. They had taken to secreting themselves, partly to hide from prying eyes, and partly in the hopes of witnessing something incriminating, or overhearing some revealing conversation. Sinbad had managed to convince them that they were the target—that it was everybody else who was out to get them.

And they had all been fed a liberal dose of Sinbad's version of the rescue—the one about how he had so cleverly duped King Noble and that boy ("that intruder") into getting Sinbad's dearest friends out of an unfortunate predicament.

Buckley was skeptical. "I thought you were the one who got them into that scrape in the first place."

"That was an honest mistake, my friend. Nothing more than that. True, we now know with absolute certainty that dwarfs cannot live outside the boundaries of Tolk. Yes, it appears that the old fairies' tales were right about that after all. But I've never been one to deny it when I've made an honest mistake, and I honestly did not know that those dwarf-humans weren't exactly like our own breed of dwarfs.

"When I invited Smoot here, and Dori, to come with me, I didn't really think that..." He winced. "Well, you get my drift. I only wanted them to see how truly wonderful it is there. If only I could show all of you! But we know now that it's too risky—out of the question."

Buckley squinted at the cat and wrinkled his nose, conspicuously revealing his two large beaver incisors. "I don't get it. Exactly how did *you* get them out of there?"

Sinbad stretched up a little so that he could look down on the doubting beaver. "It was quite simple, really. I knew that I could never rescue them on my own. And I couldn't let old Murphy think *I* was the culprit, so even though I was the brains behind the whole plan, I made it look like the others were responsible. I tell you, Frank had taken quite a shine to those dwarfs. Ha! Finest looking pair o' garden ornaments that ever sat in the sun." He chortled and cuffed Smoot with his paw.

Then his lip curled back in disgust. "Oh, I'm well aware how much King Noble fears and despises me. I've seen that look in his eyes. Why, he is practically eaten up with envy every time we meet." Sinbad ground his teeth. "He knows how powerful I've become, and in his bones, he knows that his days as king are numbered.

"As for the boy, you don't realize how much he *hates* the old man. Hates him, I say. Hates him because he wouldn't let him on his property—Frank's own property, mind you. Wouldn't let him build a clubhouse where wicked boys could meet to plan their next rampage. Oh, I keep my ears pricked, and people aren't even aware when I'm nearby listening. But I knew about that. I was there when Frank turned him down, chop-a-chop." He made a zigzagging motion with a foreleg.

"I knew it was only a matter of time before they'd come after those dwarfs, knew it as sure as dwarfs nap and fairies fly. I knew that King Noble would try to make *me* out as the villain. And I knew that boy would do anything—*anything*—to get his own back from Mr. Murphy. That's the kind of boy he is—mean and spiteful. Oh yes. Very carefully I reeled them in, playing on their weaknesses. That's how I arranged the whole thing." He grinned.

"Why, they weren't even aware they'd been playing right into my court. In the end, realizing his stupidity, King Noble even tried to thwart the rescue. Can you imagine it, my friends? What utter cowardice!" Sinbad spat in disgust. "Why, if it hadn't been for Frank, I'd have been..." He shuddered. "But never mind that. That's too terrible to even contemplate."

Suddenly Sinbad looked distraught. "Oh, but I cannot tell you how much that ungrateful Dori has let me down. And to think that I risked my life for him between the jaws of that canine brute. Just the thought of it wounds me to the heart." Sinbad slumped forward, as though he had actually been stricken. One of the bears shifted uncomfortably.

"Come along now, Chief. I hate to see you like this, way down at burrow's bottom."

"I know, Tucker." The cat sighed deeply. "But there's nothing else for it. I've been betrayed, and that's that. Still, I'm not bitter. Far be it from me to hold a grudge. I'd take the scoundrel back before sunset tonight if he'd let me. But I suppose I can hardly blame Dori. It's just that he's been taken in by that conniving duo: Dunce Dog and Barrel-Brained Boy." He nudged Tucker playfully. "You know how a barrel's big and round and full of air." They all chortled.

Then Sinbad was suddenly grave. He folded his forepaws neatly in front of him and looked at the others. "You know..." He paused. "I don't like to point a claw ... of course, I could be mistaken. Surely, I *must* be mistaken ... but..." He glanced down and scratched in the dirt with a toenail, as though reluctant to go on.

"What, Chief?"

"Aye, what?"

Sinbad rolled his eyes upwards and sighed. "Ah my friends, it's just that it is too, *too* terrible to even contemplate."

"What is it, for the love of toadstools?"

Sinbad spoke haltingly, as though he was having the greatest difficulty wrenching out the words. "What is the worst thing ... the *worst* thing you could ever imagine?"

His companions glanced at one another uneasily. "We dunno. What? What!"

"I sometimes wonder if ... if ... that dog isn't becoming ... like one of *them*."

"Like *them*? Like who?" Buckley Beaver eyed the cat shrewdly.

Sinbad pursed his cat lips. "It wouldn't be fair to come right out and accuse him. What if I was wrong? But, what he did to me ... at least what he meant to do ... what I swear he had it in his heart to do, on that fateful night. I saw it in his eyes: that hunger. He's becoming just like them ... those beasts!" Sinbad looked pleadingly heavenward, as though wanting to be absolved from what he must say next.

"Out with it, cat!" Buckley Beaver slapped his tail impatiently. "Say what you mean, and mean what you say!"

Sinbad's lips quivered and his voice sank to a harsh whisper, as though his throat had become so constricted with emotion that he couldn't speak properly. "Those ... *predators!*"

"What?"

Sinbad whispered the dreaded word again, so softly this time that it was barely audible. "Like those *predators.*"

The group sat in silence, most of them aware that some terrible news had been divulged, but not at all sure what it meant.

Finally Buckley shook his head. "No. Impossible. Couldn't be. King Noble may be a fool, but he's not ... that."

The others remained either silent and uncertain, or silent and confused. But Sinbad was satisfied. He had sowed the seed of an idea whose time had not yet come, not yet.

"At any rate, it's a great consolation to be surrounded by the likes of you." All at once he was the jovial comrade again. "Ah, if only the others were as clever and cunning as you lot. If I had *my* way, I'd see to it that every one of you got a share of the booty. And, as the booty is endless... Well, ha-ha, you see how it stands."

"What's there to stop us from bringing the advantages of the world right here, right into Tolk?" Smoot hadn't missed his cue.

"Why nothing, unless you take into account that witless dog." Sinbad clipped the last two words contemptuously, betraying his intense dislike. "Let's consider it. If there were enough of us—picture this now—enough of us who could proudly bear aloft the banner: '*LEISURE, TREASURE, AND PLEASURE, WITH IMMORTALITY FOR ALL*,' then King Noble would become a no-account. And oh my friends...!"

Sinbad groaned under the yoke of unfulfilled yearning. "My friends! There's so much there for us, so much more than you can imagine, just for the taking." He shut his eyes in rapturous contemplation of all the luxuries. "We could have it all—have it all, forever. And Tolk to boot."

Then the eyes popped open again. "Just who does he think he is, that dumb animal, saying we can only have one and not the other? That's a licked-bottom lie!" He edged nearer to the others and spoke with slow deliberation. "Tell me, my friends, have you ever wondered what lies beyond the shores of the As-Far-As-The-Eye-Can Sea or the borders of the Blue Boundary Mountains? No one that we know of has ever even tried to find out. Now, if I had an airplane ... or better yet, a helicopter..."

"Wha...?" Duff sniffed and screwed up his face.

"What're you talking about?" asked Frip.

"Airplanes and helicopters," Sinbad repeated. "Machines that can fly—with us in them!"

But Buckley and several others quickly quashed the idea. The beaver shivered.

"I'm not sure that I, for one, even *want* to know what lies beyond the borders of Tolk." The fact was that Buckley had no great love for Sinbad, as intrigued as he was by this idea of living in the lap of luxury. Sinbad backed off.

There was a slight rustling in the leaves just above them. Glancing up, Duff thought he saw a shape, a small dark shape, flit off skyward. He pointed in that direction.

"I seed something, Chief. Up there!"

Sinbad jumped up and scrutinized the branches overhead.

"It's that confounded robin!" he muttered. The orange fur stood up straight on his back. He mulled it over. "Now all of you, it's time you were off! But remember: the more of us, the better. You know the pitch. You know we're all—*all* of us—greedy at heart. We all want more than what we've got. Just make sure that our friends realize what they're missing out on. Try to convince as many of the others as you can. Now ... go to. *Go!*"

A disgruntled Sinbad was left alone. He stood in the covey, oblivious to his surroundings and deeply absorbed in his own thoughts. The truth was, in spite of his boastings, he really didn't have much of a plan at all—short of winning over new followers and stockpiling tools and implements that might be used to 'persuade' the others when the time came. But he actually had no clear idea what he was going to do next. Still, he had to keep up appearances. He realized, though, that he was going to have to come up with a workable plan, and it had to be soon. If not, he could be cast forever in the role of outlaw and rabble-rouser, running here and there, keeping out of sight, never really up or down. Why, that could go on for years! No. That was not to be his fate. He had greater ambitions than that. More and more he had come to see that, as far as he was concerned, it was all or nothing. And if it were to be nothing, then he would see to it that as many Tolks as possible went down with him.

An odd sensation suddenly crept over him: the distinctly eerie feeling that he was being watched. He turned slowly. King Noble stood only a few feet away, his steady brown eyes leveled on the cat. Sinbad hissed and shrank back.

A minute passed, and the dog did not speak. Sinbad was obliged to swallow his fear, but he quickly discovered that his potent hatred gave him a sure voice.

"What are *you* doing here? What do you want with me, *O King?*" he fawned, lowering himself to the ground in mock submission.

"Insolent creature!" King Noble growled, and a trembling Sinbad crumpled in fear. "The fact is..." the king went on, "I have come with an invitation."

"An invitation?" said the cat, still afraid.

"Yes. I have come to offer you the opportunity, along with myself, to present your case to everyone, out in the open."

Sinbad stared at him dumbly. "Present my case?"

"There will be an assembly, a meeting. It will take place in four days, midway between high sun and sunset, at the location the fairies call the *Moon's Platter*. Everyone must attend—I have seen to that. You may then state your case."

It took a couple of minutes for the cat to digest this startling information. "I'm afraid I don't understand. What *case* do I have? I have no case. And if I did, why would I share it with *you*," he sneered, "or the *likes* of you?"

The dog raised his voice only slightly, but his authority bore down irresistibly. "You do not deceive me, Sinbad. I am well aware of your doings."

The cat had to swallow his fear once again. "Should I agree to this ... to this contest," he said, a tremor in his voice, "what am *I* to gain from it? I'm not interested in a circus."

"As a result of this 'contest,' as you call it, the inhabitants of Tolk will become two distinct and separate peoples, which is only what has been happening anyway. It has never been my way to force anyone's loyalty. You know that the Tolks have always, of their own free will, accepted me as their king. But if there are those who would choose a different ruler—namely you, Sinbad—then I will not stand in their way. Indeed, I cannot."

Sinbad stared in disbelief. Then, as realization dawned, like a limp sail catching a sudden gust of wind, his whole being seemed to inflate.

"Four days isn't much time. Why was *I* not consulted about this?"

King Noble growled. "Need I remind you, cat, it was only two nights ago that I threw you ear over tail against a brick wall? Do you not realize that with one snap of my jaws I could have ended your life? I am still king, and it is only because of my mercy that you are alive today."

"And am I supposed to thank you for that?" Sinbad sneered. "You can't harm me here, not now."

"Do you not understand, cat, that at any time I could remove you bodily from Tolk? You would not live one minute."

The horror that registered on Sinbad's face was absolute. He shrank back.

"But I will do no such thing. I have much too high a regard for the sanctity of life ... even your miserable life, Sinbad."

"But why should I believe you?"

"A-a-a-r-r-g-r-r-r!"

"Yes, yes, I do believe you; I do!"

"There are only four full days, Sinbad. On the afternoon of the fourth day we will meet."

"Yes. Four days it is. You leave me no alternative."

King Noble turned to leave.

"Wait! What will happen as a result of this division? I do have my allies, you know."

"Rest assured, that not I, nor any of my followers, will interfere in any way with the power you wield over those who take your side."

"You know, of course, that I'm an *extremely* skillful orator." Possibilities were beginning to open up to Sinbad's mind. "Supposing the greater part of the Tolks choose me? Doesn't that concern you? Wouldn't you then have to bow to *my* authority?"

"It would be a gray day indeed when I should be intimidated by the likes of you, Sinbad."

"And I *must* be granted a position of honor, lawful and binding, where I may rule and reign in Tolk for always. And what lands will I be given? I insist upon the right of choice. This cannot be a one-sided arrangement. And what assurances do I have that the division will be fair and equal?" But before he had finished speaking, King Noble was gone.

This annoyed Sinbad. But only briefly. Now there was a renewed gleam in his eye and vigor in his step. How incredibly this opportunity had come to him. And in such an unexpected way! Now he had the plan, in the rough at least, that he'd been so fruitlessly seeking only minutes ago, and King Noble himself had laid it before him on a platter. What an incompetent!

He has no idea what lies ahead, thought Sinbad, smirking. Soon there would be two kings: King Noble and King Sinbad. Now, if he could only persuade the majority of the Tolks to side with him. Even if that were not possible within the four-day deadline, in due course he'd convince them, one by one. And after he brought the humans here—the *right* humans that is—then the others would see for themselves what a splendid way of life it was. It would be just a matter of time before King Noble's fate would be sealed. He, Sinbad, would be ruler of all of Tolk. Yes, he would have it all. *All!* He purred. Such a delicious idea.

Perhaps the time had come, he thought, to start giving his plan more serious consideration. *What of this scheme of mine?* he asked himself, still purring softly. Just how would it work?

Humans, he presumed, would take well to fairies, elves, and dwarfs—they were so human-like. At first, no doubt people would be awestruck by such beings. Not in the same way they adored their pets, of course. Humans, he realized, might not consider these Tolks *exactly* as equals. In fact, he thought the humans might put them to work. But then fairies, dwarves, and elves were well suited to work. For the time being, of course, he'd have to keep them in the dark about that. The dwarfs especially would never agree to a plan that involved work.

Now the giants were another matter. People would be terrified of the might and mien of the giants. *I could perhaps make use of that,* he contemplated with a sly grin, *to keep the humans in their place.* It was an interesting idea.

And what about those Tolks that humans, in their own domain, referred to as 'wild animals?' The ones that people generally ignored as long as they remained in their habitats. Although he felt some sympathy for the animals, being one himself, Sinbad was certain that such Tolks would never be revered in the same way that cats were. *But they could carry on as they do now,* he thought, *and take advantage of all the perks, the same as anybody else.*

Then there were the other animals, the ones that people used for food. Well after all, Sinbad considered, they couldn't be slaughtered in Tolk—there was no danger of that. Most of them could continue on as always. Milk cows, horses, sheep and others were useful to humans. Naturally, they would be well cared for.

The most important thing, which Sinbad firmly believed, was that pussycats would always be revered and honored above every other creature, including humans. That, of course, was the material point.

Just at that moment a dense, dark cloud passed over the sun, and Sinbad shivered. Why did he suddenly feel a prickle of unease? He studied the darkening sky for a few seconds. *Supposing...* he thought, *supposing I am wrong after all. What then?* This thought had actually been distilling upon his conscious mind for some time. Now he faced it head on.

King Noble is a no-account, of course. But these humans ... Is it possible they might be more difficult to control than I realize? And... There was something else niggling at Sinbad—a most disturbing idea. *Lately, I've noticed some aches and pains in my joints. I ... I think I might be aging.* He felt an icy droplet of fear trickle down his spine. *Slowly, yes. But I do believe it's happening. Why, only last month, I forgot about Tolk for five days. Five entire days! It never crossed my mind. And when I did recall, it was like dredging up the shadow of dream.* Now the icy trickle seeped into his flesh. *I'm beginning to ... to forget things.* It was alarming to admit that he might be in the process of becoming mortal.

"This makes it all the more urgent to proceed!" he spoke aloud. "And I could never, *never* return to the way things were before. I know far too much! And I could never surrender my immortal soul and live in the world. It's out of the question! I say, 'better to have tried and failed than never to have tried.' And if I do fail," he glared up at the sky, as if daring it to oppose him, "it is of no consequence to me how many of these ignorant vermin accompany me to defeat!"

Chapter Twenty-Five: Grandmother has Questions

Price and Grandmother tarried over a late supper of potato salad with thick slices of buttered bread and milk. He yawned. The last two days, every available minute had been spent biking around Tolk with Freddy and O.P. The fairy naturally had the bird's-eye view, and under her direction, they had drawn up detailed maps of the territory. And since she couldn't read or write human script, Price had acted as her scribe. (He'd taken a large notebook, a couple of ball-point pens, and some pencils and erasers with him—items that had proved to be endlessly fascinating to everyone they met.) Together, the three of them had interviewed dozens of Tolks and tabulated hundreds of names. They had appointed captains and assigned them the job of informing all their friends and kin about the upcoming assembly. There was still much more to do, but Price decided not to think about that. At the moment, he was so tired that the prospect seemed altogether too daunting.

Grandmother was watching him. She was not so much surprised by the boy's fatigue as she was by his attitude. Whatever it was that he and his friends were doing with so much focused energy, he was certainly taking it very seriously. It didn't seem like regular child's play somehow.

"I thought we might play a few hands of gin rummy this evening," she said, "but I can see that you're tuckered out. Maybe you'd like me to read to you for a bit."

Price smiled wanly. "What d'you want to read?"

"How about a good mystery? I walked over to the library while you were gone today. I picked up a couple of books that look very promising—plenty of intrigue and suspense. What do you think?"

"Sure."

The doorbell rang.

Grandmother patted Price's arm as she rose. "Just this once, we'll let age bow to a young man who is really and truly worn out. I'll get that."

Price could not see the front door from where he sat at the kitchen table, but he was within earshot. His grandmother had opened the door and was speaking to a man whose voice Price recognized at once: It was Mr. Murphy.

And Mr. Murphy was not at all pleased to find himself face to face with an elderly woman he hadn't expected to see and did not know—and for that matter, did not *want* to know. He had wanted to speak to that nice woman who had admired his garden the other day.

"Uh, is Mrs. Evans at home?"

Grandmother, on the other hand, recognized Mr. Murphy at once. She knew all about his prize-winning garden. She also knew that he was hailed as the town's foremost recluse and grump. But she gave no hint of this when she answered him. "No, Mrs. Evans is out right now. Can I help you with something?"

"When will she be back?"

"Not for a month, I'm afraid. She's on vacation."

This news seemed to trouble Mr. Murphy. He screwed up his eyes, and trying not to look directly at Grandmother, peered anxiously down the street. Then he cocked his head in the direction of his house. "Name's Murphy. I live next door."

"Yes, I know. Mr. Murphy, the fame of your wonderful garden is heralded all over town."

"Oh." The old man blushed. He disliked Grandmother a little less now. "Ahem. Fact is I'm going out of town for a couple of weeks. Doctor says I need to get away and take some rest. So I'm going to the coast. Uh, my daughter's there, you see."

"How lovely! I always think it's a good thing to get a change of scene. But I'm sorry to hear that you're not well. I hope it's nothing serious."

"Yes, well. No, no. Not really." He drew a long breath, as though bracing himself for an ordeal. It was the ordeal of being obliged to ask a favor of a complete stranger. "Uh, I'll be leaving tomorrow, sometime in the wee hours. I'd like someone to keep an eye on the place, you know. If you don't mind, that is. And if you notice anything unusual ... or suspicious... Do you by any chance get the local newspaper?"

"Yes, I read it every week." The community newspaper was a weekly.

"Then you must have read about the ... uh ... vandals." Mr. Murphy squinted. He seemed perplexed. He was still keenly disappointed that Mrs. Evans was away and wasn't sure that this old woman could be of any use.

"Ye-s-s, I did read about that. What a very strange thing it was, too. Quite a mystery, I'd say. It just doesn't add up, does it?"

"You think so, too?" Mr. Murphy suddenly sounded hopeful.

"Absolutely. It doesn't make any sense at all! What kind of people would tromp all over a beautiful garden and then take off with the lawn furniture? It just doesn't make a bit of sense."

"Lawn furniture? Oh yes. Well." The old man shrugged dispassionately. For a moment he had thought—but of course not. How could she possibly know anything about it?

"Uh, there is another matter." He hoisted up a weighty plastic grocery bag from where it had been sitting on the step by his feet. It was bulging with cans. "My cat. I haven't seen hide-nor-hair of him for four days. Not since... Uh, if he does show up, this is his food. Would you mind?"

"No, no. Not at all. I'll watch for the cat. What does he look like?"

"He's a big ginger fella. I wouldn't want him to starve."

"Oh no, of course not." Grandmother took the bag. "Yes, I think I saw him sitting on the wall the other day." She was pretty sure that the tough-looking animal she had seen was perfectly able to fend for himself.

"Well, the police knows all about my situation, but I just thought it couldn't hurt to have an extra lookout next door." He eyed Grandmother dubiously. "So I guess that'll do then. Thank 'ee ma'am." He nodded and headed back down the steps.

"You're most welcome." Grandmother watched the wiry, stiff-legged codger hurry along the front walk. As he turned onto the sidewalk, she could see his bushy eyebrows, drawn tightly together under the hairless pate, now creased with worry. He seemed preoccupied, muttering under his breath, mostly keeping his eyes on the ground.

"Yes, he looks like he's due for a holiday," said Grandmother, shutting the door.

Price's mood had brightened considerably as he'd caught the gist of this conversation. Mr. Murphy was going away for two entire weeks! This was great news. It meant that now he could go in and out of Tolk whenever he wanted, without having to worry about getting caught.

Early the next morning, Grandmother was surprised to find a note from Price on the kitchen table. He had gone for the day, the note explained. He'd taken some granola bars, apples, and cheese from the pantry, so she didn't need to worry about his lunch. He'd try to be home for supper. Grandmother read the note over two more times. Then she sat down at the table to think.

So, he was going to be gone all day once again. For the first time she felt honestly worried. Just who were these friends that he met at the park—friends she'd never seen and that Price didn't really talk much about? Come to think of it, he never talked about them at all, not even to mention their names. But then, he'd always been a quiet, reserved kind of boy. But what were they doing that was so important? Not merely important. Whatever they were up to, to Price, it was vital. It puzzled her. She thought that perhaps, later that afternoon, she might just take a stroll in Riverbend Park herself.

It was eight o'clock before Grandmother heard the rattle of Price's bicycle, as he put it away in the garage. She watched him from the kitchen window, striding up the walk, swinging his arms and whistling—a mostly tuneless rendition of something she couldn't quite make out. As he came through the kitchen door, he greeted her with a big, self-satisfied grin, the kind that comes in gratitude and relief at the completion of some onerous task, such as a big exam or a major school project.

"Hi, Grandma. Wow, what a day!" He headed straight for the bathroom. A few minutes later, he came skipping back down the stairs. "Boy, am I hungry! What's for supper?"

"Summer food," she said. "Why don't you set the table?"

"Sure."

He hurried to the buffet and began rummaging through the cutlery. Ten minutes later, a cold supper was laid before them. Price delved into bread and tomatoes and sliced cheese with gusto. Grandmother was unusually quiet, but Price didn't notice.

"I take it you had a good time today, is that so?" she asked after a few minutes of eating.

Price's mouth was full, so he nodded.

"Tell me where you went and what you did."

The boy chewed more slowly and seemed pensive. He swallowed.

"I was here and there."

"Well, you weren't at the park this afternoon. I know that because I went for a walk there myself."

Price studied his cheese sandwich. "No. I didn't go to the park today."

"Where did you go then?"

Behind a deadpan expression, the boy's thoughts scrambled all over themselves. What could he possibly say that would be both honest and reassuring? Of course, she would never believe the truth.

"Price, you know that I am responsible for you. I must know where you go each day and what you are doing."

The boy's brown eyes looked imploringly at his grandmother's kindly, wrinkled face. "But you know I would never do anything bad, Grandma."

"That's beside the point."

"I was with my friends."

"Who are these friends?"

"There's this girl named Freddy. And you remember Octaruse Pinecone? You made him. I had him in my pocket."

"That's all? Just the two of you?"

"Three of us."

Grandmother's eyebrows went up. "Three?"

"Freddy, me, and O.P. That's short for Octaruse Pinecone."

"Oh, I see. And just what were the 'three' of you doing all day?"

"We were ... I guess you'd say ... taking a census."

Whatever Grandmother may have expected to hear, this was not it. "A census?"

Price nodded.

"A census of whom?"

"A census of all the different animals and other ... creatures around."

"Animals!" Grandmother sat back in her chair and looked closely at Price, trying to make some sense of this. Then she threw back her head and laughed. "Well I never!" So, it was only make-believe after all. She leaned forward and placed a hand gently on the boy's arm.

"Now, I wasn't laughing at you, Price. There is nothing at all wrong with this kind of ... activity. And I can tell that you take it very seriously. It shows what a wonderful imagination you have. It's just that I thought ... you seemed so ... so caught up in it. I couldn't quite make it out."

Price forced a smile and continued to munch his sandwich, but his appetite had gone.

"And what did you learn? About the animals?"

The boy rolled his eyes. "There's a lot of them. You wouldn't believe it."

"But why don't you bring Freddy home with you some-time? I'd like to meet her."

Price swallowed again. Slowly he took a sip of milk. "She doesn't really want to come."

"Doesn't want to? Why not? Is she that shy?"

"Not exactly."

"Is it her parents then?"

"She doesn't have parents."

"Really? An orphan! Poor child. Then who does she live with?"

Price cleared his throat and examined a small, floral detail on the placemat. "With her ... kin." He began to pray that Grandmother would not keep asking questions that he knew would get harder and harder to answer.

"I'm surprised that I don't know her. Is she new in town?"

"I-I think so."

"I see." Grandmother was thoughtful. "What's her family name?"

"Fairchild."

"Fairchild? Now that strikes a bell." Grandmother cast into her memory banks, but came up empty. "No, I don't think I know any Fairchilds. But perhaps they are new in town. And naturally I don't know everyone."

They sat in silence for a moment while Price drank his milk.

"Did you know that my birth-name was Fairborn? But I believe I told you that already. My, but I hadn't thought of that name in years." Grandmother folded her arms and shut her eyes. "Fairborn. Fairchild. What clean, innocent sounding names, don't you think?"

"And Fairbe," added Price.

Grandmother opened her eyes, startled. "What made you say that?"

The boy shrugged.

"Yes, come to think of it. And Fairbe."

Price began clearing away the dishes. "Are we going to read tonight, Grandma?" He was trying to change the subject, but Grandmother did not seem to hear. When she spoke next, the words came out slowly, as though her mind was really someplace else.

"You tell your friend, Freddy, that I would be happy to meet her any time. But I understand if she can't." Her voice trailed off. Then she added brightly, "And Price, tomorrow I want you to check in at mealtime at least. After all, I might need your help."

"Sure, Grandma. Sorry for being so thoughtless."

"That's all right, my boy. I know how it is when you get together with a friend. I was young once myself. Although, I'm sure you must find *that* hard to believe. Now ... what did you say ... about reading?"

Chapter Twenty-Six:
Discretion versus
Deception

Early the next morning, Price lay awake on his bed as daylight gradually washed in through the open window. He had slept fitfully in anticipation of the great event that would unfold later that afternoon in Tolk. He sensed a kind of energy that seemed to link him in some way to every inhabitant of that land, and they to him. As if all were conscious of a great haunting presence, like a monumental question brooding in every mind.

That morning Grandmother asked him to give her a hand with the laundry and vacuuming, and to carry home the groceries from the store. He was glad of it. It would help to pass the time. The chores took all morning and part of the afternoon. They had a late lunch and by two o'clock, Price knew it was time to leave.

"I have to go now, Grandma. My friends are expecting me. I ... I might be late ... really late. But I don't want you to worry. I don't know when..." His voice trailed off, but his eyes were fixed unwaveringly on his grandmother. They were begging her to trust him.

"What do you mean by 'late?'"

"This is *really* important, Grandma. I might be ... very late. But I don't know how late."

Grandmother's jaw tightened, deepening the fine lines that etched her lips. She didn't respond right away, as though searching within for understanding. The boy's face was perfectly candid and open, but there was willfulness in his expression that surprised her.

"Supposing I say that you must be home by eight o'clock."

"I can't promise I'll be home by then."

"And why is that?"

The boy did not flinch. "I'm sorry. I can't tell you why, because you couldn't possibly understand."

Grandmother's eyebrows rose. Again, she had the distinct impression that whatever was happening was not ordinary child's play. Price lifted his chin to strengthen his position.

"So," she sighed heavily, "this is the way it is." Here was something else that made no sense: Price defying his grandmother. She would not have believed it possible even ten minutes before. She felt a warm young hand on her shoulder.

"Please don't worry, Grandma," he said. "I'm doing what I have to, and I'll come home when I've finished, but no sooner."

From the kitchen window, she watched him bring his bicycle out from the garage. The weather had softened a bit at last. There was some welcome cloud cover and a light breeze. Price slung his backpack over his shoulder, and then, as Grandmother looked on, he did something entirely unexpected. Instead of going out through the back gate, he went behind the poplar tree, where that unused gate was, the one that led down into the space between Mr. Murphy's garage and their own.

"What does he think he's doing?" she muttered. "He can't get out that way." She expected him to reappear at any moment. Finally, after waiting about five minutes, she strolled out into the yard.

The gate leading into the space opened with a slight tug. The space was empty. She knew positively that Price had not come back out again. Had he gone through the other gate, the one leading into Mr. Murphy's garden? That seemed unlikely—it wouldn't make any sense. At the back of the space, the stone wall stood as ever, quite solid and immovable. Surely he hadn't scaled the wall—with a bicycle?

"I'm floored," she thought out loud. Still, Grandmother was a practical, down-to-earth person. There had to be an explanation.

Gingerly, she made her way down the stone steps to the mossy ground. She looked for a door in the side of the garage that perhaps she'd forgotten about or that had been added since her day, but of course, there wasn't any.

"What a nice, cool spot," she said, advancing toward the stone wall at the back. She reached out a hand to steady herself. Then suddenly, as though something had startled her, Grandmother's hand went to her heart. At the same time her breathing became short and irregular, and the slanted gray eyes opened wide in alarm. Abruptly she turned, hurried up the stone steps, and without even closing the gate, ran trembling into the house. Anyone seeing her would have thought she was being chased.

In a sense, that was true. But Grandmother's pursuer was not a person. It was the surfacing of a strange and long-forgotten memory—a memory that frightened her, because it seemed to defy rational thought.

Price's first stop was the Muskins' to see if O.P. or Meepy were about. But, as Millie explained, they'd had important business to deal with; he'd likely find them with King Noble at the Bollum Bears' cave. Price had no difficulty remembering the way and soon stood before the overgrown thicket of honeysuckle. He glanced around quickly, then slipped inside.

Just then Timmins Arbuckle and a tall, lean beaver that Price didn't recognize emerged from the cave entrance. The beaver was stooped over, his wide, toothy mouth close to Tim's small gopher ear.

"I'm convinced it's all a pack o' lies, myself," rasped the beaver in a hard-edged whisper. "But I can't persuade young Brundle o' that."

"Look sharp now, Williger. We're steppin' out. You'd better mind your this 'n thats. Sometimes I think even the trees are listening. Sometimes I think even my thoughts are too loud. 'Course, that could be because I have the bad habit of talking to myself." He laughed.

Then he saw Price. A grin spread over the portly gopher's furry face and the small, black eyes almost disappeared into his round cheeks, like two raisins on a rising bun.

"Well, well! Look who we have here. Come to report to King Noble, I suppose." He took a quick look around; then cupped a paw to his mouth. "He's in there all right. Been attending to all and sundry the whole day long. We left him alone just now for the first time since dawn. If it was me, I'd be as worn out as a dancin' shoe the morning after Fairies' Jamboree. So take it easy. Don't rush him too much."

"Okay." Price smiled. "I'll do everything in slow motion. I'll even talk in slow motion."

"That's the spirit! Now, this fine fellow you see here is a chum of mine, Williger Beaver by name. And this lad you see before you is the boy, Price. I suppose you've heard about him."

"What? Tim, you beetle-head. D'you think I've been in hibernation? It just happens that I've seen the lad, too. Although we've never been formally introduced." The beaver extended a paw. "Pleased to make your acquaintance, boy."

Reaching down, Price took the paw and shook it firmly. "Me, too."

Tim Arbuckle folded his hairy 'arms' and slowly shook his head. "Yes, there's sparks flying in the air today, that's certain. It's as though we're all standing at the brink of a ravine waiting to step into thin air."

"I know what you mean."

"Dot's been stirring up a cloud of wheat flour as big as a giant's belly. Her method of handling the suspense is baking raspberry tarts. She'd filled every corner of the kitchen before I left, and I wouldn't be surprised to find some in my bed tonight. It just happens that's where we're headed now. I figure a dozen or two of raspberry tarts between us, with some fresh cream, will do a good deal to calm these nervous tremors."

"Sounds like a great idea," said Price.

"Come and join us later, if you have the time."

Price waved to the pair as they waddled off—Mr. Broom and Mr. Dustpan.

Like the great sphinx, King Noble was stretched out in the middle of the cavern floor. For the moment, he was alone. Although his head was erect, his eyes were shut, and Price thought that he must be asleep. But then the deep, bass voice spoke.

"Come in, Price. Sit down."

Price did as he was told. The dog opened his eyes.

"I'm sorry I'm late again. I had to help my grandmother." Price crossed his legs trying to get comfortable on the hard, stone floor.

King Noble cocked an eyebrow. "To sit in comfort here you need a heavy fur coat and a thick layer of bear blubber."

"You're right about that!" They both smiled.

"She's getting suspicious," Price said, "my grandmother, that is. I didn't know what to say to her. I couldn't tell her the truth."

"Are you saying that you lied?"

"Oh, no. I told her that I couldn't say what I was doing, because she wouldn't understand. It's a hard thing, King Noble. I've never before had to deceive anyone." He looked away sadly.

"Oh, but what you're describing, my boy, is not deception. People, you know, are not always ready to hear the truth—or worthy for that matter. Then all you can do is share as much of the truth as is right and fitting."

Price wasn't sure he understood. He leaned back on the palms of his hands and studied the dog's gentle face. King Noble had again shut his eyes.

"King Noble, are you ... worried about what will happen today?" He had been going to ask 'are you afraid?' but somehow the idea didn't seem to fit.

"The truth is that I care deeply," the dog answered without opening his eyes. "And sometimes I admit that I am very, very sad. But I'm never worried ... or afraid."

"Why is that?"

"Because I already know what the outcome will be ... and its consequences."

Price wanted very much to ask him to explain, but had the feeling that in this case, *he* was the one not ready to hear the truth.

"And now that you are here, my boy, any concerns I might have had are gone with the wind. But then, I knew you'd come."

"What do you mean?"

The king's eyes had opened and were smiling again. "It's no great mystery. You knew that you were needed here today, and I know that you're the kind of boy who does his duty. So here you are."

"No, not that. I mean, if your concerns are gone away, what's that got to do with me?"

"Ah. As to that, you shall see. And, as it happens, that is no great mystery either."

But to Price it was a mystery, though he dared not say it aloud.

He thought about the second part of the agreement they'd made, when he'd first been summoned into Tolk. 'You must expose Sinbad,' Timmins Arbuckle had said. But the way things were turning out, with the assembly and all, it looked as though the matter had been taken out of his hands. That was okay with him, but did it mean that he was no longer needed, or that he had somehow failed?

At that moment, King Noble leapt up and shook himself out. "I think it's time," he said. "And there are others who are anxious to see you. Come. We must go to our friends." The dog inhaled deeply. "Ah, Price! The dam has broken and there is nothing in Tolk or in the heavens above that can stop the flood now, as it surges into the great river of mortality. Only follow me, and we can ride the waves. They will carry us safely into eternity itself!" With a bound, he stood at the cavern door and signaled for the boy to follow.

Now Price was thoroughly confused. But he knew that the answers would have to wait.

Chapter Twenty-Seven: Sinbad States his Case

The Moon's Platter was that same large grassy mound that Price had discovered when he'd first entered Tolk. (He'd since learned that the meadow was called Fiddlers' Field.) Only a couple of weeks had passed since that day, but somehow it seemed much longer. Now the appointed hour had arrived, and here he was again.

An immense crowd—almost too large to be believed—was gathered in a great half-circle before the Platter's broad circumference. The sea of grass was now barely visible under the thousands of bodies spread across it. In spite of the crowd, an intense, brooding suspense hung in the air. *Like smog*, Price thought. Even the insects were ominously silent.

Price knew from the data that he and Freddy and O.P. had so painstakingly collected that there were around five thousand dwarfs, giants, birds, and animals present. There were, in addition, about half that number of fairies and elves, who in typical fashion had congregated in two separate bodies. Only a couple of captains—a giant and a giantess—were at that moment still going over their lists. With the eager persistence of children assembling a complicated new toy, they were checking off the last of the names. Finally, with a toothy grin, the giantess signaled to Freddy that all on their lists were accounted for. With a great sigh of relief, the fairy sank down onto the grass next to Price and O.P.

Suddenly, everyone who was seated stood, and a seam opened up through the middle of the crowd. King Noble had arrived and was making his way to the flat rock at the top of the Moon's Platter. An imperious Sinbad strolled along behind him, deliberately leaving a large gap between himself and the dog. After all, he didn't associate with dogs any more. Also, he didn't want to draw attention to the fact that he was so much smaller, or that he was indeed in the rear.

But what he didn't possess in mass, he took great pains to compensate for with sheer presence. His tawny coat had been groomed to a sheen and fluffed out to make him look as large as possible. He stretched himself to the limits of his size and raised his full, handsome tail. There was just a slight, inward curl at the tip. And he strutted. Like all cats, he was designed to strut, with his dainty, silent feet and keen, beautiful face.

King Noble stood on the flat stone and looked out over the crowd. Sinbad came up beside him, standing to the right, and just a little ahead of King Noble. He also turned to face the crowd.

"Please, everyone, be seated," announced the king. He waited a few minutes until all had settled down. Then, in a loud voice, he addressed the entire assembly.

"Before we begin, Sinbad, you are to sit here, on my left." He indicated a level, grassy spot.

Inwardly Sinbad bristled. But he held his tongue, and as he took his place, thought to himself, with some bitter satisfaction, *This may be the last of your commands that I ever obey, O King!*

King Noble looked out over the crowd, directly at Price, "And now I call Price Evans to come and take his place on my right."

An animated buzz rose from the assembly. But strange as it may seem, Price was not surprised, even though it had never occurred to him that King Noble might call on him. Not that he felt somehow entitled to a place of honor. Not at all. But if King Noble wanted him at his side, that's where he would be. And if anyone had asked him what he was doing there, he would have answered, "Just wait and see," and *he* would have been waiting to see along with everyone else.

But Sinbad was clearly annoyed. "What is the meaning of this?" he sputtered. "This boy has nothing whatsoever to do with the affairs of Tolk. He is an outsider, an intruder. His presence here was never part of our agreement!"

"You are mistaken. It was always part of our agreement, only neither you nor he knew about it."

"I was never consulted!"

"You were never consulted, because I chose not to consult you. I am still the king, Sinbad. Our original agreement was that you and I would each have a chance to state our case, and so we shall. Nothing has changed on that score." He turned abruptly. "Now Price, and Sinbad, please sit down!"

"If you think that I—!"

"Sinbad, our agreement still stands! And I warn you, if you back down today, you will not have a second chance." The king looked steadily at the cat as he spoke.

Sinbad remained standing for a few more seconds, rigid with anger, but then grudgingly sat down in the designated place. Price stepped to the right of King Noble and sat cross-legged on the grass.

King Noble faced the assembly. "Good citizens of Tolk ... thank you for coming today.

"As you all know," he went on, "certain false rumors and accusations have been circulating amongst us, creating much confusion and division. The truth is, because of this, we have reached a state of crisis!" He paused, giving the crowd a moment to reflect on the gravity of the situation. "I will *not* allow this problem to continue unaddressed. Please everyone listen carefully to what I have to say."

He raised his voice then and spoke very distinctly and deliberately.

"To begin with, my friends, believe me when I assure you that there has *never* been any danger that vicious predators might enter Tolk. Such creatures have no place in an immortal sphere. And even if that were not the case, the doors leading into our land are ancient, closely guarded secrets. Only a very few Tolks know the location of any of these portals, and only I know them all. You can trust me perfectly when I say that no outsider can enter Tolk unbidden, for it is an eternal law decreed from the foundation of time. And the one portal that has become a risk, the one around which all of this business revolves, is soon to be sealed off from the outside world forever!"

Sinbad looked up in alarm. This was news to him. Now he began to suspect that King Noble might have more in the bag than he had first imagined. Oh yes, it appeared that he would definitely need to be on his guard. Perhaps he would have to sway a good many more citizens today than he had thought. But then, he was so clever with words. It was not impossible.

The king shut his eyes and inhaled deeply. It was evident that he had come to the disagreeable part of his address.

"Secondly, citizens of Tolk," he went on, speaking more quietly, his meaning all the more gripping, "I am fully aware that we are becoming a divided people. This is not to be tolerated! I will not allow us to break into petty, warring tribes. Thus, I declare unto you, that on this day the nation of Tolk will become two nations! Two peoples who will exist completely separate and independent of one another!"

The crowd gasped. Then instantly fell into a stunned silence as every ear strained to hear.

"It will fall on each of you today to make a difficult and *irreversible* choice. I will no longer allow hostility and confusion to erode the safety and peace of our land. In the past, you have always freely accepted me as your king. But there are now many who want a new ruler, namely this Sinbad that you see here beside me—this rightful citizen of Tolk, who was previously known as Flame. Today you each must decide for yourself. Today you must choose between Sinbad and me!"

There was a murmur of surprise all around, and many anxious faces looked up at King Noble.

"Friends..." His voice had now grown tender and imploring, "I know each of you so well—you are like the many cozy rooms of my den. I know all your good sides as well as your dark places and hidden passageways. I know your dreams and your schemes. I know your pleasures and sorrows. And all of you have known me your entire lives. Indeed, you *know* that I love you—each one of you.

"I ask you to consider this: Have I ever deceived you? Have I ever taken from you that to which I was not entitled? Never! And have I not labored along with you and stood by you whenever you were in need? I have—at any time or place. Would I deceive you now? No. Never would I deceive you. Never! Then hear me and believe: Bringing humans into Tolk would only open the door to death and corruption. In the same stroke, it would bring about the end of our way of life, and an end of all of us as we are now—all of us! In a very short time, our beloved Tolk would cease to exist!

"I plead with you to believe me—to trust me. Today I implore you, for the sake of our country, our homes, and our loved ones, stand by me, King Noble, rightful monarch and ruler of Tolk!"

There was a long pause. Then the king resumed. "Now ... I have stated my case," he declared.

He turned to the cat. "Sinbad, you now have my permission to speak."

The cat looked up in surprise. *That's it?* he thought. *That's all he has to say? No flattering words, no veiled threats, no idle promises, no bargains? Well then, this is going to be easier than I thought.* And to demonstrate his contempt, Sinbad drew himself up slowly and stretched.

King Noble retired to the grass next to Price while the cat leapt up, replacing him on the large, flat rock.

"Fellow Tolks, my oldest and dearest friends..." he began, pointedly ignoring any courtesy owed the monarch, and certainly ignoring Price. His cat voice, if dry and thin, was very precise. "Nearly three summers have passed since I first made a lucky venture into the world of humans. You may recall that it was the summer of the high wind that toppled five dwellings in Drumbleton." (It was a well-known fact that the giants were terrible engineers.)

"Ah, now I believe that you do remember. I want you to remember, for I am about to take you on a journey.

"On the same day that I entered the town of Clareburn, I met a man—the first man I'd ever seen—Mr. Frank Murphy. Straightaway, he opened his door and invited me in." Sinbad cast his eyes skyward and sighed, as though actually reliving this pleasant experience in his imagination. "He extended to me the privilege of sleeping on his own personal easy chair, and thinking I might be hungry, he opened a can of—" He stopped himself from saying 'tuna,' and paused for a second before continuing, "...stewed beet root, and in a china dish, served me a generous portion along with fresh cream. Mm-m. That cream was as cool and light as new-fallen snow. I wondered how the cream could be so cold, because it was a warm day. Did Frank have a stream running through his garden, where he'd left the cream to chill in a sealed tumbler? Not so, I soon discovered. He stored the cream, I learned, in the *refrigerator*. 'Refrigerator' was the first of many exciting new words that I would soon come to know and love.

"'What is a refrigerator?' you ask. Well, hear this. A refrigerator is a wonderful cupboard that stays as cold on the inside as a brisk winter morning, no matter what the temperature is on the outside. Just think of it, my friends. On any day of the year, Frank and I can sit together and sip apple punch that's as cold as ice even though we live, oh, at least two miles from a streambed."

Barlow Bear stood up. "Go away with you, Sinbad! That can't be true, and you know it."

"Can't be true? Thundering thunderbolts! Do I have to answer for every word that I utter? But..." he lifted his chin and looked down his nose at Barlow, "now that I think of it, having the boy here might prove to be of some use after all."

He turned smugly to Price. "Boy! Tell this bear here that what I have said about refrigerators is the truth."

All eyes shifted to Price. "Well, yes," he conceded. "The part about the refrigerators, *that's* true. But as for the rest...?" With a one-shoulder shrug he left the thought hanging.

Sinbad filled his lungs and carried on. "Please, *no* further interruptions. It will only make this whole journey far too long. Now where was I? Ah yes, refrigerators ... and ovens that bake without burning peat or wood. You simply turn a dial and there is heat. And you need only push a lever right at the kitchen basin and out comes hot water. And washing machines wash your clothes without wetting a hair on your paw.

"And television! Ah, those wonderful moving picture screens that I've mentioned so many times before. And automobiles, vehicles that on their own run faster than Barlow Bear with nettles in his nose!"

Everyone laughed. Barlow glowered uncomfortably, as though he felt somehow betrayed.

"Now, all of these things and more I have already described on other occasions. I won't go into that now. Only, I will say this: Imagine a life where you don't have to haul water from well or stream; imagine a life where you don't need to chop firewood, or plant corn, or card or spin or weave!" He waved his arms enticingly at a bevy of sheep. "Or milk or churn, burrow or build. Simply by bringing a few select humans into Tolk, all of these things could be done for us. Without anyone having to lift a finger or claw.

"Imagine walking into a bookshop with, not dozens I say, but shelves of thousands upon thousands of books. Not one of them did any fellow creature have to copy out word upon word, line upon line, by hand or paw."

"B-b-but ... stop right there. I say *stop!*" Everyone stared. Derbin Dreckle, the hermit dwarf, was actually standing before them in plain view. He was considered an 'odd body' who kept to himself as much as possible. "But hand-copying the fairy poesy and elfin song is what I love doin' best! I'd be terrible lonesome if it weren't for that. If you had your way, cat, what would I *do?*" Both fists were clenched tightly at his sides.

The cat purred softly. "Oh, I am so-o-o glad that you have spoken up, Derbin, even if it did take you ninety-nine years to get around to it. Heh, heh. You misunderstand me entirely. I only said that you wouldn't *have* to do any of these things, not that you couldn't do them if you wanted to. Of course, in *my* kingdom we will all continue to do any of the things we really want to."

Now Freddy jumped up. "Sinbad, you scoundrel! You know as well as the rest of us that some humans are a bad lot. They'd just come here and spoil everything!"

Sinbad eyed the fairy coldly. "Strange counsel coming from *you*. Aren't you the fairy I see here daily, clinging to the arm of a human, like an adoring infant? *That* human no less, who is nothing more than an ignorant boy." He stopped and began to fastidiously examine the claws of a front paw. "There's a name for the likes of you," he said without looking at Freddy. "You," he looked directly at her, "are what is known as a *hypocrite*. Not to mention a poor judge of character. Who but a fool would associate with an interfering boy who is good for nothing but causing trouble? Just ask Smoot, if you don't know what I mean. Smoot?" He looked around for his most trusted ally.

"Aye!" The obliging dwarf jumped to his feet. He pointed an accusing stumpy finger at Price. "That boy didn't care a hoot about rescuing Dori and me. He was just out for revenge! For himself, because he hates the old man, and for that ... that *dog!*" The finger swung to King Noble. He made a fist. "*That's* what he came here for!"

"Ah yes," Sinbad resumed, "there's more mixed up in this stew than what's plain on the surface of the pot. Too many secrets by far in some circles." He glared at King Noble. "I've even heard of clandestine gatherings and secret meetings. It makes me mightily suspicious. Personally, I would never trust anyone who can't be perfectly honest and upfront!"

Freddy continued to stand, speechless and trembling. Furious, Price made to rise, but King Noble restrained him with a paw. "Not yet," he whispered.

"And so, my friends. I think you can plainly see why you need *me*." The cat leapt up, circled, and stretched himself as tall as he could. "For *I* am the only creature here who can rule you honestly. And the only one who has any experience in dealing with humankind. Three full years I have lived among men. Yes, it's Sinbad, and Sinbad alone that you can trust to bring the right humans into Tolk: only those men and women who have proven that they love and cherish and devotedly serve their pets, the little creatures."

"The little creatures?" boomed out the voice of Zoltora, a prominent giantess. "Well, I'd like to know, what's about the *big* creatures?"

"Ha ha!" Sinbad chortled with glee, and cuffed the ground playfully with a hind paw. "Why, those humans would be so terrified of you giants, you'd only have to raise a finger and they'd grovel before you like weeds before the wind." He narrowed his eyes. "If you simple giants only knew the power you could wield with those massive bodies of yours. Yes, I can assure you that every giant would hold a very high position in *my* kingdom. In fact, I'd make the giants my army. And Bran could be a general ... if he saw things my way."

"Army? General? Is that so?" These unfamiliar words confused Zoltora, and she consulted with her friends in low whispers. "Is that something good or what?"

"Why yes. Armies are tremendously important—armies and police. All giants would be eminently notable people in *my* kingdom. Eminently." Sinbad paused and watched for a few seconds while the giants talked this over. "Now, if you don't mind, I'd like to continue without further interruption. We can't stay here all night, and I haven't yet told you about the gardens and crops. But most importantly I haven't yet spoken about the *supermarket.*"

He rocked back slightly on all four heels and looked dreamily off into the distance. "My friends, how can I describe the life of a pampered pet?" He shut his eyes and sighed aloud. "To begin with, there is the food. Such a quantity! And the variety. All planted, harvested, carted, prepared, and served up without one lick of creature labor. Humans and their machines do it all. For some reason, humans just love to work. They thrive on it.

"There are fruits and vegetables, grains, the likes of which you've never seen in Tolk. Believe me, you'd need to enlarge your pantries just to hold them. Cherries as large as plums, plums as big as apples, and apples the size of melons. Ach! There is hardly any point in describing them, there are so many, most of which you've never before set eyes on, much less tasted. How could you even begin to understand? It would be wasting words ... wonderful words such as luscious, succulent, sweet, honeyed, dripping, oozing, juicy, savory, and plump, all in exciting new shapes, textures, and flavors never before experienced!

"But I have experienced them, my friends! And you could, too. If, on this very day, you choose to side with

Sinbad, the sumptuous and bounteous repast of human-kind could be yours."

Sinbad paused and shut his eyes, as if in deep contemplation. But through narrow open slits, he slyly observed the expressions on the faces grouped before him. Many, their mouths slightly open, looked very hungry indeed. He went on.

"Milk, juices, honey—flowing as rivers. Dozens of kinds of savory cheeses. Confections, pastries, and cakes like snow-topped mountains. Gardens the size of villages, granaries lined up row upon row, as broad as this knoll and nearly as tall as the pines in Shadowfir.

"But this is only the food. What of the rest? What of the soft beds, comforters, and cushions? What of the endless varieties of entertainment on television and the movies? Trips in the car to the lakeside, to the park, to the mall..." He stopped suddenly. "Ah yes ... the mall.

"Now, you're all wondering 'What is a mall?' My friends, a mall is a vast building filled with dozens of rooms. Rooms that are warm in winter, and cool and fresh in summer. These rooms are all linked to an enormous chamber—a vast cave of sorts (he nodded to the bears)—having a tiled floor in all the colors of the rainbow. A place of luxury dotted with glittering fountains and crystal pools filled with scores of fish, as bright as polished copper. Exotic trees and shrubs bloom and flourish year round. Sunlight streams in from above through domed skylights. Ah, it is a beautiful sight.

"The rooms I mentioned, surrounding this exquisite space, are brimming with goods of every description, piled from floor to ceiling. Compared to the mall, the markets of Tolk are like some grimy little puddle next to the As-Far-As-The-Eye-Can Sea.

"But!" To focus their attention he raised a single claw. "By far the most compelling attraction at the mall is ... the *supermarket*. Augh, my friends! This place is almost indescribable! And yet, here and now, I will attempt to describe it."

The cat inhaled deeply and began again. He spoke of the vast abundance of foods that a creature could select at its leisure. He spoke of meeting any need or desire, however trivial, at any hour. He spoke of shelves that, as if by magic, instantly replenished themselves.

"My friends, if humans were admitted into Tolk, they could build a supermarket. Never again would we need to cultivate, to scavenge, sheer, spin, weave, burrow, or build. In short, never again would we need to work! Life would be as a dream—one long and eternal celebration of happiness and ease."

His tone suddenly softened and sweetened. "There's only one condition, though." His eyes roved from face to face, pausing just long enough for each person to wonder what that condition might be.

"There is only one being who can bring this to pass." He stretched up on his hind legs. "That one is *I*, King Sinbad, lord of all of Tolk! You *must* choose me as your new king—all of you, everyone, without exception. In choosing me, you open the doors to knowledge, to untold pleasures, and to happiness we cannot even conceive of. I will bring humans to Tolk—humans who can instruct us, wait upon us, and adore us." He stopped mid-speech, as though something quite unrelated had just occurred to him. His voice dropped almost to a whisper. "And who can also *protect* us."

He began to pace nervously. "What can I tell you, my friends? What can I say that might impress upon your minds the very real dangers that could spring upon us at any time? Even immortality could not save us from destruction. To be immortal is to live forever in our present condition." He lowered his voice and adopted a conspiratorial tone. "But supposing someone, or something were to *alter* our present state."

An unsettled murmur arose, like dry leaves driven before a stiff wind.

"Tell us what you mean!" someone shouted.

Sinbad sat down on his haunches and faced them squarely.

"Imagine, if you can, cats of such immense size that even a giant would quail at the sight of the muscle and claw." Dramatically he leapt up and unsheathed his own front claws. "Imagine claws sixteen times the length and breadth of these! Why, in only minutes such weapons could shred Barlow Bear there—even Bran the giant-man—into shreds, ripping them into so many pieces they could never again be reconstructed in all of time!"

Duff, the great redheaded oaf of a giant, moaned aloud.

"Imagine this, if you can! Lizard-like reptiles as long and as broad as felled trees. Jaws like heavy trunk lids lined with hundreds of sharp, jagged teeth." A young beaver nearly fainted and had to be held up by her friends.

"Imagine," he said, his eye on a group of dwarfs, "snakes as thick across as ripe squash, as long as the fairies' flagpoles are tall, capable of coiling around a body and crushing it to pulp, like mashed corn.

"Imagine," he went on, "enormous grizzly bears that slash and maim. Ferocious wolves—those mangy canines that hunt in packs. Why, they'd tear us apart limb from joint, tongue from toe, as soon as they laid eyes on us. They'd take over our homes and despoil the hard-earned work of our paws!

"But that, my friends, dreadful as it is, is not the worst of it. Oh no! I've not yet told you the worst. Now, why do you suppose these terrible creatures would want to tear us to bits in the first place? For what possible end would they perform such despicable and cruel acts?" He paused, leaving the question suspended in the air like a dark cloud waiting to unleash its torrent. "Why, simply to gratify the most basic of appetites, of course. After all, we all have to *eat*, don't we?"

Several hundred voices gasped in unison. "No!" "Never!" "It's not possible!"

"Even if such creatures do exist, Sinbad, which I doubt..." the speaker had to shout over the rising clamor, "they couldn't do us any harm! It's impossible. Here in Tolk, we're all immortal. And that makes us indestructible. And besides, they can't get into Tolk in the first place. King Noble has said so!"

The cat raised his tufted brows and looked down his nose in disdain. "*No*, you say? Well, I say, *Why not?* We've never had to contend with such creatures—Predators!—so how do we really know? And there need be only one entrance into Tolk discovered..." His eyes wandered knowingly across to Price. "Or *revealed*. And after all, whom can we trust?" He looked out again at the crowd. "Just *one* entrance could mean a life of chaos and terror. Maybe even annihilation!"

This time there was no rebuttal. The very idea was so frightening and so completely alien that no one knew what to think. Thousands of pairs of eyes riveted on the orange cat, hanging on what he would say next.

In a loud voice, he declared, "Do any of you suppose, for even one minute, that this canine seated here—this "king," as you call him—could protect us from such a menace? Let me assure you, as one who knows, even if he is not the coward I imagine him to be and did not seek outright to protect his own hide, then believe me, in the face of such enemies *he would be the first to be destroyed!*"

As he spoke these last words, Sinbad directed a forepaw accusingly at King Noble. For a second time, fists clenched in anger, Price made to rise, but again the king restrained him with a heavy paw. King Noble himself looked sober, but unconcerned. He met the cat's accusation with a steady, unflinching gaze.

By now the entire company was writhing in anxiety. Whisperings and murmurings had risen to an excited babble. But Sinbad, assuming the role of one who is in full command, quickly shouted down the ruckus.

"Silence! Silence, my friends!" He extended both 'arms' overhead in an all-encompassing gesture. "Hear me out! There is someone, my friends, someone who stands on this very spot, someone you can trust, who knows and cares about each of you ... someone who is only concerned about your safekeeping and happiness, and *the only one among us* who can bring into Tolk trustworthy humans to protect us from vicious predators *and* attend to our every delight ... to our every comfort.

"We *can* have it all, my friends. We can have immortality *and* the variety and richness of human experience. But only King *Sinbad* knows the way. It stands at the door, simply waiting for you to choose. Today—"

"That's it, Sinbad! I can't listen to another word!" Without realizing it, Price found himself on his feet. "That's the biggest pack of lies I've ever heard! And now *I've* got a thing or two to say!"

Chapter Twenty-Eight: The Debate

It took Sinbad only seconds to gather his wits. "I object to this! I object. You, boy, have no right to even be here! This is a matter between King Sinbad and King Noble. You are an intruder. *You* go back to where you came from and stop meddling in our affairs! We don't want you here!"

"Aye!"

"Aye!"

A number of Tolks, mostly animals and dwarfs, jumped to their feet and joined in the rebuke, some angrily shaking fists in the air.

"Go back where you came from, boy!"

"We don't want you here!"

"We don't need you!"

"Now, wait a minute. Wait a minute! Citizens of Tolk!" Price had to shout to be heard over the ruckus. "Listen to me!" He raised his arms and waved the crowd down to a tense silence. "Remember! I was born and raised in the outside world! You shouldn't close your minds to someone's first-hand experience. After all, Sinbad is asking you to give up a life that you already know for something completely unknown.

"King Noble said the decision you make today is *irreversible!* How could you make such an important decision without hearing *all* the facts? Citizens of Tolk, you *do* need to hear what I have to say, because believe me..." His voice darkened dangerously. "I know things about humans and the outside world that Sinbad hasn't told you!"

He paused, breathing heavily. "I say that you'd better listen to me and *beware!* Some of what Sinbad has told you is only part of the truth. Some of it's complete nonsense, and..." he looked at the cat, "some of it's out-and-out lies!"

"What?" Sinbad leapt up in defensive anger. "And who are you to accuse *me* of lying? You're nothing but a meddlesome *child!* You're a nobody here in Tolk. Your opinions aren't worth a cricket's song and dance."

"You're wrong. I've got nothing to lose. I'll go home tonight and nothing will have changed in my life. But here in Tolk everything will be different. Citizens of Tolk, you have a *right* to hear what I've got to say. You *have* to listen to me!"

"Aye!" Dori sprang to his feet. "I, for one, want to hear the boy! You let him speak, Sinbad—you scheming, triple-sided fur ball!" ('Triple-sided was a common Tolk expression referring to someone who was not just front-side and back-side, but who also had a hidden agenda.)

"Aye! Let's hear what the boy has to say!" bellowed Barlow Bear. "Then we can make up our own minds!"

"Aye! We'll decide for ourselves!"

"Hear the boy! Hear the boy! Hear the boy!" Freddy was on her feet again and began to chant loudly. She motioned to the other fairies to follow her example. "Hear the boy! Hear the boy!"

In almost no time, most of the crowd had joined in, and it was obvious to everyone, even Sinbad, that the majority wanted to hear Price's side of things. But Price did not wait for Sinbad's approval. Again he waved his arms, raising them high over his head.

"Thank you. Thank you, citizens of Tolk. Thank you for allowing me to speak." He glanced over at Sinbad.

Now that he'd begun, Price dared not pause, not even to collect his thoughts, for fear his antagonist would again jump into the fray. "You see," he went on, praying silently that the right words would come to him, "there are some things you need to know about humans. You have to understand that people—by that I mean humans—are much more powerful than you realize.

"In my world, animals aren't like they are here in Tolk. They can't speak, or read and write, or make things, like you do. Where I come from, humans are the only really intelligent beings, and have power over all the others. Sure, maybe some humans, coming to Tolk, would think that animals that can reason and speak should have rights like people. I think that way. But there'd be those who wouldn't.

"Humans have a hard enough time getting along with each other. And I hate to say it, but most of them think it's their right to hunt and kill animals. Many people have great respect for wildlife, but there are lots of others who don't care. And even responsible people will kill animals that threaten them or stand in their way.

"Now, maybe it's true that people couldn't do that here in Tolk. But it's an attitude. It's the way people are used to thinking about animals—the way they're used to treating them. And you should know..." Price looked away, paused for just one second, and then went on in a rush, "where I come from people raise animals for food. They slaughter them, and they eat them!"

There was one brief moment of stunned silence. Then...

"What?"

"Never!"

"That can't be true!"

"Sinbad never told us any such thing!"

Sinbad donned an expression of shocked denial, as though he couldn't believe that even a wretched boy would dare to say anything so wicked and false.

"Is that true, Sinbad?" someone shouted.

"Certainly not!" The cat spat, with a great pretense of righteous indignation. "Not true! Not a word of it!"

"Well, supposing it *is* true," sounded a booming voice from the back. "Supposing humans *do* kill and eat beasties, then does that mean that *you* kill 'em and eat 'em, boy?" This cunning question came surprisingly from Duff.

Sinbad sniggered, thinking that Price would certainly be caught in his own trap. After all, how could any decent Tolk countenance a self-confessed flesh-eater? But Sinbad was disappointed.

"No, I don't actually," Price was happy to declare. "That's because my grandmother is a vegetarian. She would never eat meat ... er, animals, even when she was a kid. And since that's how my mom was raised, that's how we eat, too."

"Well, if he don't eat animals, then I say *no* peoples eats animals! That's what I think." Duff brought his right fist down resolutely onto the palm of his left hand. He grinned at Sinbad. "Isn't that right, Chief?"

"Certainly any human *I* brought into Tolk would *never* eat flesh."

Price shut his eyes. He could see that this was a no-win situation. He decided it was time to change direction, hoping that the giant's flawed logic would be obvious. But before he could continue, Freddy jumped up to the rescue.

"Don't be foolish, Duff!" she said. "When was the last time you ate a mushroom pie?"

"Mushroom? Mushrooms is for dwarfies! Duff, he never eats mushrooms. Duff eats big stuff, like punkins and melons and scrambled up goose eggs."

"Yes, but dwarfs do eat mushrooms. You see!" With a succinct nod of the head Freddy sat down again.

Price knew that the issue had not been resolved but, at the same time realized that he had to move on. "Sinbad talked about having an army of giants," he said. "He didn't tell you that armies are for fighting wars. Wars happen when humans kill and enslave one another, usually trying to take away property or lands, and sometimes trying to force their beliefs on others. I'm ashamed to admit it, but in my world, wars are common. If I were you, I'd be asking Sinbad what *he* wants an army for!" Folding his arms across his chest, Price faced the cat, keeping his feet firmly planted on the rock. He had no intention of giving up his prominent position on the platform while calling Sinbad to account.

The cat was quick to take advantage of the situation. He hopped up next to Price, invading his space. But the boy refused to budge. He looked down his nose, challenging the cat.

Sinbad hissed under his breath and flashed the assembly a self-conscious grin. "I'm glad you brought up this subject." By now he realized that he had no choice but to share the stage. He relaxed and assumed a very serious and knowing air.

"War, my friends? Here in Tolk? There could never be war in Tolk. And should some misguided humans, brought here to serve and indulge us, have other ideas, my valiant army of giants would see to it that each wicked person ..." he glanced at Price, "was escorted promptly out of the country and never admitted back again. I'm afraid, boy, that you have an exaggerated notion of the importance of humankind. No living human would be any match for the might and valor of a giant from Tolk—a giant of such noble mien as Duff, here, for example."

Duff drew himself up, puffing out his massive chest.

"Yes," Sinbad shook his head sadly, as if reluctant to reveal something that pained him. "Yes, I will allow that there is the possibility, even after the most careful screening, that some person or persons might be disloyal—considering the fickle natures of *some* humans. Of course, I would choose only those who are trustworthy and hardworking, and who love their pets more than they love their own lives. Such humans are not rare, I have found.

"Nevertheless," he quickly went on, "I admit that it's possible that an unfortunate situation might arise. But that only shows how essential my army would be."

Sinbad regarded Price haughtily. "You've done me a great service, boy, by allowing me to clear the air on this matter." He bowed insolently to Price and then, with a more courtly gesture, to the crowd.

Price swallowed hard. He had to think quickly. "Oh, Sinbad!" he exclaimed in exasperation. "Your plan is so full of holes ... if this wasn't so serious, I'd be laughing!"

Frustrated, he turned to the others. "Citizens of Tolk," he pleaded, "Sinbad can't possibly give you all the things he says. People grow gardens and crops for *human* food. Most people work hard for what they've got. It's not like here in Tolk. Where I come from, failure and success go together. You don't earn success without dealing with failure first. It's built right into our way of life.

"And like I said before, people are so much more powerful than you realize. They would never in a million years pander to animals. Why would they? Sure, some people love their pets almost like they were their own kids, and some people honestly respect the lives of all animals. But even then, it's not equal. Always the human is dominant. Nev—"

"Not correct!" Sinbad interrupted. "This boy is lying, and I know it." He directed a claw at Price. "It *is* a fact that pets are not on an equal footing with humans. The truth is that humans *adore* their pets. Frank treats me like a king, which of course, is exactly what I am. And he is my devoted servant. And today, my friends, *you* can choose to be princes and princesses, all of us members of one great royal household. Why, serving his pet is a human's greatest joy in life. Believe me. *I* should know."

"That's all and well for the beasts, but what about us dwarfs?" someone shouted.

Once again the cat had become the focus of attention. He pulled himself up. "Ah yes. Now that is a very good question. What *about* the dwarfs, and also the elves and the fairies? Even though there are no such beings living in the mortal world, humans *are* aware of your existence. In fact, people are so fascinated by the very idea of elves and fairies and dwarfs that many books have been written about you. Yes! You are featured in stories, paintings, and in moving pictures. I've even seen your images carved out of wood and stone.

"Now, if humans so revere even the *idea* of fairies and elves and dwarfs, imagine how it would be to meet you in person. Why, they'd be as thrilled as explorers who'd just discovered a wonderful new country. You would be worshiped almost as much as any pet!"

Price interjected. "Sinbad, that's nonsense. Sure, at first people would be in awe of fairies and elves. I was. Imagine it. Boys and girls that can fly, tiny people only a foot high, and cute roly-poly dwarfs—" This comment provoked some rumblings and a resentful grunt from the audience. Price quickly moved on. "Um ... you-you'd all—*all* be a huge novelty. But you have to understand that people are independent—they take care of themselves. And they'd expect you to do the same. Why would they cater to elves and fairies, or anybody?

"And I'll tell you something else. People are used to getting what they want. It wouldn't take long before some greedy person would swindle you out of your lands and take them over. To most people, Tolk would seem a pretty attractive place to live. I've said this before and I'll say it again: You don't understand just how powerful humans are."

"No! It's you who doesn't understand, boy!" Sinbad was really angry now. "You underestimate the cunning of us Tolks! My giant army would dispose of any human corruption with such speed. Believe me, we'd spit out the bad like a mouthful of sour milk. And the sweet cream would remain to fatten us."

"You couldn't do it, Sinbad. People wouldn't serve you. You couldn't make them."

"I can, and they would. I have done it already."

"You're lying. Mr. Murphy is not your servant. He's your master, and you know it."

"My so-called master has provided me with every comfort. He feeds me and coddles me. Can you deny it?"

Price compressed his lips. "No," he admitted.

"There. You see. Mr. Murphy bows to my every whim. *I* am the master."

"Sinbad, you know full well that Mr. Murphy only keeps you because you kill the mice that get into his garden!"

"What? *What!*"

There was a full moment of shocked silence. "Now this has gone too far. Are you accusing me of—"

"Murder."

"I deny it—absolutely and completely. This is cruel and despicable, and you're a loathsome coward to even suggest such a thing. Oh-ho, you're pretty desperate now, aren't you?"

"It's not a lie. It's the truth. And what's more—"

"Do you have any evidence to back up this preposterous accusation?"

Price thought hard. "Yes! Yes, I do. Meepy! You tried to *kill* him!" The cat betrayed only the merest flinch at the mention of the popular mouse's name. "He can tell us about it. And there were other witnesses. Meepy!" Price called out loudly, "you've got to come up here right away! We need you."

Eagerly he scanned the crowd. There was a long pause, and many necks craned and heads turned in all directions trying to spot the well-known little rodent. But Meepy was nowhere to be seen.

"Come on, Meepy. You have to come up here ... now." Price's eyes continued to search the crowd. "He *must* be here. Meepy!" For a moment all was silent while everyone watched and waited. "Meepy?" But no mouse came forward.

Now, Sinbad was as surprised about this as anyone. It was impossible that Meepy, of all creatures, would not attend the meeting. Then it occurred to him that perhaps some of his own trusted cohorts had clapped hand or paw on the mouse to prevent him from showing. *Well*, he thought, smiling to himself. *Whoever they are, I'll see to it that they're duly rewarded.*

Sinbad drew himself up, giving the impression that he'd known all along that Meepy would never dare to stand before his own friends and kin, never dare to perjure himself before all of Tolk. For the moment, he had the advantage and knew that he must act quickly to turn the tide. Otherwise, there was a good chance that all would be lost.

"Well, boy!" he gloated. "Where's the evidence? Where are your witnesses? Hm?" Mocking Price, he cupped a paw over his eyes and pretended to search for Meepy. "To his credit, your little mouse friend appears to have chosen *not* to support you in this terrible deceit. You seem surprised, but it doesn't surprise me at all. It's one thing to blindly follow a king you know—a fellow Tolk—however incompetent he has become, but it's quite another to support a bald-faced lie. Perjury! At the behest of an intruder! All that this little exhibition has proven, boy, is what a liar *you* are."

The cat narrowed his yellow eyes and menacingly wagged his head at Price. "And now there is something *I* want to ask you, boy! I hear from a reliable source that you don't want to stay in Tolk, that you prefer your own kin to the friends you've made here. Is this true? Answer me!"

"That's only partly true." Price folded his arms across his chest. "I *can't* stay here in Tolk—because of my family. It doesn't mean I don't care—"

"How is it...?" Sinbad interrupted. "How is it that, if humans are so terrible, so warlike, so cunning, as you say, how is it that you'd rather remain with your own wicked fellows than stay here with us? After all, Tolk offers you unending peace, freedom from all of the so-called evils of human society. It even offers you eternal life. From what you have said about humans, I must conclude that you don't want peace—that you actually prefer pain and suffering and hardship. You enjoy these things so much that you are even willing to die for them. Now, I'm sorry boy, but there's something here that doesn't add up, something that smells peculiar, like the inside of Barlow Bear's den in mid-hibernation. I don't think that humans can possibly be as bad as you let on, or why would you be so eager to run home to them? Ah yes, I say you've been stringing us a yarn, boy."

Once more the crowd began to murmur.

"Dat's right, boy," said Duff. "If peoples is so bad, then why don't you want to stay here? I guess you just don't like us none, huh?"

Smoot leapt up. "You know, Duff's right. For once he's hit the scuttle with the scuttle ball. That boy doesn't care a britches' button about us, and he's been lyin' about the true nature of humans. I say he's a liar!"

"Smoot!" Dori's round face was so red with anger that he looked like a tomato about to burst its skin. "Have you forgotten that if it weren't for this lad, you'd still be pro-vidin' a spot o' shade in the garden? What's wrong with you anyhow?"

"Aw. That weren't the way of it, Dori. Sinbad just made an honest mistake, and he's admitted to it. I tell you, King Noble's mightily afraid of Sinbad. He knows that when the sun comes up, the crickets stop their music, and that's what's got him so scared." Smoot pointed accusingly at the king. "The sun's comin' up on him right now!"

"Why, of all the brain-empty prattle—"

"Hold on now, both of you!" Barlow's big voice cut through this exchange of insults, halting it instantly. "It comes to my mind that we ought to find out what the boy has to say. How's about it, boy? Fact is I can't make any sense of it either. Why would anybody want to live in such a place as you do, where people are mean and corruptible, when you could live with us forever, all peaceful and harmonious? To me it looks like two halves of a broken kettle that don't match up. There's just no way you can put 'em together to make a thing that works. So, what's the meaning of it, boy?"

"Aye! We're supposed to be your friends, aren't we? Guess you think we're not good enough."

"I think you just don't want to share all what you got!"

Price looked out over the sea of faces, many piqued and irate. *This is crazy!* he thought. How was it that *he* was suddenly the one on trial? And what could he possibly say to help them understand?

Chapter Twenty-Nine: War

"Y-you don't understand," Price stammered. "Most people aren't bad. Most people are just living their lives, doing what they can. Sure, *some* people do terrible things ... but ... there's reasons for that. It's not that simple."

No expert on human vice, Price felt really adrift. "It's true, it can be a hard life, but there are choices. And it-it's the challenge. Where I come from, you can decide for yourself and then work hard to become whatever you want. Well ... maybe you can't always be *exactly* what you want ... but there *are* choices. Everyone has choices."

Price looked away. He was grasping for some solid foothold, some real traction. "And when you *do* achieve something," he went on, "when you figure something out, the feeling is so great—like a huge light coming on in your mind."

He scrutinized the crowd. Many blank faces stared back at him, but there were some who looked interested.

"It's like this. One day at school, some guys were laughing at me, because I'm no good at running. We were playing soccer—uh, that's a game where you have to run and kick a ball into a goal. Then one of the guys tripped me, and I fell. He made out like it was an accident, but I knew better. Even the coach turned a blind eye, because even *he* didn't want me there.

"I felt really crushed, like I was a total failure. But the next day, a teacher chose one of my drawings for the cover of the yearbook. I'd worked hard on that drawing, and I was ... thrilled. What's more, one of the guys who'd been laughing at me the day before came up and said, 'Great drawing, Price.'

"Right then I realized something. It didn't matter what those guys thought about me. My happiness and success didn't depend on anybody else, but only on me and *my* choices."

In vain Price studied the crowd for some kind of reaction. "I know it doesn't sound like much, but that *changed* me. I felt ... stronger."

"Oh well! After hearing that gripping tale, I feel stronger myself," mocked Sinbad. "In fact, I feel a strong inclination to yawn." The cat dropped his jaw and patted the open cavity. "Ya-ya-ya..."

"But there's more to it than that," Price went on, ignoring Sinbad. "It has to do with my family, more than anything else. You see, they love me, and I love them—even more than I love my own life. If I stayed here in Tolk, it would break their hearts. And the truth is, I would rather die than hurt my parents or my grandma like that." He bit his lower lip and looked thoughtfully out past the edge of the crowd.

"It's all the great times we've had together—camping and hiking, laughing, and playing games, even working together. Dad helping me with my homework and delivering my flyers. Mom looking after me when I'm sick. They've always been there for me."

Price looked out over the rows of upturned faces. He could tell that he had made a connection. Love and loyalty to kin seemed to be something that the Tolks understood.

"It's as if we're somehow bound to each other. Do you see what I mean?" Many silently nodded.

Sinbad spat in disgust. "Love? Challenge? Hah! You cannot arm or defend yourself with love, boy. And why would anyone want to work hard when you can get somebody else to do it for you?"

Price looked steadily at the cat. "You missed the whole point, Sinbad. Meeting the challenge is what makes you stronger and better, and love is what makes it worthwhile. If you take those away, there's nothing left. Is that what you want? For yourself? For the Tolks? Nothing? You all deserve better than that."

"Deserve better? *Better!* What could be better than to be freed from every care, freed from every common drudgery, freed from the necessity of bumbling along, figuring it all out on your own? You can fall into error that way, boy. Why would anyone do that if they didn't have to? Come now, you've got to come up with something better than that." The cat pointed a claw at the boy and laughed.

"Oh, Sinbad, Sinbad. You talk about enemies that can't even exist here, while at the same time trying to make everyone subject to you. You're the real enemy."

Exasperated, Price appealed to the others. "Tolks, you already have a king—a great king. And who loves you more? Who can you trust more? King Noble, who you already know is a good king, or this lying..." he glanced contemptuously at the cat, "*villain*, who's only looking out for himself?

"Look, he tells you that sooner or later predators are going to get into Tolk and destroy you, but at the same time, he wants to throw open the door to humans? Believe me, you have *way* more to fear from humans than you do from any predators, no matter how wild or ferocious. Before you even knew what was happening, humans would take away everything you have, and evil and death would move right in. That's the way of the world, but it's not the way it should be here.

"Tolks, I'm begging you ... I'm pleading with you ... today every one of you should stand behind King Noble." Price felt hot tears prick behind his eyelids, and he was breathing hard. "It will be the best thing you ever did!"

Suddenly he felt very tired. His shoulders slumped and his head dropped forward. Wearily he flopped down onto the grass beside King Noble, and buried his face in his arms.

Sinbad wasted no time assuming center stage. "All right. Side with King Noble if you want!" he cried. "Stay just as you are now and always have been and always will be! Let Tolk remain forever the same—a place where nothing ever changes from one day to the next, from one age to the next. A place where there's no improvement, no adventure, no excitement, no fun! But as for me and my friends, we're going to have the best of both worlds. We *can* have it all: all the variety and richness of human experience with no need to sacrifice our immortal condition!

"I, King Sinbad, can make it happen. Tolks! The time for debate has ended. The time to act is now! Come!" With outstretched arms, he beckoned earnestly. "Come over to my side. Follow me!"

About ten seconds lapsed in silence, and then there was a collective shout and a wave of bodies began to surge across the grass. Many, like excited children, scampered happily over to Sinbad's proximity. Some turned back to smugly face the remaining Tolks, as if they defied anyone to challenge their decision. But others were simply delighted, as though they were expecting a treat, like children who've been invited to see the circus. With a burst of renewed energy, Sinbad motioned wildly for more to follow.

He had just opened his mouth to cry out again when, like a thunderbolt, King Noble's voice resounded from the rear of the crowd. "Hear me, O citizens of Tolk, and *hear me well!*"

No one had noticed the king slip to the back, where he had joined his flock, now rallying round him. Neither had anyone noticed the many Tolks who had crept out of the woods where they'd been hiding, or those who had already quietly disengaged themselves from the others, radiating to the outer edges of the gathering. Under Meepy's direction, the king's army had closed in. The large assembly was completely surrounded. Everyone was stunned—especially Sinbad.

"Hear me, O citizens of Tolk, and hear me well," the King solemnly proclaimed. "On this day, Sinbad and anyone allied with him *will be driven from Tolk forever!* Take heed, I say, for surely you will *never return!* The choice is yours!"

A hiss arose from the crowd like a great gasp of steam. In both camps, all were now genuinely shocked and appalled. For a moment, even Sinbad looked worried, but then he threw back his head and laughed derisively.

"Ha! And what do you intend to do? Remove us all bodily? You couldn't do it! We are too many and we are much too powerful. And who would do the dirty work? Our own kinfolk, our life-long comrades? Do not be fooled, my friends. He would not, could not, *ever* drive us from Tolk. It is impossible."

"*Choose!*" shouted King Noble in a terrible voice.

As the enormity of what was taking place began to register with the Tolks, shock quickly transformed into horror.

Dozens frantically scampered back to where the king's followers were gathering around him.

But there were many others who were still wavering.

"*Choose!*" shouted King Noble again. More souls slunk over to the king's side, as though they were ashamed, but whether they were ashamed to be deserting Sinbad or to have been allied with him in the first place, was uncertain. There were even a few who, on consideration, decided that they simply could not forgo the temptations Sinbad proffered after all, and they scuttled back over to his camp.

The cat remained upright and defiant in the midst of his followers, but by now he too was actually beginning to be afraid.

"Sinbad." The king's voice softened. "Flame. Do you want to reconsider?" He lowered his eyes, giving the cat the chance to save face should he have a change of heart.

But, once again the focus of attention, Sinbad drew himself up like a broken reed striving to be a tree. "*Never!*" He spat to one side. "Why *should* I reconsider? You will never get away with this!" It was impossible not to sense the rank hatred emanating from his being and even contaminating those surrounding him, like a foul odor.

"Then it's time!" shouted the king. He barked out a sharp command.

Meepy, perched in the brim of Barlow Bear's cap, where he had a periscopic view, signaled to his captains and began calling out orders.

"Trumble, to your left. Miftup, close ranks *now!*" The piping mouse voice was augmented with a system of arm and hand signs—not to mention indispensable help from Barlow. "Pull forward! Pull forward! Bootle, take up the rear!"

King Noble's army was made up of bears, giants, many of the more sturdy dwarfs and animals, and thanks to Freddy, all of the fairies. They moved in, as though well rehearsed, and before the rebels were even aware of what was happening, the 'soldiers' had neatly cut off Sinbad's cowering entourage. They now formed a tight-knit barricade around the rebels in two concentric circles. The larger, more powerful creatures made up the inner circle. Each of these soldiers carried a stout pole, which they grasped tightly in both hands. These were to bar the escape of any enemy, great or small. They could prod a victim if necessary to keep him in line, or stop him if he tried to break through.

The purpose of the outer circle, which consisted of the fairies and many of the smaller, more agile creatures, was to catch and drive back any small animals or others that might escape between the cracks. King Noble himself trotted around the periphery, ready to catch in his teeth any rebel who made it through the ranks, and toss the offender back into the circle.

Slowly and methodically the entire company began to creep as a body across the meadow. From above it must have looked like a giant beetle inching its way towards the stone wall. It didn't take the rebels long to see where they were headed, and with that came the horrifying realization that they might actually be driven through the portal. Frantically, they tried to resist, but their efforts soon degenerated into the chaos of panic as they found themselves being relentlessly propelled along.

Now such a howling and wailing arose from their midst that it chilled one to the bone to hear it. It was the heart-rending cry of the doomed, and it caused even some of the king's soldiers to falter in their purpose.

Perched lightly on his shoulder, Toorilla watched with Price from the flat top of the Moon's Platter. The robin immediately sensed the confusion in the ranks. At once, she soared up into the air and swooped down over the heads of the fumbling soldiers.

"Don't look back, my friends!" she cried. "If you do, we'll all be lost. Lost! All of us! Think of your homes. Your loved ones. They're depending on you! They're counting on you!"

Price stood watching, his face drawn with anxiety, fists clenched tightly at his sides. Finally, unable to restrain himself, he thudded down the Platter's incline and charged through the tall grass toward the scene of action.

O.P. was in the act of grabbing two small belligerent mice by their tails, when he caught a glimpse of the boy careening towards them. He dragged his squirming quarry to the red-headed fairy, who caught hold of them and chucked them back into the inner circle.

"Hey!" O.P shouted, waving his arms and jumping up and down. "Over there!" He pointed. Then with a jerk, he caught a scrappy little vole by the scruff of the neck and slung him off to the red-headed fairy.

Price couldn't hear O.P. over the din, but he got the message and made a quick right-angled turn. In the shelter of some low hanging willow, he found Drusilla, the rabbit he'd met in the market, sitting on a cache of sturdy poles. The rabbit's eyes flicked over the boy. She singled out a pole just the right size. She would have rolled it to him with her large hind feet, lumberjack-style, except that three broken-off branches stuck out at one end—like spikes.

"Especially for you," she said.

Price took up his weapon. Drusilla grabbed a smaller pole, and with hind legs apart and forepaws clutching it

285

near each end, demonstrated how to use it. Her movements were quick and deft.

"Keep the paws—er, hands—at least two foot-lengths apart," she advised. "More leverage that way." She rotated the pole as if turning a large crank. "And you can prod ... like this." She put her right forepaw firmly over the top end, and with her left grasped the pole about two-thirds of the way down. "You can make a powerful thrust, like this— Aha!" She lunged. "Hard to resist." With a satisfied grin, she made a little grunting sound and her nose quivered.

Nodding his thanks, the boy rushed off.

"Good luck!" Drusilla called after him.

By now, hundreds of birds had joined Toorilla, crying out their warnings as they flew back and forth over the ranks. Their words had found their mark. With renewed courage, the Tolks had managed to tighten their grip. Barlow Bear and Meepy had been particularly vigilant in hounding Sinbad, making sure that he, of all creatures, did not escape. Slowly, but inevitably, they were advancing nearer and nearer to the wall.

Price pushed his way through the outer ring of fairies and smaller creatures and soon gained the inner circle. He found himself between Fender and another dwarf he didn't know. Fender glanced his way, and after a start of surprise, nodded his approval. Almost immediately the boy had to stave off a large badger. He was glad that his pole had spikes.

Most of the rebels were too terrified and desperate to be fully aware that Price had joined the battle—but not Sinbad. He'd spotted the boy almost right away, and it caught him off guard. In fact, he took quite a blow to the back of the head from Barlow as a consequence. The cat quickly ducked out of sight, leaving the bear goggling in confusion.

Sinbad slunk down, almost on his belly. He snaked his way through the maze of legs, claws, and clashing poles, intent on a pair of boy-legs that were now his object. True to form, the wily cat had slithered out of sight and singled out Price's most vulnerable part.

But Toorilla spotted the orange serpentine shape from above and could see where he was headed. Instantly, she dove down, and dropping onto Price's shoulder, cried a warning in his ear. The boy jerked to attention, his eyes frantically searching the jungle of bodies for a glimpse of orange fur. Then he saw it, about six yards to his right.

Others nearby were quickly becoming aware of the impending confrontation and an incision began opening between cat and boy, even as the battle continued to wage on around them. No longer undercover, Sinbad rose up on all fours. He advanced stealthily, dangerously, eyes riveted on the boy's—radiating contempt.

Price felt fear such as he had never felt before. How, he wondered, had he become the target of such intense hatred? But he was also aware that he was facing the final argument in a long debate—and he knew that he must win. With a great force of will, he stanched the fear and braced himself. He now pitted all of his mind and physical strength against the cat.

Aware of the contest developing, others of King Noble's followers hedged around the boy as best they could, shielding him from attack by any of Sinbad's minions, while at the same time driving them along. By now they had nearly reached the portal.

Price had the advantage of being larger than the cat, and of having a weapon. Sinbad, on the other hand, had dagger claws and greater speed and agility. He continued to move steadily towards the boy, their eyes locked in mutual combat. Sinbad was finally near enough that he shifted his weight to his haunches, almost in a sitting position. Price tightened his grip on the pole, senses white hot. The cat made a powerful lunge, leaping about a yard higher than the boy. Price responded instantly, raised the spiked pole and thrust it at the animal. The pole caught the cat on his underside and with a mighty heft the boy flung the creature into the crowd.

Sinbad was on his feet in a second, and rushed at him. Hop, hop—gaining momentum—he leapt, feet-first, aimed right at the face. Instinctively, Price's head went down while his arms went up, still grasping his weapon. Clenching the pole tightly, on impact he flung his arms out and away from his face and body. The cat was down again, but not without having clawed deep, bloody gashes in each of Price's arms.

Now Price charged and caught the animal on the end of his pole. With all the energy he possessed, he drove him, striking front, then left, then right, keeping him down. Sinbad began to cry out as he was helplessly propelled along. But then, with a great sinewy wriggle, he righted himself. Back on his feet, he darted away a few yards, then circled back and faced the boy again, ready to spring.

By this time, the entire body had reached the portal where the soldiers were breaking rank. One by one they began shoving the rebels through. Absolute panic set in and the howling and wailing rose to a deafening pitch. Instinctively, Sinbad's head cranked in that direction.

Price didn't miss his chance. He cannoned forward, caught the cat on the end of his pole, and running with all the speed he could muster, flung the creature through the portal. Sinbad landed on his feet. In shock, he turned himself around and stared at the boy, as if in disbelief.

Just then King Noble appeared at Price's side. At the sight of him, Sinbad flinched back in fear. By now many terrified animals were fleeing past the cat, and bodies had begun to pile up around him. Coming to himself, Sinbad shot back one last lingering hateful glare, as cold and hard as stone. He turned then and bolted out of sight.

Exhausted, Price slumped forward, the spiked pole dropping to the ground. Others quickly moved in, leaving the boy in their wake, where he stood motionless and past feeling, not even aware of the open wounds on his arms.

Soldiers now took up positions at the entrance, to make sure that no rebel re-entered Tolk. Among these was Bran, who had been very efficient at dealing with many of the rebel giants. As soon as the last enemy had been prodded and pushed and flung out of Tolk, he rolled a huge boulder, prepared in advance, across the opening. The portal was now completely blocked. Bran then climbed up and sat astride the immense slab of granite. In triumph, he folded his arms across his massive chest. Here he would remain, keeping guard, until the time came to seal off the portal permanently.

Everyone else, meanwhile, had watched and followed at a distance. Now a loud cheer rang out as one and all rejoiced.

Chapter Thirty:
Freddy's Choice

Jubilant Tolks began to romp and dance and sing. Fairies appeared overhead trailing colored lanterns, spotting the dusky sky like many pastel inkblots. Even the shy elves danced along with the rest, playing their pipes and other instruments that they struck or rattled. Seemingly out of nowhere, tables appeared, laden with food and drink. Price could hear laughing and shouting, and nearby one dwarf hailed another.

"Hie! Smucker! You tell Tealeye we want some of his peppered mushroom pastry. My mulled cider isn't the same without it. And you must all come over and join the party."

"B-but..." Smucker fumbled awkwardly. "Didn't you know?"

"Know what?"

"Tealeye. He-he's gone, you see."

"Gone? Oh—Oh yes, of course."

The sweet joy of victory began to lose its savor as many suddenly became aware of beloved friends and kin who were absent—those who'd chosen to follow Sinbad and had been banished from Tolk forever. Very quickly the festive mood paled. Many stood thoughtfully by the wayside, alone or in small groups, or trudging along quietly with others. Price moved along too, clutching his bleeding arms, still dazed by all that had happened, and very much aware that he did not have long to remain in Tolk.

Suddenly, reverberating across the meadow like the toll of a great bell, they heard the loud, deep baying of a hound. It was King Noble who had returned to the Moon's Platter. He stood silhouetted against the sunset, heralding his subjects.

"Awoo! Awooo! Awo-o-o!"

Everyone was drawn to the sound. Like lonely travelers lured by the glow of a fire and the promise of food, they began to drift towards it from every direction. A feeling, almost of reverence, had come upon them as the enormity and finality of what had taken place became apparent. They stood by, quietly waiting for the king to speak.

Once again, he stood on the flat, protruding rock, facing them.

"My friends," he began, "I want to offer you comfort. Be assured that our banished comrades would never have been content to remain in Tolk as it is. They would have caused more mischief and misery than you will ever know. They would have destroyed the happiness of all those who did not agree with them. You are not familiar with the ways of the world outside, the wiles and the wickedness of men. You cannot fully appreciate the great tragedy that has been averted today. Yes, there are wonders out there to be sure, but no such things come without a price. And here in Tolk, it was never meant that we should pay that price. The loss of our friends is a terrible blow, but not as terrible as would have been the loss of *all* of us, and of Tolk as well.

"We've shared in a momentous event, one that has forever altered our destiny. And yet I say, be glad! You may think that this tragedy has torn us apart, but you are wrong. In time you will find that it has united us in a way that would never have been possible otherwise.

"The pain of loss is sure to linger for some time. But there is peace to be found in knowing that we have acted well. We will rebuild our lives. We will strengthen the old friendships that remain and build new ones. We must be grateful for what has been preserved and look ahead with the brightness of hope.

"My friends, victory *is* sweet and we must enjoy it to the fullest. We have a right to rejoice. And we have a right to celebrate. Come! Let us all rejoice and make merry together!"

With that, the king threw back his head and howled. But this was no cry of agony; nor was it the lonely, plaintive cry of one who has been rejected by his own. Full, rich, and resonant, it was a howl of triumph.

Gradually the laughter, the music, and the revelry returned, and soon began again in earnest—only this time even the air seemed to smell cleaner and sweeter. Some attributed this to the setting sun and the natural cooling of the atmosphere at day's end, but others said it was due to a purging rendered by the timely words of the King.

Many now hailed Price and stopped to clap him on the shoulder or to shake paw or hand. All were brimming over with praise and congratulations. And nearly everyone commented on his wounds. "King Noble will take care of those," they advised.

Looking around, Price noticed the German shepherd stealing away to a place by himself. As soon as he had the chance, the boy followed him. He found the dog couched out of sight behind a clump of bushes, watching the moon rise in the east over the long, black band of fir trees. The animal turned to him. Without a word, Price wrapped his arms around the king's neck and hugged him tightly.

Then the dog began licking the boy's wounds. The warm, rough tongue seemed to draw out all the pain, and when Price looked, the deep, red gashes were barely visible. Having finished the treatment, King Noble, stretched out on his belly and looked out over the night scene.

"Four summers ago," he said, "Flame and I sat on this very spot. We watched the same moon rise and talked of sailing on the As-Far-As-The-Eye-Can Sea. Oh, that our friendship had been as constant as the moon."

"But *our* friendship is constant, isn't it?"

"Yes, indeed. I know that it is, for it has been tested and proven. But I also know that you must soon leave us."

Price buried his face in the dog's luxurious neck. "I couldn't go without thanking you, King Noble. Thank you ... thank you so much."

The animal clucked his tongue. "Isn't it *I* who should be thanking you?"

"Thank you for bringing me to Tolk. I wouldn't have missed this adventure for the world. As long as I live, I will never forget it. And I'll never forget you."

King Noble knew that Price would forget, but he said, "Nor will I forget you. And I also must thank you. It's because of you that so many of our friends are still with us."

"I'm happy about that, too." Price smiled. "But the truth is, King Noble, on my own, I was nothing. If it wasn't for all the help from you and the others, I couldn't have done what I did. And it took every one of us to defeat Sinbad and his followers."

"Yes," agreed the dog. "And speaking of that cat...!" What could they say about Sinbad? The animal would never trouble the waters of Tolk again. "I will always be grateful."

He licked Price's cheek. "But I also want to thank you for being our friend ... *my* friend." The dog's tender brown eyes were moist. "I love you, boy."

Price felt a catch in his throat and for a moment couldn't reply. Then he said, "I love you, too. You're a great king. Soon everything will be back to normal. Everything will be like it was before, but we will always have our happy memories to hold on to."

"I'm afraid things will never be the same in Tolk." The dog licked Price's cheek again. "You have no idea, my boy, how the seeds that were sown here today will bear fruit—as is only right. But I know."

"What d'you mean?"

The animal nudged him affectionately. "Now that is something for you to wonder about."

Price shut his eyes. "I don't really understand," he said, "and right now I'm too tired to care." He thought of his bed and then of his grandmother. He knew that she would be very worried by now. "How am I going to get home, King Noble?"

"Bran can roll aside the stone one last time and let you through. But before the sun sets on another day, that portal must be sealed off forever."

"Will I have time to say goodbye to my friends?"

"Of course."

They sat for a few more minutes, contemplating the moonlit scene—so serene and undisturbed by the remarkable events that had happened there so recently.

At last Price said, "Then I guess I'd better go and do it."

He left the king and began wandering about amongst the revelers, searching for his friends. It wasn't long before he spotted O.P. and Meepy at the hub of a large group.

With sprightly antics and plenty of drama, they joked and laughed, swapping war stories. O.P. had center stage.

"It was that big dwarf—Truthers—you remember him. The one who said that all dwarfs ought to live in shopping malls and be in charge of doling out the food. Ha!" O.P. slapped his (sort of) knee. "We all know what he meant by that! Well, I saw him wrest the staff from Dori here, like this. Then he was going to switch sides, and make out that Dori was the enemy. But, I tell you, nothing gets past General Meepy here." He clapped his mouse friend roughly across the back. "Meepy signaled the magpies. They swooped down in a flock and attacked Truthers' face and hands. He dropped that staff quicker'n the twitch-of-a-tom's-tail. Dori caught it on the first bounce."

"Aye." The dwarf nodded enthusiastically. "Those magpies never let him be after that. They followed him and tormented him right to the bitter end."

"Which reminds me, did you see that scab of a cat at the last moment?" Meepy shuddered at the thought. "Did you see the look on Sinbad's face? I was sure we were going to have a mid-summer freeze up. When he looked me right in the eye, I felt my heart stop. Whew!"

"Aye. He was a bad'n, that one," said Dori. "Turned as cold as a stone at the bottom of a bottomless well. The sooner I forget his face—nay, by jiggers! The sooner I forget every bit of him, the better!"

"And there was that nasty she-beaver, Bartooth. Just take a gawk at the battle scars she left here on this staff. See that?" Barlow Bear displayed his deeply gouged weapon. O.P. in particular, having much to fear from beaver's teeth, shivered at the sight of it.

"Guess she thought she could devour the whole thing," Barlow went on. "Figured she'd gobble it right up to my armpits. Ha, ha!"

"Aye, aye."

Price turned away. At the moment, he didn't feel he would fit in well with a crowd of jubilant conquering heroes. He ambled on, wondering where Freddy was.

Suddenly he felt a tap on the top of his head and a pebble bounced onto the grass at his feet.

"Freddy!" he called, looking up and around.

She hovered just above him holding a rose-tinted lantern. It cast a pink glow on her face and her silvery dress. Behind her back, the vibrating wings looked like a glittering pink mist. Laughing, she fluttered down to his side.

"I've been looking everywhere for you!" she cried happily. Price grinned. "Isn't it wonderful, Price? Our work is finished. Tolk is safe again. And the fairies—Price, not one was lost! We are all—*all* of us—still here!"

"That's great, Freddy."

"You know ... we fairies stick together."

Price laughed. "So I've heard."

"And Price," her voice softened. "You were so brave. I was so afraid for you. But I thought you were wounded?" She grabbed an arm, and when she saw the faint marks, looked up at him questioningly.

"King Noble treated my wounds," he explained.

"Yes, wounds never last long in Tolk." She smiled. "They're having a dance right now in the Bluebell Bower. Won't you come with me?" Eagerly she caught his hand.

But Price looked away. "No, Freddy. I'm sorry. I can't. I have to leave pretty soon."

Freddy promptly released him. Her face fell. It was as though she had just turned to the final page of a wonderful storybook only to find that the ending was missing. There was no 'happily ever after' written there.

"Of course." She nodded dully. "I knew it would be soon."

"I'm really going to miss you, Freddy. You and O.P. are the best friends I've ever had."

"Same. I'm going to miss you too." A single pink teardrop formed under one gray eye and rolled down her cheek.

"You understand that I have to go, don't you?"

The fairy nodded again. "Yes, I know." Then she had to quickly hide her face under her free arm. She couldn't stop the flood of tears that suddenly welled over. Price relieved the girl of the lantern that now seemed to weigh her down.

"Remember the day that you and O.P. and I went to Drumbleton?" Price spoke brightly, by way of distraction. "Remember, how we saw Duff trying to fix that broken fence, propping it up with corn stocks? He was so proud of himself. Then the wind blew the whole thing over. I can still see him stomping on his hat."

A sort of muffled giggle came from under the fairy's arm.

"And remember, that same day you took us up into your tree house and we had a picnic? Boy, what a climb that was. O.P. was so scared. He shook like the last leaf of summer. You know, before my dad went on vacation, he said that he and I are going to build a tree house in our poplar tree. But it won't be as great as yours, Freddy. I'll always remember that tree house of yours. And in the winter, I'll think about you living there."

Freddy sniffed. A tear-stained face emerged. "Me, too. I'll think of you always." Bravely she wiped her eyes with the sash of her dress and sniffed again two or three times, but the flow of tears had stopped. Gently Price took her hand, and they wandered about reminiscing, sometimes stopping to chat with someone they met.

Price was even introduced to some of the elves. And King Noble was right. The people *had* been united in a way that had never happened before. Even the elves had come out of seclusion and celebrated victory alongside the others. They were not entirely emancipated, though. The shy, diminutive elves would only speak to Price through an interpreter, one of the dwarfs whom they trusted, none other than Derbin Dreckle, the hermit.

The time went by so quickly, it seemed only minutes when actually over an hour had passed. King Noble came up beside them with Meepy and O.P. lounging comfortably on his back. With them were Dot and Tim Arbuckle, Spark and his friend Sparkle, Toorilla, Bootle, Barlow Bear, Priscilla Smallpatch, Millie Muskin, Dori, Laefay, and many others.

No one actually declared it outright, but they began to make their way across the meadow, heading in the direction of the portal where Bran still faithfully stood guard. A number of fairies flew overhead, lighting the way with their lanterns.

For such a large company, they were remarkably silent. Even O.P. seemed at a loss for words. The small, piping voice interrupted only once. "Wait! Stop!" he said. King Noble stopped, and so did the others in quick succession.

O.P. looked up at Price, his black painted eyes round and sad. "Can I ride in your pocket one last time?"

"Sure." The boy reached down, and the small wooden man settled in the cupped palm of his hand. Carefully Price put him into his breast pocket. They continued on in silence. The only sounds were the humming of fairy wings and the swishing of many feet passing through the grass. Even the insects were respectfully silent.

All too soon they arrived at their destination. Bran had been watching their approach for some time and hailed them now with an energetic wave. He seemed to be the only one who was glad that the end had finally come.

"I guess this is it, O.P." Price lifted the little man from his pocket and held him at eye level. The pinecone man's lower lip quivered and he could not quite look the boy in the eye.

"Thanks, O.P., for all the jokes and the good times. I know you'll be happy here with your new friends."

"Sure, I will. But if it wasn't for you I wouldn't even... You've been a great pal!" Price knew that, coming from O.P., this was a huge compliment. Tenderly he placed him on King Noble's back.

"So long, Meepy."

"So long, Price. We couldn't have done what we had to without your help. And that cat—you sure took care of him. We can't thank you enough for that."

Price looked fondly at the German shepherd dog. Then, setting the lantern on the grass, he dropped to his knees and hugged him quickly.

"Goodbye, King Noble."

"Goodbye, my boy." The dog kissed his face. "I will come with you and see that you get home safely. Heaven only knows what awaits you on the other side of the wall."

Last of all Price turned to Freddy. But, overcome with grief, the poor little fairy couldn't even look at him. She buried her face in her hands. Price gently touched her arm.

"Goodbye," he said. But Freddy could neither see nor speak. Picking up the lantern, Price and King Noble faced Bran.

The giant jumped down from his post. Straightaway he set his mighty shoulder against the stone and heaved— once, twice. The stone rocked slightly, then sank back into place. He tried a third time. Then, red-faced and grunting, he dug his heels into the grassy turf. He heaved again. The ground began to crunch loudly under the shifting weight of the huge boulder.

"Wait!" It was Freddy. "Wait!" she cried.

Everyone looked at the fairy. She stared hard at King Noble and the dog's kind gentle eyes gazed steadily back at her. He nodded.

"I'm coming too!"

"But Freddy. Are you sure? Do you realize what you're doing?" asked Price.

The fairy tossed her golden curls. "Yes. I know exactly what I'm doing, and I *am* sure."

"But why?"

Freddy lifted her chin. "You were right, Price. There *are* some things worth dying for."

There was a loud grunt as Bran heaved again. They heard a grinding noise and a dull groan of protest as the huge boulder was rolled back. The dog went through first. Then, with a final salute to their friends, hand in hand, the boy and the girl slipped out of sight.

Chapter Thirty-One:
Home Again

It was an awesome sight that met them on the other side of the wall. Cast in the pale, pink glow of Freddy's lantern, the stiff, wooden bodies of the rebel dwarfs littered the space. Heaped with them were at least two score of granite boulders, each about the size of an apple box—all that remained of those giants foolish enough to enlist in Sinbad's 'army.' Seven slender saplings were crowded together in a corner, the unfortunate remains of the elves, Maebry and her friends. King Noble was nowhere to be seen.

"Follow me," Price whispered to Freddy. Taking the handle of the lantern in his teeth, they clambered over the mound on hands and feet. As much as possible they avoided looking directly at the grotesque shapes, wincing every time they had to place a hand on a boulder or one of the misshapen dwarf-logs. At its peak, the pile reached nearly to the top of the garage walls, and they soon discovered it had pushed right through the open gate and spilled into the yard.

Grandmother had left the backdoor light on, and they found King Noble in plain sight on the lawn, confronting a crowd of desperate, cringing animals. The dog was crouched down, glaring fiercely at the wretched creatures.

Who would have thought that eyes so full of love only a short time ago could now be so terrifying? Lips curled back, baring his long, sharp teeth, he snarled. Savagely he snapped his powerful jaws and lunged. This was a side to King Noble that these animals had never seen, and almost instantly they scattered in fright. Price searched for Sinbad among the fleeing beasts, but saw no sign of him.

In the shadows, near the east wall, they could dimly make out the shapes of three large bears. King Noble lunged in their direction, growling and snarling with such ferocity that Freddy jumped and clutched Price's arm. The bears fled, scrambling over the stone wall and onto the street.

The dog circled back and pointed with his snout towards the house, as if to say, "It's safe now; you must go in."

"Are you leaving us?" asked Price.

The animal shook his head 'no.' Then something caught his eye. They could barely hear the deep-throated growl as he padded off into the darkness, but it was filled with malice. He disappeared around a corner of the house.

"We'd better go in," said Price. Taking Freddy's elbow, the boy steered her towards the back steps. She hurried up the walk ahead of him.

"Freddy! Freddy!" Price called in a harsh whisper.

The girl turned sharply and found him staring at her in shock. "What is it?" she asked nervously.

"Your wings!"

She glanced over her shoulder—then gasped. The wings were gone! One of her small hands instinctively reached back to the place where they had always been, but the beautiful, delicate fairy wings had disappeared forever. "Oh, no. No!"

"And you're taller ... and bigger," said Price.

Freddy looked down at her tunic, which now seemed several inches too short. With frightened eyes, she looked up again at Price. Then, like a curtain rising on a new day, the anxious feelings seemed to vanish, and she smiled.

"It's okay," she said. "I'm human now ... like you."

Grandmother was in bed, and although it was very late, her lamp was still on. Price tapped on the bedroom door and looked in. She was lying propped up against the pillows with her eyes shut, her needlework discarded at her side.

"I'm home, Grandma," he said.

Immediately, the eyes fluttered open and she sat up.

"Price! Thank heavens." She started to pull back the covers.

"Wait! Don't get up. I'm tired. I'm going right to bed. We can talk in the morning, okay?"

Grandmother put a hand to her throat, and her mouth opened, as if to object. But then, letting out a deep breath, she relaxed. "Yes, yes. I'm just *so* thankful you're home. I've seen the *strangest* things outside the window, and heard such dreadful noises. Price, there are animals running all over our backyard!" She met his eyes with a searching look. "I've been half-afraid to stir from this bed. I thought of calling the police, but ... that ...didn't seem like the right thing to do. Somehow I thought that *you* might have an explanation."

Price did not want to do any explaining or make any introductions just then. It was all too complicated, and he needed some time to think things over.

"I'll explain everything in the morning," he said. "It's too late now. But I promise," he looked her in the eye, "there's nothing to worry about."

Grandmother studied his face for a long minute. "All right," she said at last. "I'll trust you for a full account in the morning." Gratefully, she sank back into the pillows.

"Thanks, Grandma." He turned halfway to the door. "G'night then."

"Good night, Price."

Quietly, he closed the bedroom door. A few seconds later, the bedside lamp switched off.

Price shut and fastened all the windows and made sure that both the front and back doors were bolted. Then he and Freddy got sleeping bags and pillows and spread them out on the living room carpet. Wearily, just as they were, they flopped down on top of the bags to sleep.

At least they tried to sleep. But outside the secure walls of the house, the night air was punctuated with strange sounds—pitiful moaning and wailing sounds, sounds that were definitely not human. In the darkness, they lay listening to the cries of anguish and distress. There were sounds of things thumping and bumping against the walls. Sometimes, they heard scuffling and scraping noises, followed by growling and snarling. Later they heard sirens and the voices of men and women—excited, surprised, but decidedly confident, taking charge.

Finally, there was silence, and from sheer exhaustion, they each sank into a deep sleep.

The next thing Price knew, sunlight was streaming in through the living room sheers, and he could hear dishes clattering in the kitchen. He could also hear two voices conversing together in hushed tones. He sat bolt upright. Freddy was gone.

Uh-oh, he thought, and was at the kitchen door in a second.

Freddy was wearing an apron over her silvery tunic and stood at the counter wiping dishes. Grandmother was stirring a bowl of pancake batter as she spoke. "I'll tell you this much, I won't be leaving out any food for that cat. Price! You're up!"

There was a full moment when no one said a word. Price just stood there, staring, wide-eyed and slack-jawed. He looked expectantly from one to the other and back again. At last Grandmother turned and ladled a spoonful of batter onto the griddle.

"Have you noticed the time?" she asked casually.

He glanced at the kitchen clock. Five past one. "It's late," he said.

"I should say so. Freddy's been up for three hours. But then we fai—uh females tend to be light sleepers ... compared to males, that is." She ladled out two more pancakes. "Did you sleep well?"

"I guess so. Not at first."

"I should say not. How could you? Lucky for me, I don't hear too well. Even so, many of those awful creature sounds did not escape my ears."

Price couldn't help glancing over at the window.

Grandmother anticipated his thoughts. "It's quite all right today, though. Everything was very quiet this morning."

"Whew. That's good." He said this to himself, under his breath.

"I expect the German shepherd dog I saw early this morning, sitting on the walk, had something to do with that. He's gone now."

Grandmother turned from the griddle. She looked directly at Price. "Freddy and I had a long conversation this morning, Price. She has told me everything."

There was absolutely nothing he could say in response to this announcement. His brown eyes met Grandmother's as he waited for her to continue.

"Strange as it may seem to you, I believe every word she said." She wiped some batter from her hands onto the apron. "I'm proud of you, Price. You and Freddy were both valiant in a good cause. And I hear you gave that dreadful cat quite a beating. Well, he asked for it, I'm sure." She leaned back against the counter. "Sometimes the bad ones have to be stopped or they'll spoil it for everybody else."

Then she looked at Freddy and smiled. "And I'm also happy that Freddy is here with us now."

Price heaved a huge sigh of relief. "But what are we going to do about it?" he asked.

"First of all, we're going to eat a good breakfast—or I should say, brunch. Then we'll see about cleaning up the yard. Eventually, we'll have to make some legal arrangements for Freddy." She put an arm tenderly around the young girl's shoulders. "Don't you think this child looks as if she could be my ... say ... long lost grand-niece? Just look at those eyes, the spitting image of mine." She smiled with such sincere warmth that all clouds of apprehension cleared away. For the first time that morning, Price and Freddy exchanged a grin.

"Oh course, I could never actually *say* such a thing," Grandmother went on, "but people might *think* it all the same. And I wouldn't discourage them if they did. In fact, I would feel honored. And how can the girl possibly remember her parents if she never had any? It may be tricky, but if she stays with me for a while, and later becomes a ward of the province, I think there's a good chance they'll leave her in my care." Grandmother turned her attention to the griddle and flipped over a couple of pancakes.

"But now the question is: What are we going to do with those horrible wooden monstrosities piled up by the side of the garage? And those rocks? The saplings I think I can use in my own garden. Price, d'you mind getting three grapefruits from the pantry? Come, then. Pancakes are ready. Let's sit down and discuss the matter over brunch."

Later that day, they found Price's bicycle and backpack, which he had left behind in Tolk, leaning against the garage. How they came to be there, they never knew. But all incriminating evidence, such as the pulley, twine, and sticky tape, leftovers from the rescue, had been removed. And as for dealing with the mess in the yard, it turned out to be less complicated than they had first thought.

To begin with, they got some old jeans and a T-shirt of Price's that were too small for him and Freddy put them on. Then they set to work. It took two full days to sort through the great heap of rubble and dislodge all the wooden dwarfs. Grandfather's crowbar and some two-by-fours proved invaluable as levers.

But it was a morbid task. Just looking at the misshapen dwarfs with their awful, contorted faces was disturbing enough, but actually handling them was positively repellent. Eventually, though, they managed to extract them all, and there were 167 altogether.

Now, Grandmother no longer owned a car, but she did still have a valid driver's license. A few days later, the three of them walked to a car rental place, where they rented a half-ton truck. They loaded as many of the dwarf-logs as they could into the cab and drove to the local garden center, hoping the proprietor would agree to sell them as lawn art. He laughed out loud when he saw them.

"Where the heck did you get these?" he marveled.

"Oh, now," Grandmother gave him a sly look, "*that's* a trade secret. Let's just say they sort of ... appeared out of nowhere." She lifted her eyebrows and nodded mysteriously.

"Uh-huh." He didn't sound convinced. "Say ... aren't you the lady who knits all that stuff for charities? Blankets and things?"

"Yes, I am," said Grandmother, smiling.

That seemed to clear things up. "Well, you've outdone yourself this time." He grinned. "These are pretty hideous, but Halloween's not far off. Sure, I'll take them," he said. "They oughta sell like hot cakes."

"Good!" said Grandmother, grateful that she lived in a small town where everybody knows your business. "And I've got a few more back at home," she added.

And so, it was all arranged, with Grandmother donating her share of the profits to the local food bank: her favorite charity.

The boulders, though, were another matter. These they could not remove without help. Grandmother had to have men come with a crane and a dump truck. The crane was to lift them over the wall, one-by-one, and the dump truck was to haul them away. It might have been a costly operation, but as luck would have it, the outfit they hired just happened to need some boulders of that size and appearance (there were 42 of them altogether) to landscape a large rock garden outside a new office building in town. If the workmen were at all curious about how they came to be there in the first place, they didn't let on. After all, boulders don't just drop out of the clear blue sky—yet, there they were, plain as day. The only logical explanation was that they had always been there, lodged between the two garages, and now someone was finally getting around to removing them.

There was one particularly large one that Grandmother took a fancy to. It was bigger than the others, with a reddish granite hue, and had the attitude of a giant curled up asleep. That one she had the men deposit in a corner of her front yard. She planted shrubs and perennials around it. Everyone who saw it admired it and praised Grandmother for her artistic flare.

The seven saplings she planted in a row across the far end of her backyard. In time they grew into tall, slender birch trees that provided a windbreak and welcome shade on hot summer evenings.

For quite some time, reports circulated about the strange behavior of animals in the area. Grandmother read in the newspaper that thirteen bears had been discovered roaming the neighborhood, raiding garbage cans and dumpsters. Bears! And thirteen of them! Five were dressed in clothes, so obviously they'd had a recent connection with humans. It was generally thought that they must be circus animals. But, oddly enough, no one ever claimed them. In a short time, all were apprehended, and according to the newspaper, deposited many miles away on a wildlife reserve, far from any town.

Everyone in Clareburn had a story to tell about some squirrel or skunk or rabbit they'd seen acting in odd ways. A businessman on his way to work one morning found five wild hares stretched out asleep on his patio furniture. Sheep, goats, and cattle were herded off people's lawns and taken to farms (or to other places far less inviting). A few animals had been caught peering in windows or taking things that normally wouldn't interest them, such as note-paper and pencils, tools, and even books. Some of them, when confronted, had become unusually aggressive.

One day, a crowd of wild animals—squirrels, mice, badgers, raccoons, gophers, and even a couple of beavers—entered a shopping mall en masse (through the automatic doors, of course), flooring the local retailers. The animals headed straight for the supermarket, in particular the produce department, where they'd frightened the customers half to death. Freddy, Price, and Grandmother had to chuckle when they watched the report on the evening news.

But sadly, these creatures were dealt with much more severely than the bears. No wildlife reserve for them. The local exterminator quickly solved the problem. Photos taken by customer's cell phones were posted online, but were naturally considered photo-shopped. The incident was so bizarre that it actually made headlines in the tabloids. And of course, when that happened, nobody believed it any more. The whole affair was generally assumed to be a hoax.

For quite awhile, the reports kept people speculating about all kinds of reasons for the unusual animal behavior, and had the S.P.C.A., the fire department, and the wildlife authorities hopping. But in time the occurrences became less and less frequent, and people began to forget about the animals, moving on to other topics of interest, such as poltergeists, UFOs, extra-sensory perception, or the weather.

Of course, Price's parents were astonished when they returned from their vacation and found a totally unexpected and previously unknown addition to the family. They puzzled over it at length for many days. Eventually they decided that Freddy really *must* be related to Grandmother in some way. Since Grandmother was adopted, her native background and history were a complete mystery. Even more mysterious was that Freddy, also, would somehow appear seemingly out of nowhere, much as Grandmother herself. But, my goodness, those unusual eyes. What a striking resemblance! The similarity was remarkable.

But besides that, Mother had always wanted a daughter—in addition to Price, that is. And Freddy certainly needed a family. Almost from the outset, Mother and Father accepted Freddy and loved her as if she had been their very own.

And yes, Grandmother did in time become Freddy's legal guardian (the DNA tests happily confirmed a close family relationship). And as it turned out, having the care of a sprightly and determined (if somewhat teary) young grand-niece, gave Grandmother a renewed lease on life. Almost all of the lonely feelings, and even much of the frailty, were dispelled. Of course, she still missed Grandfather. But she knew that she would see him again one day ... when her turn came.

And what about that tiny wooden box that Price brought home from the market? Well, somehow it found its way into Grandmother's cedar chest, along with Freddy's lantern and clothes, and soon Price had forgotten all about it. And Mother never mentioned Octaruse Pinecone. She seemed to have forgotten about him as well.

As for Mr. Murphy, he never came back from the coast where he'd gone to visit his daughter. It seems that he met an elderly widow there, and instead of coming home, married her and moved into her house, which was located in a much more desirable climate for gardening. One day a moving van pulled up to his property. The contents of the house were loaded onto it, and a *For Sale* sign appeared on the front lawn. Not long after, a family with three youngsters of various ages (and with active imaginations) moved in, much to the delight of Freddy and Price.

The children often get together in the space between the garages, which is now shared by both families. It's become a kind of headquarters and refuge—always holding such wonderful possibilities.

One spring day, months later, when she and Price were alone in the space, Freddy scrambled up the stone wall at the end and peered over the top.

"What're you doing?" asked Price.

She hoisted herself all of the way and sat down. "I was just imagining," the girl replied wistfully. "I was imagining that there might be a fairyland on the other side of this wall. But," she sighed, "there's nothing here but the alley."

Price climbed up next to her and took a look for himself. Something stirred in his memory, and he half expected to see that big German shepherd that used to live in the neighborhood. He'd really liked that dog. But then, as quickly as the impression came, it vanished. He looked at his friend.

"Freddy, you don't believe in fairies, do you?"

"Well, I'm not sure."

"That's ridiculous. That's just for little kids. But I'm glad you came over today," he said. "Come on. Let's get Grandpa's toolbox and start on the lean-to. It's supposed to rain this afternoon. Nick's bringing his tarp, and Amanda's bringing their camp stove. Mom said we can cook beans and pancakes for supper."

"The camp stove? Are they really going to let us use that?"

"Their dad said he'd supervise. Come on." He jumped down. Then, light as a fairy, Freddy landed next to him, on her toes.

As for Sinbad, no one knows what became of him. He was never seen or heard from again. It may be that King Noble had something to do with that. Or it could be that the cat went somewhere far away, and never came back, because he simply couldn't bear any encounters with his past—anything that might remind him of his defeat. Whatever his fate, Price and Freddy never knew it. But they really didn't care, and certainly no one missed him. Not even Mr. Murphy.

The End

About the Author:

For many years, Lesley Renton has enjoyed working with hundreds of youth, from school age to young adult, and believes strongly in their innate desire and ability to make good choices and succeed in life.

"Our youth today live in challenging times," she says, "and my aim is to create stories that are both captivating and empowering. In "Cat Between Two Worlds" there are no magical solutions to problems. The main character resolves conflict using his wit and ingenuity. At the same time, he must rely on the contributions of all, right down to the smallest person.

"As a mother, reading with my two children was part of the family adventure. Throughout their childhoods and even into their teens, we explored together many wonderful books. These were warm, comfortable times, close to the heart. It's my hope that this story will inspire, in those who read it, that same sense of wonder, adventure, and inclusion."

Lesley and her husband, Bruce, live in Calgary Alberta, where she teaches private piano lessons at a performing arts school.

Watch for more books by Lesley Renton—coming soon

Printed in Canada